QUEEN OF NORTHERN ICE

ABIGAIL ADDISON

first edition 2023

IBSN Code: 978-0-578-38916-5

For those who have a dream but hesitate to go for it—may you find the courage to chase what sets your heart on fire

"Behind every sweet smile, there is a bitter sadness that no one can ever see or feel"

~ Tupac Shakur

Prologue

I remember that morning as if it was yesterday.

Getting out of bed and walking toward the small window in my room. I could hear my parents downstairs talking to each other and I could see other children running and laughing outside. I remember smiling as I looked into the forest that surrounded our village and how I had fallen asleep to the Wisps flying in it the night before.

As I walked downstairs, the aroma of my mom's cooking filled the air. Some mornings, she was gone before I woke up, but that day, she was there. She had made pancakes–mine covered in blueberries, my dad's in bananas.

While we ate, my mom and dad talked about their plans for the day. My dad was going to go hunting with the others later so that they could store food to cover the rest of the town over winter. Whilst my mom was going to see the children in the orphanage, to read them stories, and give the ladies who cared for them blankets so they could stay warm over winter.

My mom was a Phoenix, and she made sure that I as well as others always had a smile on our faces and that nobody in our town was treated unfairly or poorly. My dad, on the other hand, was a wolf; this was always odd to me because wolves tended to marry into other packs for alliances or they'd marry people in their own packs. My dad always said it was fate's choice that he married my mom; so I never had a reason to question it.

I wish I did.

I listened to them as we ate before I chimed in that I was going to go searching for berries in the forest to use as paint for my art. I would have asked one of the Wisps for help, but they usually only came out at night and my dad had told me not to get too close to them in fear of what might happen if I did. I never listened, of course, because when the Wisps did come out in the daytime, they'd help me pick out all kinds of flowers and then braid them into my hair. Sometimes, they'd even chase me around the forest until I was laughing so hard that I couldn't breathe.

My mom told me to be careful before I left for the forest, listing a bunch of do's and don'ts so I wouldn't get hurt. She gave me her coat telling me to be safe before she kissed my head and lightly pushed me out the door.

When I reached the forest, I noticed how the clouds darkened and covered the sun. I had this feeling that something wasn't quite right, but I decided to shake it off and continued to look for the berries I needed instead.

I wish I could go back and warn them all.

Wanting to find the blueberries first, before the red and yellow ones, I set off through the forest, carefully scanning the ground for any sign of the small blue fruits. The thought of them—fresh and ripe—made my mouth water. I waited for the Wisps to appear, to help me gather them as they always did. But today, nothing. No flashes of light, no soft whispers in the air, just the rustling of leaves and the quiet hum of the forest.

Without them, it took me longer than usual to find the blueberries. Each step seemed to stretch out, every turn feeling like it led me further into the thick of the trees. It took almost an hour to gather them all, and every time my hand brushed against a particularly plump berry, I had to fight the urge to pop it into my mouth. They were so tempting, so sweet, but I had a purpose today. I needed enough to make the paint, not just a snack.

Finally, when I had a good pile of them, I began the walk home. The sun was beginning to dip lower, casting long shadows on the forest floor. As I neared the edge of the trees, I glanced back, and that's when I saw it—a black Wisp, trailing just behind me. Its form was barely more than a flicker in the shadows, but I knew what I had seen. The Wisp froze when it realized I had noticed it, then hurriedly slipped back into the forest, disappearing as quickly as it had appeared.

I frowned, standing still for a moment, feeling a strange unease ripple through me. But there was no time to dwell on it. With a quick shake of my head, I turned back to the path and raced home, clutching the blueberries tightly in my hands.

Once inside, I set the berries down on the kitchen counter. The quiet of the house surrounded me, and I focused on what needed to be done. First, I needed to turn these berries into something that would bring the painting to life. I gathered the small mortar and pestle, the one my grandmother had used for years, and set about mashing the blueberries. The dark, rich juice spilled out as I ground them, their vibrant color staining my fingers and the stone beneath. Slowly, the blue began to take shape—a deep, almost velvety shade that would be perfect for my canvas.

Next, I mixed the juice with the other colors I'd brought from the forest. The red berries would give me the crimson I wanted, and the yellow ones would brighten things up. I worked carefully, mixing the colors in separate bowls, each hue placed beside the other, just waiting for the moment I could start painting.

When everything was ready, I set up the easel, the wooden canvas resting there in front of me. I took a deep breath, then dipped the first brush into the blue paint. The bristles caught the color and I could feel the weight of the moment—the quiet anticipation of creating something new, something raw. As I lifted the brush to the wood, I didn't know exactly what I was going to paint. I never did. The colors just flowed, spilling from the brush, guided by some instinct I couldn't quite place.

I dragged the paintbrush across the wood, sometimes hard, sometimes soft, feeling the weight of the color as it pressed against the grain. Each stroke revealed a new layer of the image in my mind, though I didn't quite understand it yet. The blue seemed to swirl, the red adding splashes of intensity, the yellow brightening the edges. Slowly, the painting began to take shape, though I couldn't quite tell what it was. There were no clear lines, just layers of emotion, of feeling.

When I finally stepped back, my heart raced as I blinked at the painting in front of me. The colors seemed to shimmer, blending together in a way that almost made them feel alive. I hadn't set out to paint anything specific, but now, as I took it all in, I realized it was a reflection of something deep inside me. What that was, I couldn't say, but I could feel it in the air—something had shifted, though I couldn't yet understand why.

As I stepped back to look at the painting in its entirety, I noticed the blend of colors, each corner holding a different energy. The top left was a deep, swirling blue with hints of black, while the bottom right was bright yellow with traces of pink, like the first rays of dawn. The colors seemed to dance, swirling around the canvas in a chaotic but mesmerizing way. The lower half of the painting was soft and light, bathed in hues of pink, yellow, and orange. But as the painting rose, the tones deepened, darkening into blues, blacks, and reds, as if the mood was shifting.

In the center, where all the colors converged, there was a mess—a swirling mix of light and dark, bleeding into one another, not quite defined. The way the colors tangled together made the middle feel like a point of conflict, something torn between two worlds, two emotions. The more I stared, the more I realized the contrast between the top and bottom: the bottom half was gentle and vibrant, while the top was heavy and oppressive, as if some unseen force was pulling the light away.

I frowned as I looked at it. This wasn't like any painting I had done before. Usually, my work was bright, full of life, with the dark colors reserved only for shadows. But this—this was something else entirely. The darkness wasn't just a background, it was part of the message, woven through the very heart of the painting. I couldn't fully grasp what it meant, but I knew it was something I had to understand. Something was speaking through the colors, and it was telling me a story I wasn't sure I was ready to hear.

And the funny thing is, I really wasn't ready.

I left the painting on the easel to dry, knowing I'd place it with the rest of my works later, after showing it to my dad. I was fairly certain he would tell me it was great, just like he always did. But I also knew he'd be a little confused—this one didn't look like the others. It was different. The usual vibrancy and lightness that filled my paintings was absent, replaced by something deeper, more complex. He'd probably talk to my mom about it, and that would lead to her having a conversation with me, trying to figure out if everything was okay.

I turned my head to the right, where the rest of my paintings sat against the wall, leaning gently on each other in a messy pile near the window. Dad always called them masterpieces, which made me laugh. I'd jokingly tell him that they were just as good as anyone else's work—except, of course, for professional artists.

I wish I would've listened to him more.

Later in the day, I decided to take a nap in my room – a quiet and peaceful environment – feeling secure and safe in my own home. It was so quiet that I couldn't even hear the birds chirping outside or the children screaming. The clouds covering the sun made it seem like the perfect time to sleep.

I wish I would've known that it meant something else entirely.

Unfortunately, a few hours later, I was jolted awake by the shrill screams of the people in my village—my home. I remember the bloodshed that greeted my eyes, innocent lives lost in an instant. The snow was falling heavily outside my window, thick flakes swirling in the wind. I remember thinking it was far too early for snow to be coming down that hard. The chaos, the fear, the violence—it was all too much for me to process. It overwhelmed me so completely that I blacked out, losing track of everything around me.

I'm glad I did.

I couldn't remember how I got here, or why. I had no recollection of what had happened, or who might have been after me. All I knew was that I had woken up in an unfamiliar room, in a building that was definitely not my home. The air felt thick with something I couldn't quite place, and the walls... the walls were smeared with blood. It was a dark, haunting red, slowly dripping down to pool on the floor below, staining everything it touched.

The only thing I could clearly remember was someone telling me to run. So I did.

I ran—through the dense forest, weaving between the trees, my breath sharp and ragged in the frigid air. Every step was a battle against the snow, which fell relentlessly from the sky, blanketing the world in a thick layer of white. It clung to the branches above me, coating the leaves, turning everything into a blurry white mess. I had to be careful—spiked branches reached out like claws, and the thorn bushes threatened to tear at my skin, but I had to keep going. I had no choice.

The ground beneath me was slick with snow, packed down hard from the weight of the storm, making each step feel like I was pushing against an invisible force. Winter had come early, too early, and I was unprepared. My legs burned with the effort, and the cold seeped into my bones, but I couldn't stop. I was alone, and I had no idea if I was being chased, but the fear in my chest told me I had to keep moving, or I'd never make it out alive.

As I kept running, the scent of smoke slowly began fading away the further away I got. I didn't bother looking back as I knew if I did, it would have made that day even worse than it already was.

My parents were gone. My home was gone; everything was.

My hood had long since fallen away, and the snow was relentless, sticking to my hair, coating my eyelashes like tiny shards of ice. My body had gone numb, every inch of it—from the tips of my fingers to the sharp ache in my nose and ears. The cold was unbearable, the air biting at my skin like a thousand tiny needles. I could feel the pain of my nose and ears stinging with the frost, the blood rushing to them, making them burn in protest. But none of it mattered. I couldn't stop. I couldn't afford to.

Around me, the Wisps were near. I could feel their presence—an energy, a whisper on the edge of my consciousness—but I couldn't see them. The snowstorm was too fierce, the temperature too cruel for them to emerge. They were hidden from view, retreating into the shadows, and in some strange way, I was too. But even if they *were* visible, it didn't matter. They didn't need me. They had survived long before me, long before anyone, and they would survive long after.

I pushed myself harder, my breath a cloud in the frigid air, my lungs burning with the cold. Every exhale felt like it froze before it could escape, and my legs—heavy, stiff—kept moving as though they were being controlled by some force beyond my own will. The pain in my chest was unbearable, a tight knot that screamed at me to stop, but I couldn't. I couldn't stop for them. I couldn't stop for anyone.

The snow whipped around me, stinging my cheeks, but I didn't slow. My body ached, every step felt like dragging myself through wet concrete, but I pushed through. The cold air tore at my face, numbing me even further, making it harder to breathe. But still, I ran.

The world around me grew distant, fading in and out of focus as my strength drained away. My legs wobbled, my breath ragged, and just when it felt like I couldn't take another step, my vision blurred. The earth beneath me tilted. The sounds of the storm—the wind, the snow, the crackling branches—became muffled. I could feel the air thickening around me, the weight of exhaustion pulling me down.

And then, it all went black.

When I came to, the air was still and damp. The sharp smell of mildew and decay assaulted my senses, and I blinked into the dim light, trying to gather my bearings. I was lying on something hard, rough beneath me. The cold floor of an abandoned cabin. I could hear the faint drip of water somewhere in the distance, but the world outside was silent, distant. The walls were crumbling, cracked wood and peeling paint, but at least it was shelter.

Wood covered the windows as if bolted up with nails, whilst cobwebs engulfed every corner I could see. I wasn't sure how I had gotten there or if it was real or not. All I know is that the last thing I saw was a black Wisp by the window, causing me to release a gasp in surprise. Once it realized that I'd seen it, it flew away. I wanted to get up and chase after it, but I was too weak to do anything. Instead, I released a sad sigh, sat up, and pulled my knees towards my chest to warm myself up. Then, I simply let my thoughts wander in an attempt to recall everything that I remembered before I blacked out. All I hoped for was that I had run far enough.

All I could remember was the blood, so much blood. Everywhere I looked there was blood. I just couldn't remember seeing any bodies to go with the blood. I faintly remember the smell of death and the metallic iron that invaded my senses. I remember having to hold my hand against my mouth in order to prevent myself from vomiting. As I knew if I did, I wouldn't be able to stop, so I held it in.

I had to.

Eventually, someone – I don't remember who – rushed into the building I was in looking confused and worried. They twisted and turned as if they were urgently searching for someone, but when their eyes landed on me, I realized that I was the person they were searching for. They rushed over to me as soon as they spotted me, almost as if it were the most important thing at that exact moment. Once they reached me, they slid on their knees in front of me and gripped my shoulders tightly, all the while I stood there in complete shock. All I remember thinking at the time was where were my parents? I was knocked out of my shock when the person started to shake my body. They had been trying to get me to listen, but all I could focus on was the blood staining the walls, the tears were pouring down my face and my breathing as I felt like I couldn't breathe. They placed their hands on my face, turning my head so I was focusing on them and only them, and like a switch being flipped, I could finally hear what they were saying.

"Run, Sephy, run, and don't you dare look back. Never come back! Run, and stay hidden. Don't stop moving. Go!" they said in a quiet yet demanding tone.

I didn't want to listen, as the child in me wanted to run home and ask my parents what was going on. I wanted to fall back into my dad's embrace and cry on his shoulder as he whispered nothing but kind things into my ear. He would tell me that everything was going to be ok, and that he was there for me. I wanted to find my mom and sit at the table eating the waffles she'd always made, just for me. But I couldn't, and the hands gripping my shoulders wouldn't let me as this person kept telling me to run. I didn't want to listen. I didn't want to be alone.

The person looked back at the door before looking at me again; I assumed they had had enough and were worried about not having enough time. I remember feeling myself being pushed towards another exit on the opposite side of the building from wherever they had come in from.

I turned back with tears still falling down my face; I didn't want to leave. As I was about to take another step back toward the person, they shouted at me to run and not look back again.

That time, maybe I had realized that I wasn't going to find my mom or my dad. Maybe I thought my parents were outside waiting for me or maybe I thought that when I walked out the door I would wake up and find out it was all just a horrible nightmare, but either way, I listened. I listened, thinking they would follow behind me. So with tears streaming down my face and painful sobs making me choke, I turned and sprinted out the door, not daring to look back. I stopped for a second once I'd made it a couple of feet from the building and turned around. I looked around for my parents, but there was no one around. In the distance, I could see glowing embers and I could faintly smell the burning wood; it made my eyes burn more than they already were, knowing what the embers meant. I remember knowing I wasn't going to see my parents again, and that if they had been with me, they, too, would have told me to run. I glanced back towards the building to see if the person who told me to run was coming along with me, but I didn't see them following me. Tears began to pour from my eyes at a faster rate than before, but I decided to take a deep breath to calm down.

After I did, I turned around and sprinted into the forest towards the next town, hoping to get help and I didn't stop. Not when I heard the monsters who destroyed my life ask the person who saved me where I was. Not when I heard their screams and pleas, begging for them to stop. Not even when it got too cold for me to feel my toes. I just kept on running.

I had to.

I ran, tears streaming down my face, only to freeze as they fell from my chin. I ran, knowing my ears would grow numb and my nose would turn as red as the cold would allow. I ran, fully aware that I'd probably catch a cold, but I didn't care.

No matter how far I went, I couldn't forget the metallic stench of blood that still lingered in my mind, the smell of it so thick, it felt like it was still suffocating me. I couldn't forget the scream—the one that tore through the room, the scream of someone who chose to protect me instead of saving themselves. That scream followed me. It haunted me.

In my dreams, the shadow of the person who saved me appeared, their voice accusing me: *It's your fault. You caused all of this.* Maybe they were right. Maybe I was the reason for all the bloodshed. They told me I should end my life, for causing so much pain, so much suffering. But I couldn't. I couldn't end it. I had to live with the heartache. I had to live for the lives that were taken—for my parents, for everyone who died.

I had to live.

That was the last day of my happiness. The last day I wasn't constantly running, the last day I had a real home, a place where I stayed longer than just a couple of days or months. The last day I didn't have to look over my shoulder, waiting for someone to leap from the shadows. The last day I wanted revenge for something as meaningless as a flower—one that took me hours to pick because I wasn't sure if it was the right one.

I've never really understood why they were after me, but I don't want to know. If I find out, it means they've already found me—or worse, I'm asking questions, which would lead them right to me.

But one thing is for certain: if they find me, I'll make them suffer. Not only for what they did to me but for the trauma they caused my family and friends in their final moments. They'll suffer for not allowing me to say goodbye to my mom and dad, for ripping that chance away from me.

And because of that, they'll pay. They'll suffer the same fate as those they killed, no matter the cost.

The one thing I can say about that night is that I wish I could remember what happened in that room—the one drenched in blood, where death hung in the air like a heavy fog, so thick I could almost taste it. I wish I knew who had been there before me, how they met their end, and where they were taken before I stumbled into that place. I don't even remember how I ended up there. Why did I go inside? Had I been there before, my mind wiping it clean because the violence was too much to bear? Or had someone told me to go in there, unaware of the danger, or worse, knowing exactly what awaited me?

But above all, I want to know who told me to run.

I wish I could thank them for saving my life, even though their sacrifice probably cost them theirs. But I can't. I'll never have those answers. Not all of them, at least.

The only way to find any of them is to go back to where it all began—the place I promised never to return. The place I swore, to the person who told me to run, that I would never look back. If there's any control I still have over my life, it's that promise. I won't break it. Not now, not ever. I won't go back. Not until my last breath.

For the rest of my days, I'll keep running. I'll fight for myself, and I'll always be watching my back. The least I can do is survive—for those I lost. Even if their screams and calls echo in my head, telling me I should've died with them, I won't stop running. I won't let their deaths be in vain.

But deep down, I'll always wonder. Why was my home attacked? Why was I the one they wanted? What did they see in me that made me the target, the one they came for? I'll never know, and that is the one question I wish I could answer more than any other.

Chapter 1

It's been about 144 months since I started running.

About 625 weeks since that day, and yet I still get nightmares about it.

About 4,380 days since I've been completely and utterly alone.

About 105,120 hours since I've lost everything and everyone I've ever loved in a single day.

About 6,307,200 minutes that I've been in and out of towns, making sure to avoid all Abolystics because I have no other choice.

About 378,432,000 seconds since I began having to explore the forests to find ways to escape from the people who are after me.

I hope for the day that I eventually lose them, but I know it will never happen as there is nowhere for me to go. I will forever be trapped in the country of Karsindel. Knowing this, I know that the only way for me to survive is if I know every inch of the entire country, every hiding place, every watch area, every small tiny detail, even where the squirrels live; not that there are any. I know that if I didn't, I'd be caught and I refuse to let that happen.

It's not all bad though. I mean sure being alone for a couple of years as well as being on the run seems like an awful way to live and, in all honesty, it is. Unfortunately, it's something I've had to live with and will continue to live with until I die; or at least until I decide that I cannot fight anymore.

My life is like a maze. Sometimes, I get stuck behind a wall and I have to turn around and find another way out. Other times, I find the right way, where there's no barrier or wall in my way. For me, the wall appears when the people who killed everything and everyone I love find me. The right path, the one with no barrier, is when I leave before them and make it somewhere safe, or at least to a new town where I'm able to stay for a while. As long as I stay one step ahead of them then there will be no barrier blocking my path, but I know it won't always be like that as eventually, they will catch up to me.

Unfortunately for my maze, it has no end. At least not one where I would come out alive. It's as if this maze is full of creatures who want to see me fail. Regardless, if there was an end and I do come out alive, I'm not entirely sure if I'd be the same person I was before.

If I could go back in time to prevent what happened that night, I'm not entirely sure what I would change. Mainly because I still don't know why those cruel, murderous people came to my home looking for me, killing everyone else in their path. I am thankful though that they didn't get what they wanted, that doesn't mean it will stay that way forever as I know they could show up at any moment.

The real question that I ask myself daily is: how many people are going to die until they finally have me in their grasp?

I can only hope that nobody else gets killed because of me and that it stays that way for a while longer. Even just a few more years, because the only reason I'm still out on my own without having been caught is that I haven't been publicly exposed; nobody knows to look for me or to tell the authorities about me. Part of the reason could be that they don't know what I look like, they may have small details, but not enough to create a wanted sign of me; which works in my favor.

The thing that continues to bother me since I've been on the run is the bloodshed and pain that I witnessed that night. The smells that intoxicated my senses are to no end; I can still smell iron when I close my eyes. Of course, with the smell comes the images. The images of pain in the person's eyes when they told me to run and never look back. The images of the fire burning down my home as I could hear screams of agony from those who were still alive and burning to death.

The terror in their eyes told me an unspoken story that, if I didn't listen, I wouldn't be who or where I am today. I would be a completely different person. It told me that with that different person would've come a lot of pain. Pain that wouldn't even be comparable to what I have already gone through; pain that would be far worse than not knowing what would happen to me. Worse than being forced away from my family, and worse than being thrown into a life that I didn't choose.

A life that I didn't want.

But I guess that choice was already made when seven-year-old me ran into the forest with tree branches twisting and turning in every direction covered in snow. The seven-year-old who didn't turn back for her family, hoping that they would be okay and eventually find her, even if she knew the truth. The seven-year-old who was forced to grow up too fast.

To this day, I can still see and smell all those things when I spot a rotting deer or even the glow of a Wisp in the forest. Though every year I see fewer and fewer colors glowing in the forest, almost as if the Wisps are dying just as I am.

The only thing that seven-year-old learned over the years was how to survive alone. How to build walls so high no one could climb over them. How to never trust, never let anyone close enough to betray you. How to always expect the worst, because people could turn on you in an instant, for no reason at all. She learned how to navigate through forests, how to live off what the land offered when money was something she would never have.

That same seven-year-old had to learn how to lie, how to take without being seen, how to make choices that would keep her alive, no matter the cost. She had to learn how to sacrifice others without hesitation, to do what was necessary—even if it meant causing harm. And perhaps the hardest lesson of all, she learned how to bury the pain. How to lock it away deep inside, in a place no one could reach, so that she could keep going without showing a single crack in her armor.

Years passed, and that seven-year-old, now hardened by everything she'd endured, kept pushing forward. No matter how much it hurt, no matter how exhausted she became, she kept moving. Kept fighting. She didn't know how to stop, not even when her body screamed for rest and her mind begged for release.

She's a fighter, that seven-year-old. Broken on the inside, tough as iron on the outside. She might feel like she's dead inside, but she keeps walking through the world, with nothing but a mask of emptiness. Inside, she screams. She cries. But no one hears it. No one ever will. Not as long as she keeps that blank, emotionless face in place.

Nevertheless one day, one day I'll be able to find out what they wanted. I'll know why they choose to kill everyone except for me. One day, I'll get my revenge, but for now, I need to keep away and come up with a plan. I need to be smart and continue to watch out for myself. No matter the cost. One day, that seven-year-old will finally be at rest.

One day.

Until then, I won't let everyone I've lost die in vain. I won't let the voices in my head go unheard, even if they claw at my mind every time I hear their maddening whispers. The guilt, the rage, the grief—they tear me apart. But I won't listen. Not anymore. Not when there's still a reason to fight.

I've endured too much to give up now. Too much to let this dark hole swallow me whole. I've seen things no one should ever witness, felt the weight of loss like a stone crushing my chest, yet I keep moving forward. Even when it feels impossible. Even when every part of me wants to collapse, I keep pushing because I can't afford to stop. Not yet.

But more than anything, there's one thing driving me—finding out who took everything from me. Who was behind the destruction of my home, the slaughter of my family. The attack that shattered my world into pieces. And I will make them pay for it. For everything they've stolen.

The need for answers consumed me. It wasn't just a desire—it was an obsession. I couldn't move on, couldn't breathe without knowing. I didn't care how long it would take. The truth had to be out there, and I would find it.

At first, I had no idea where to begin. The pieces didn't fit, and the truth felt like it was slipping through my fingers. The more I searched, the more I realized that the answers I needed were buried beneath layers of lies and secrecy, hidden behind walls of power I could never hope to breach. But the longer I searched, the clearer it became. The whispers became louder. The signs started pointing in one direction.

And years passed. Slowly, frustratingly, I pieced together the truth—until it hit me like a hammer to the chest.

The King.

It was him.

It had to be.

The same King who swore an oath to protect his people, to defend his kingdom. The same King who now rules through fear, his grip on the land forged from terror and bloodshed, all to fulfill his twisted vision of control. He's the one who shattered my world, who ordered the massacre that destroyed everything I loved. I don't know why. I don't know what drove him to commit such atrocities. But I know this: He's the one who murdered my family, my friends, my home. And now, he's hunting me.

But I won't let him win.

I won't let him have the satisfaction of seeing me broken. I can't just charge in, blinded by rage. No. I need to be smarter than that. I need to know him, understand him—learn his weaknesses, his patterns. I need to find a way to get close to him, to slip unnoticed into his world, and get the answers I need. Every fiber of my being tells me to stay away, to keep my distance and slip into the shadows, but I know I can't hide forever. He will answer for what he's done.

The King will pay for every life he's stolen. For every innocent soul he's crushed under his heel, for every life lost to his tyranny. He's the King who punishes the smallest of mistakes with death, the King who hides behind iron walls and an army of fear, manipulating everything in his grasp to maintain control.

He won't get away with it.

I'll make him pay. For everything he's taken from me. For everything he's destroyed. Even if it means I have to rip it from him with my bare hands.

But not yet. Not until I know what he wants from me. Not until I understand the full extent of his plans. I need to be patient, to play my cards carefully, because if there's one thing I've learned, it's that rushing in blind is a quick way to end up dead.

Once I know what he's after, once I know exactly how to strike, I will make him regret the day he decided to cross me. The day he took everything from me.

Until then, I'll continue running, because if I just give myself up, it will be too obvious that I know what he did. Unless he knows that I know. Not that that matters as it makes running even better; he'll believe that I'm running from him in fear of being killed. Even if that's not the case, running just gives me more time to make a plan and think of ways to make him suffer tremendously. To make him suffer the same way everyone else has since he began his rule.

I have thought of many ways to kill him throughout the last few years. Probably the most painful years of my life since the bloodshed. I haven't been able to come up with a painful enough way to kill him. If he dies without pain, my entire plan will have been ruined.

I want his death to be bloody, but painful and slow. I want to drag a knife down his skin, from his collarbone to his ankle. I want to make gashes everywhere, from the tips of his fingers to the bottom of his toes. I want him to die with the names of all the people he's killed carved into his body. I want him to scream in pain, and I'm going to listen as he begs me to let him go, for mercy, to stop. Even so, I won't give him that, because he doesn't deserve it. Once he realizes that his cries for help won't do anything to change my mind, I'll cut off his tongue and watch as the blood drips down his chin. I'll make sure he chokes on his blood. I want to see tears streaming down his face as he realizes what he's done, and I want him to beg me to forgive him. I want to see and hear all of it as I watch him take his last breath. Maybe that makes me a monster, but I'll be the monster he created when I was seven.

I want- no, I need him to feel the pain that I feel every night. The nightmares that I have to relive over and over never end. I need him to see all the pain he's caused me. All the tears that haven't spilled. All the blood I have on my hands. All the regret I'm holding inside of me for running away from a battle I had no chance of winning. All the truth I've had to hide. I need him to see it all. It'll be like a wound being ripped open again, unable to close. I need him to see that he didn't win. I need him to know and see with his own eyes that he had, in fact, finally lost.

Above all of that, I need him to be sorry for what he's done. I need him to beg for his life. I need him to give me some sort of explanation as to why he did what he did. Why would he go through all of this trouble just for me? Why all the bloodshed? Why all the guards? Why all the pain? Why couldn't he just come to my village and ask for me?

I want answers. And after I get them, I'll be sure to cut the head of the Basilisk and lock him in a room of mirrors so he can see for himself what he had become; before I burn everything to the ground until it's all ash.

And ash it will be.

Chapter 2

I woke with a start, my heart pounding in my chest and tears streaming down my face. My breaths came in short, ragged gasps, each one more desperate than the last. I shot upright, hands shaking as I wiped the tears away, trying to convince myself it wasn't real. Just another nightmare. *It wasn't real.* I whispered the words over and over in my head, clinging to them as my chest heaved. Slowly, my breath began to steady, the tightness in my lungs easing. Finally, I let out a shaky sigh, the tension in my body loosening, even though the terror still clung to me.

After a minute or two, I let myself fall backward, my head landing back on the pillow below me. I closed my eyes for a moment before letting out a low sigh. Once I was relaxed, I reopened my eyes and stared at the ceiling for a couple of minutes, trying to decide if I should get up or try to get more sleep, though I knew I needed to get up anyways. Thus, I got up and threw the blanket off of me, deciding that I wasn't going to be getting any more sleep tonight. I never do after my haunting nightmares, anyways. I could still hear the screams and pleas of innocent men, women, and children, prompting me to close my eyes tightly and shake my head to get them to go away and think about something else.

I was staying at a place called *Celia's Cottage*. It was a cozy, modest building—nothing extravagant, but it had its charm. The structure had two floors, with around twenty to twenty-five rooms in total. Fifteen of those were on the ground floor, nestled near the dining area where guests gathered for breakfast in the mornings. A comfortable seating area by a crackling fire near the front desk offered a welcoming spot for guests to chat and unwind. I was in room seventeen on the second floor.

My room was simple but inviting. A soft, homely space with a bed large enough for two, though you could squeeze in three if you didn't mind getting a little too close. A decent-sized closet offered just enough room to hang my things, and a small desk in the corner gave me a place to set down my belongings. The air always smelled faintly of forest trees after the rain, a fresh, earthy scent that felt grounding. It was the kind of smell that made you feel at ease, and one I could easily grow fond of if I were to stay longer.

But I wasn't...

I let out a heavy sigh, trying to push the memories from my mind, if only for a moment. Even a brief moment of peace felt like a relief.

I glanced at the clock on the wall, the soft glow of the digits telling me it was almost dawn. The quiet urgency of the hour tugged at me, and without hesitation, I swung my legs over the side of the bed, feet hitting the cool wooden floor. I pulled on my black dress, the fabric flowing smoothly as I slipped it over my head, the long sleeves hugging my arms as the hem brushed the floor. The dress was practical—loose enough to move freely, but still elegant in its simplicity. I added my shawl, wrapping it snugly around my shoulders, the weight of it comforting against the chill creeping through the air.

I stood in front of the small mirror, brushing through my hair with deliberate care, fingers working slowly to untangle the knots, trying to avoid the painful tug of strands coming loose. When I finished, I let my hair fall freely, the dark waves cascading over my shoulders and down my back, a curtain to shield my face from prying eyes.

I pulled my boots from the closet, the leather cool against my fingers as I slid them on, lacing them tightly for the long walk ahead. With one last glance around the room, I stood and moved toward the door. My hand lingered on the handle for a moment, the quiet of the cottage pressing in on me. I turned the handle slowly, pushing the door open just enough to slip through, then paused. The satisfying click of the lock echoed in the stillness, a small but important reassurance.

Today was my last day at the cottage. If fate's on my side, and my luck doesn't betray me, maybe—just maybe—I'll be able to stay in my next destination longer than I have anywhere else.

It had been years since the incident, and the constant flight from my past was taking its toll. The strain of moving every few days, never staying in one place long enough to settle, was wearing me thin. I couldn't remember the last time I had a full night's sleep or felt even a flicker of true peace. Every time I thought I could pause, take a breath, the shadows of what happened would claw their way back into my mind, the screams of the lost and the bloodshed echoing through my thoughts. But even so, I couldn't stop.

I'd gotten used to the pattern—set up in a new town, try to blend in, and when the whispers grew too loud or danger got too close, pack up and disappear. I'd let myself stay for a few days, maybe even a week, if it seemed safe enough. But every stop, every quiet moment, felt more like a fragile illusion than anything real. And now, the illusion had shattered.

The news had reached me through the usual channels—the half-hearted chatter of the townsfolk, their voices barely above whispers, telling each other about the King's guards. They'd be coming in a couple of days, they said, for a town search. My stomach dropped as I overheard one woman mention it, her voice tinged with both fear and confusion. The villagers had no idea why the King had chosen this place. But I did. The King didn't send his men to randomly comb through a town without a reason. And that reason was always one thing: me.

I had no doubt the people here had no idea what the real reason was—they just thought it was another routine search, one of those things the King did every so often to remind his subjects of his power. But I knew the truth. I was a ghost to them, a shadow they couldn't even see, and I was being hunted.

I didn't have much time.

If I moved fast enough, I could get out before they arrived. East. I'd head East toward Direcrest, a place far enough to keep a distance between me and the King's men. The Bloodthorn Forest lay between here and there, thick and dangerous. It would slow them down—most likely make them hesitate to take that route. I couldn't afford to stay in one place any longer than I had to. The King's men were relentless, and with each passing day, they grew closer.

West was no longer an option. Not that I could go that way even if I wanted to. Heading West would be like walking into their trap, like offering myself up for capture. I'd been running from that direction for years, always moving away from it. It was the last place I could go without getting caught, and I wasn't about to hand myself over.

But the more I ran East, the closer I came to a problem. Eventually, there would be nowhere left to run. The land would curve, the paths would shrink, and I'd be forced to turn back West. And when that time came, I knew there would be no more avoiding them. I would have nowhere to hide. Nowhere left to go.

Unless, of course, I was caught before then.

I didn't think about that. I couldn't afford to. The only thing I could focus on was getting out, staying ahead of them, and maybe—just maybe—finding a way to stop running. But as the hours passed and the search got closer, I realized one thing: no matter how far I went, the past was never far behind. And sooner or later, it would catch up with me.

My bag was packed, a careful mix of essentials for the journey ahead—enough money to bribe my way if necessary, a few changes of clothes, some dried food, and enough water to last a few days. I wouldn't have to worry about those things for now. What I did need to worry about was the temperature. It had already begun to dip below forty degrees, a sharp bite in the air that made the harsh winter feel like it was already here. The sky was clouded over, a heavy gray mass that hinted at snowstorms, and the ground was starting to frost over as I stepped outside.

I knew I'd be crossing freezing landscapes soon, the kind of cold that numbs your bones and steals your breath. The thought of it gnawed at me. Hopefully, I could make it far enough East to avoid the worst of it, but as I neared Everwater, there wouldn't be any real escape from the winter. The cold would follow me, like a shadow, until I reached the cliffs of the North. That is, unless I got caught before then.

I was pulled from my thoughts when I heard the sound of voices, hushed but sharp, drifting toward me as I neared the front of the cottage. I stopped dead in my tracks, instinctively letting my hair fall forward to shield my face. My pulse quickened, but I forced myself to remain calm, pressing my back to the wall as I slowly turned my head down. I needed to listen, to gather any information that could give me an edge.

I crouched behind a large pillar near the stairs, hoping they wouldn't spot me, praying that the shadows would conceal me. My breath caught in my throat, muffled by the sudden tension. I didn't dare move, only straining to hear their conversation as it carried across the air, every word a potential clue to the next step in my escape.

"We need six rooms for the next..." one of the voices said, their tone clipped as they spoke to the woman at the check-in counter.

I frowned, wondering why they would need so many rooms. I kept listening, hoping for an answer, and sure enough, it came.

"The King sent us..." another voice, deeper and more commanding, cut in.

My heart skipped a beat, and I froze, the sudden rush of panic threatening to betray my presence. If they were paying attention, they'd hear it—my heartbeat hammering in my chest like a drum. But I held my breath, praying they wouldn't notice.

I dared a quick glance over the pillar, keeping my movements as subtle as possible. I let out a quiet, shaky sigh of relief when I realized they were too preoccupied with the check-in to look my way.

As I scanned them, my eyes quickly picked out the telltale signs of who they were: guards from the castle. The dark uniforms, the insignia of the King stitched onto their shoulders—there was no mistaking it.

I pressed my back against the pillar and strained to hear more. They were talking, yes, but it didn't seem like they were going to give anything up that easily. If the King hadn't told anyone about the purpose of their search, it was unlikely the guards would. Still, I couldn't help but hope—maybe, just maybe, they'd say something I could use.

Swallowing hard, I steeled myself for whatever came next.

"No, we will bring our things in later, we just need the rooms..." The first voice said, its tone smooth but edged with an underlying impatience.

I assumed the lady at the counter must've offered to have their luggage taken to their rooms—nothing out of the ordinary. But, I couldn't help but wonder if there was anything in their bags that might give me the upper hand. Something that could give me a clue about the King's plans... or anything to help get him off my trail. But I knew better than to think I could get anywhere near their luggage without drawing attention. I wasn't willing to risk that kind of exposure.

"Thank you," a new voice cut in, and then the sound of footsteps echoed in the room, approaching my hiding spot.

My heart skipped a beat. I quickly, but carefully, pressed my back against the pillar, feeling the cold stone against my skin. I shifted around it, stepping quietly to the other side, holding my breath as one of the guards walked right in front of me, headed toward the entrance.

I kept my head down, hoping my simple presence in the building would be overlooked. Thankfully, he didn't seem to notice me, his focus was more on whatever task lay ahead. He could've easily assumed I was just another local, though I didn't trust that assumption. It was too easy to slip up in moments like this, but I didn't let my nerves show.

"We..." I snapped back to the conversation, eager to catch any details, but the voices were too muffled. I was too far from the source now to catch every word.

I took a slow step forward, positioning myself closer to the center of the room, where I could hear better without making it obvious I was eavesdropping.

"Nice meeting you," I heard just as two sets of footsteps started to move in my direction.

A wave of anxiety washed over me as I realized the King's guards were already here. They weren't supposed to arrive for at least two more days. The timing didn't add up—either the King had lied about when they would come, or the townspeople had been notified too late to prepare. Either way, it didn't matter now. What mattered was that everything had just gotten ten times harder for me.

Normally, when a town search was called, I was already long gone before the guards even stepped foot inside. From what I'd gathered from other places, the King's men made sure no one left without permission. And if you did manage to get out, you had to be checked—interrogated, really. These days, even that rare chance of slipping by had become almost impossible.

But this time, it was different. They were looking for someone specific—me. If I tried to leave now, they wouldn't just let me go. They'd question me. And if I got caught in that lie, I'd be marked as a target. A bigger one. And that's something I couldn't afford. The last thing I needed was to draw attention to myself, especially now.

The sound of footsteps grew louder, snapping me out of my thoughts. The market was no longer an option—I had to get back to my room, and fast. My heart raced as I ducked into the corridor, moving swiftly but carefully, determined not to draw any attention.

When I reached my room, I didn't waste a second. I darted to the right side of the bed, furthest from the door, and grabbed my bag from where I'd left it. Without hesitating, I swung it open and moved to the closet. My hands moved quickly, grabbing the two outfits I had yet to pack, and shoving them inside along with my tennis shoes. The zipper bit down with a sharp snap, but I didn't pause to check—I needed to keep moving.

I darted to the end table next, yanking open the drawer with a quick motion, my fingers brushing over the cold edge of the book lying inside. I pulled it out and flipped to page sixty-seven, where I had hidden the envelope. It was tucked between the pages like a secret waiting to be uncovered. I didn't hesitate, snatching it and shoving it into the bag with the same speed. The drawer slammed shut with a muffled thud, leaving the book behind as I zipped up my bag, flinging it over my shoulder in one swift motion.

Without a glance back, I stepped toward the door, moving as quietly as possible. I didn't want to risk anyone hearing my footsteps, or worse, seeing me hesitate. A glance over my shoulder could have been enough to alert someone, so I kept my eyes forward, my heart pounding louder than my steps.

The hallway was eerily silent as I passed each door, no voices drifting from within. The guards weren't in sight, and I couldn't help but feel a small sense of relief—at least for now. My shoes barely made a sound on the wooden floor as I made my way to the stairs, the soft creak of the boards beneath my weight the only sign of my movement.

I stopped at the top step, my hand gently touching the worn railing, feeling the grooves and bumps of the wood as I leaned over slightly to listen. No voices. No movement. I took a slow breath, then descended, my steps as light and cautious as I could make them. Every sound around me felt like it could betray me.

As I reached the ground floor, the soft crackle of the fire filled the room, but the place was eerily quiet otherwise. There were no guards in sight. The only figure present was the same concierge I had seen earlier, her back to me as she leaned against the counter. She was engrossed in something, her chestnut brown hair spilling over her shoulder, resting loosely against the counter as she skimmed through a book.

I moved carefully, my eyes flicking between her and the door, making sure not to make a sound. I had no intention of drawing attention, but as I approached, something about her caught my eye. Her sleeve shifted, revealing a tattoo peeking just beneath the fabric. It was only a flash of it—two sticks overlapping each other—but that was all I needed. It was enough to make me stop for a brief moment and process what it meant.

She must've sensed my gaze because she snapped her book shut as soon as our eyes met. Her posture straightened instantly, and she placed the book aside with a small, almost calculated motion. Pulling her sleeves down to cover her arm, she asked, "Can I help you with something?"

I didn't answer her. Instead, I walked past, making sure to pause just before leaving. Without breaking my stride, I flicked the keys onto the counter. She caught them effortlessly, her eyes sharp—until her sleeve fell back for just a moment. In that instant, I saw it: the tattoo. Two sticks, overlapping like a crisscrossed pair of twigs.

Her hand jerked back, pulling the sleeve down hastily, her confusion masked but not quite convincing. Her gaze flickered between me and the keys, and for a split second, I caught something in her eyes—a knowing. But I didn't give her a chance to question me.

I locked eyes with her briefly, not enough to give her a chance to speak, before turning on my heel and heading straight for the door.

The chill of the morning air hit me as soon as I opened it, but I didn't waste a moment. I stepped out, pausing for just a heartbeat to check the street. I scanned both directions, looking for any signs of trouble. Seeing nothing, I moved swiftly into the cold, making sure I wasn't followed.

I kept my gaze fixed ahead, walking steadily toward the forest at the edge of town, deliberately avoiding the market. Not a single glance backward. My hood slid up over my head, and I let my hair spill forward, covering my face to shield myself from any curious onlookers—if there were any awake this early. I couldn't be sure, but I guessed the guards, now settled into their rooms, would either be resting or discussing how to carry out the search. Still, I wasn't entirely certain of that assumption.

As I moved forward, the wind picked up, sending leaves tumbling and swirling through the streets like ghosts in search of an escape. The town itself felt like a shadow of its former self, its buildings hunched and weary, as if the weight of years had begun to take its toll. The wood on the homes was chipped and weathered, the paint flaking like peeling skin. Dirt and weeds crawled up the sides of the buildings, a quiet rebellion against the neglect they had suffered. The streets were empty, save for the occasional scurrying leaf, and the air felt too still—too heavy.

I glanced around, my eyes scanning the desolate streets, searching for any sign of life. No movement, no voices, just silence. No one to see me, no one to stop me. My heart gave a small thud of relief. I pressed on, my footsteps the only sound now.

It was a relief, but also... unsettling. On one hand, it meant I could keep moving without interruption. No one would question me, no one would stop me. But on the other hand, I couldn't shake the feeling that something was wrong. The stillness could be an advantage... or it could be a trap. I wasn't naive enough to believe the guards weren't watching. Even now, they could be lurking, eyes hidden, waiting for someone to slip into their carefully laid snare. The thought of being caught and questioned made my chest tighten.

I'd heard a story once that made my skin crawl, and it kept me moving faster than I cared to admit. A wolf, thinking the coast was clear, had slipped out for a run one night, assuming the guards wouldn't be watching. There were no guards in sight, so he figured he had a window of freedom. But the quiet wasn't a blessing. A Rytian guard had appeared out of nowhere, demanding to know what the wolf was doing. The wolf had tried to explain himself, to beg for just a moment of freedom, but it was no use. The town search was underway. No one was allowed to leave.

When the wolf refused to comply, the Rytian guard didn't hesitate. He attacked. I didn't know the details, but the next time anyone saw the wolf, it was too late. His body was drained of blood, unrecognizable. What had once been a living, breathing creature was now nothing but a husk—completely stripped of what made him who he was.

And the King? He didn't care. He called it an example. He said the wolf should've obeyed orders and waited for the search to be over. No remorse, no acknowledgment of the senselessness. He simply buried the story, like everything else, under a blanket of indifference.

But to me, it was one more soul lost—one more death that I couldn't stop, one more death I blamed myself for. Because if I hadn't been on the run, if I hadn't been a target, would that wolf still be alive? Would all these deaths still haunt me?

The silence around me felt suffocating. No one emerged from the shadows to stop me, which made me wonder if I'd somehow slipped under the radar, or if the guards were too distracted by their own tasks. If someone did confront me, I'd have to think fast. I'd need a lie, some excuse to explain why I was heading straight for the forest—the one place no one in their right mind would enter, especially not at a time like this. But I wasn't sure I'd be convincing. Not to a royal guard, especially not now. The forest was a dead giveaway, the last place someone would go unless they were trying to escape. And that's exactly what I was doing.

I was almost at the edge of the woods when I felt it—*the presence* behind me. It wasn't the crunch of footsteps, the rustling of leaves, or even the telltale breath of someone sneaking up behind me. No, it was the feeling of being watched, of someone's gaze digging into the back of my neck. The hairs on my skin stood on end, a chill crawling through my spine as my heart started to race. I didn't need to hear the footsteps to know who it was. A guard. I could feel it, as if his presence had attached itself to me, making every nerve in my body scream.

I froze, instinctively, like prey sensing a predator. But I didn't turn around. I couldn't face whatever was behind me—*not yet.* A few tense seconds passed, thick with the weight of silence, until I heard it: the sound of movement. A low step. The guard had stopped too, and now we were both frozen, caught in a dangerous moment of stillness.

Then, just as I took a shallow breath, his voice cut through the stillness. Low. Gruff. The kind of voice that commanded attention and respect, the kind of voice that belonged to someone who had seen things no one should ever have to see. A royal guard's voice.

"I wouldn't do that if I were you," he said, the words deliberate, carrying the weight of a thousand threats unsaid. "I'm sure you've heard what's beyond those trees."

His steps were slow, measured. Each one brought him closer, and with each step, the air seemed to tighten around me. I could feel my muscles coil with tension, my body instinctively bracing for something I couldn't quite name.

"We wouldn't want you to get yourself killed, now, would we?" he added, his tone still cool, though with an edge that hinted at something darker. I didn't need to turn around to know the look on his face would be as unmoving as stone—cold, unfeeling, and as blank as the rest of the King's men.

His presence loomed over me like a shadow, so close now that I could almost feel his breath on the back of my neck. I tensed even more, my body rigid, willing myself to stay still. The faintest stir of air brushed past my cheek, and I felt him move a strand of my hair. The sensation sent a tremor down my spine, a strange, electric shock that left my skin tingling in a way I didn't know how to react to.

Still, I refused to turn around. I couldn't risk it—not when a single glance could give him something to hold on to, something to recognize me by later. I couldn't afford to be recognized. Not now. Not ever.

I didn't answer. If I did, the truth would have slipped out—that I knew exactly what lay beyond those trees. I could feel the scar that ran across my nose and through my eye, the constant reminder of what I'd survived. But I kept my silence, nodding slightly, my gaze fixed firmly on the ground, letting my hair fall more fully over my face, shielding it from his view.

I couldn't afford to reveal anything more.

"Good." He said before he continued again, "Now why don't you turn around, drop the hood, and explain to me why someone such as yourself is trying to go on a suicide mission into that forest?" he all but commanded me, his voice somehow getting rougher than it was before.

Despite his words, I couldn't bring myself to turn around. I wouldn't. The forest ahead was my only way out, my only chance, but even that was no longer certain. I inhaled deeply, bracing myself for the inevitable.

But before I could move, he grabbed me, turning me around so suddenly that my hood fell from my head. The cold night air hit my skin, and I gasped, the sharp sound escaping before I could stop it.

I couldn't control my reflexes, and my eyes betrayed me. They shot upward, locking onto him. For a split second, I forgot to breathe. His face was so close—too close. My heart hammered in my chest as my hair cascaded down around my face, falling away and exposing me completely. I took an instinctive step back, but we were too close. His presence loomed over me, his nose almost brushing mine.

The world seemed to pause at that moment.

Neither of us moved, neither of us spoke. The only sound was the breeze weaving through the leaves, stirring the air around us. We just stood there, staring, an invisible tension hanging between us, thick and unspoken. I could feel the heat of his breath, the weight of his gaze, but I couldn't look away.

It was as if time had frozen, leaving only the space between us, fragile and full of unspoken understanding.

Chapter 3

What I saw when I looked at him sent a chill racing down my spine. He wasn't just any guard—I could feel it. He could've passed for one, maybe, but something about him felt different. A griffin, I realized, as I studied him closely.

The man stood a full foot taller than me, his posture rigid and commanding. His guard uniform was standard, but instead of stripes down the sides of his jacket, there were stars. The unmistakable mark of a royal guard. My suspicion was confirmed. He was no ordinary soldier.

His curly brown hair, wild and untamed, hung just low enough to cover his eyebrows, in desperate need of a trim. His face remained unreadable, a blank mask, as his dark eyes scanned me from the jagged line of my scar down to the worn tips of my shoes. I couldn't help but mirror his gaze, my eyes sweeping over him in return.

His boots were spotless, gleaming despite the dirt that clung to everything else around us. I couldn't help but wonder how that was possible. Mine were already caked with dust from the road. But his? Perfectly clean. It only took a moment to connect the dots: *he's been flying*. He had to have been, watching from above, making sure no one slipped out of town unnoticed. And I was leaving. Which meant, I assumed, he was here to stop me.

Finally lifting my gaze to meet his, I caught him staring at me with wide eyes. For a moment, his mouth opened and closed, but no words came. It wasn't the first time I'd seen that expression. People who weren't used to me often reacted this way—whether it was the strange scar, the odd way I carried myself, or just the way I looked. Most of the time, it was from food vendors or innkeepers, their faces frozen in surprise when they first laid eyes on me.

I knew the shock wouldn't fade quickly, and I wasn't about to give him the chance to recover. With a quick shift, I turned on my heel and sprinted into the forest, the sound of my boots pounding against the ground as I made a break for it. I didn't look back. All I cared about was getting out alive, and hoping I could do it without a single scratch.

"Come back here!" he yelled out, but I chose to ignore him. "If you don't come back, you won't appreciate the consequences for it later!" I heard him shout again.

I didn't slow my pace until his voice became a mere murmur, lost in the distance. Only then did I allow myself a quick glance back. No guards. No pursuit. He wasn't following me—not immediately, anyway. Either he'd decided against chasing me into the forest, or he was waiting for backup, calculating his next move.

The forest itself felt suffocating, the towering trees closing in as I pushed further into the shadows. The Bloodthorn Forest. A name that carried weight, a place known for its dark history—a history that stretched back long before the events that had unfolded in my lifetime.

The old books I'd read when I was younger spoke of a world before this one, a peaceful place where people had the right to vote, to shape their own destinies. At the time, I'd found it hard to believe. It seemed so distant, almost like a fairy tale. But now, looking at the forest's endless darkness, I wished that world still existed.

But, of course, all good things come to an end. The world froze over, leaving a wasteland in its wake. Almost everything was wiped out, save for a small country that remained untouched, preserved like a forgotten relic of the past.

And that's when it all changed.

The Bloodthorn Forest didn't exist then, not in the way it did now. It came long after the devastation, after the first King had claimed his throne and named the land. The King was a visionary in many ways, establishing laws and rules that were meant to create order—something that, at the time, seemed almost too hopeful to be true.

Under his rule, every village had a lord, someone to govern and hear the people's voices. A noble idea, one that I longed for even now. But things had gone terribly wrong, and it started with the King's first council meeting.

All the Lords were gathered, save for one. A village Lord, missing, absent from the meeting. Concerned, the King had sent guards to check on him. When they arrived at the village, the people had found the Lord's body torn apart, mutilated in the forest.

From that moment, no one ventured into the Bloodthorn Forest at night. Fear gripped every heart. The creatures that had killed the Lord—whatever they were—were still there, waiting. And the people weren't wrong to fear.

The forest was a place of death, a place where no one truly returned unscathed. The longer I ran through it, the more I could feel its darkness closing in around me.

And I guess they weren't wrong. The last time I entered this forest, I barely made it out alive. The creatures that lurked in the shadows left their mark on me—a scar that ran down my face, a permanent reminder of how close I came to never seeing the light of day again.

Eventually, I made it far enough to where I couldn't see where I had entered from. Luckily, I knew where I did, as all I needed to do was turn around and go back the way I came. However I wouldn't be doing that, so it didn't matter. Regardless, if I was unsure of where I was, it wouldn't take me too long to find a way out of the forest.

I slowed down to a walking pace and began walking, being extra cautious as I knew it'd be getting dark later in the day and I'd need to find a good place to stay overnight. This time, I wouldn't be stupid and sleep in the open. That cost me too much last time.

Too much.

As I walked, I took in my surroundings and listened to the birds chirping and the wind blowing. It blew the leaves from the trees as well as the leaves that were already on the floor away into the vast forest. It was almost peaceful... too peaceful.

I wasn't sure what lived in these woods; no one truly did. All anyone knew was that whatever it was, it was bloodthirsty and had no tolerance for trespassers. I couldn't blame it, though. The last time someone entered *my* home, they killed everyone except me. To this day, they're still hunting me, and I still don't know why.

I froze, a sudden realization crawling up my spine. I turned to look back the way I came, but everything seemed the same. No movement. No sign of anyone following. A breath I didn't know I was holding escaped me.

I continued walking, my mind racing. How could I have been so careless? The guards had come to search the town—obviously for something, or someone, in particular. I should've stayed in my room, found another way to slip out, and avoided risking everything.

That guy. That damn guard... *if* he was a guard. I still hoped I was wrong. But he had to be from the castle, that much was clear. What mattered more was that he saw me. He knew what I looked like, which could spell disaster if he decided to go back and report it.

I cursed under my breath. They were searching for someone. If they put it together, I'd be the obvious suspect—the idiot who ran into the forest instead of staying put. If that guard had any brains, he'd figure it out and follow the trail. Or worse, gather the rest of the guards and bring them after me.

I clenched my fists in frustration. *Please don't tell anyone,* I thought. *Please let it go.* If he had any sense of self-preservation—his job, his family—he'd keep quiet. There was no reason to risk his neck over a runaway girl. At least, that's what I told myself. I couldn't afford for him to raise an alarm. If he kept his mouth shut long enough for me to slip into the next town... then maybe, just maybe, I could stay one step ahead.

I forced myself to believe the search would die down soon, that the guards wouldn't bother continuing it, especially now that they were here. *But what if I'm wrong?*

Releasing a heavy sigh, I tried to push away the swirling panic in my chest as I continued walking. My mind was so clouded with thoughts that I didn't notice the thick tree root in front of me. Before I could react, my foot caught on it, and I pitched forward.

I landed hard on my hands and knees, the impact sharp and sudden. I quickly adjusted my posture to catch myself before I could get mud on my clothes, but when I looked down, I saw the bottom of my dress completely caked in dirt.

"Seriously?" I whispered, frustration bubbling up in my chest. As if things couldn't get any worse.

I closed my eyes for a moment, took in two deep breaths, and exhaled slowly, trying to center myself. No time for frustration. No time for distractions.

Opening my eyes again, I rolled over to sit on the ground, facing the tree root that had tripped me. The sight of it made my stomach churn. The root was smeared with dried blood, patches of animal fur stuck to it like a sickening reminder of the forest's dangers. Moss had started creeping up its sides, adding a layer of decay to the grotesque scene. I fought back the bile rising in my throat, quickly turning my head away and pushing myself to my feet.

I straightened my dress, brushed off the dirt from my hands, and adjusted my bag. With one last glance at the twisted root, I forced myself to move forward, making sure to keep my attention sharp this time. No more distractions. The last thing I needed was another misstep.

I focused on walking, my mind drifting between the need to find shelter and the urgency of locating a source of water. I couldn't ignore the dried mud on my hands and forehead, but I knew it would have to wait until I found a river or lake to clean off. For now, I had to stay focused on survival.

As I walked, I scanned the area for any sign of shelter—something to protect me before nightfall. The forest seemed endless, the trees thick and dense, and I knew I couldn't risk waiting until it got dark to figure out where I was going to sleep. The sinking sun only added to my unease, the light already beginning to fade.

I glanced up, my stomach tight as I saw the sun starting to dip below the horizon. My nerves tightened. I needed to find somewhere to settle soon, before the night fully arrived. The forest was full of dangers I'd rather not face in the dark.

A few hours had passed since I entered the forest, and the sun was sinking lower in the sky, casting long shadows that stretched across the dense underbrush. The chill of evening was settling in, and my heart quickened as I realized how much time had slipped away. I hadn't found shelter, and the night was coming fast. A wave of panic washed over me, but I fought it down, refusing to let my fear control me.

I couldn't afford to waste time. The creatures that roamed this forest didn't follow a schedule, but one thing was certain: they were always hungry. I shuddered at the thought, remembering the last time I'd stumbled through these trees, nearly torn to pieces. I had to keep moving. Maybe, just maybe, I'd get lucky and avoid them tonight.

I came across a small watering hole a little while back, but the hairs on the back of my neck prickled as I looked at it. There was no way I was going near it, not with the chance of something lurking beneath the surface, waiting for the first sign of movement. So, I turned my attention to the ground. I dug my hands into the soft earth, pushing dirt aside until I hit a small trickle of water. It wasn't much, but it was enough to rinse my hands, scraping away the dried mud. I splashed my face too, the cold water stinging my skin, but I didn't care. At least I could breathe again, even if only for a moment.

The sun was almost gone now, leaving behind only the last remnants of light, and with it, the first bite of night's cold. I stood there for a moment, my gaze darting around, searching for any sign of a place to rest. But there was nothing. Just endless trees, twisted and gnarled, like something out of a nightmare. I clenched my fists, frustration and dread tightening my chest as I took a step forward.

Every creak of a branch, every rustle of leaves, felt like the forest was closing in on me. I couldn't shake the feeling that something—someone—was watching. My breath quickened, my pulse thrumming in my ears. Sweat dripped down my forehead, mingling with the dirt on my face, and for a moment, I stood frozen, scanning the darkening woods for any sign of movement.

But there was nothing.

I swallowed hard and took another step. I had to keep moving.

Just as I went to take another step, the unmistakable snap of a twig echoed through the silence, followed by the rustling of bushes. Goosebumps prickled my arms as the hair on the back of my neck stood up. The forest fell completely silent. My breath caught, and I cursed under my breath, my heart thumping against my ribcage. Without hesitation, I bolted forward, sprinting as fast as I could, desperate to put as much distance between myself and whatever was lurking behind me.

I didn't need to look back. The sharp, rhythmic sound of heavy footsteps was enough to tell me everything. Something was chasing me. The crickets, the birds—all of it had gone silent. I could feel the presence of whatever hunted me, growing closer with every step I took. My legs burned, but I pushed harder, adrenaline fueling my flight. The sound of whatever was behind me was deafening, closing in with every breath I drew.

I wasn't going to make it. Not if I couldn't outrun it. My only hope was the trees, the thick underbrush, but the forest was vast and unforgiving. And worse, it seemed to feed off the fear that thrummed in my veins.

These creatures didn't care about the chase; they thrived on it. They wanted the hunt, the struggle. They wanted the terror in your blood.

The wind, which had been light moments ago, turned against me now, gusting in my face, slowing me down. My breath came in ragged gasps, and I had to blink rapidly, fighting the sting in my eyes as the wind dried them out. The branches seemed to reach out of nowhere, scratching at my arms, my face. I hissed every time they cut into me, the sharp pain only driving me to move faster, but it was useless.

I leapt over fallen branches, dodged around jagged rocks, anything to try and slow the pursuit. But no matter how fast I pushed, I could still feel it gaining on me, the hot breath of the beast on my neck, almost a physical presence. Each breath it took was closer to me, as if it could taste the air around me, waiting for the moment to strike.

The branches continued to tear at my skin, leaving thin trails of blood on my arms. I could feel it, the sting of open wounds, but there was no time to stop. Every part of me screamed to keep running, to get away, but my strength was beginning to wane.

Then, I heard it—a sound from behind me, something like a snort, deep and guttural. It made my blood run cold. The creature was still right there.

The snorting continued, almost mocking in its rhythm, as if the creature was amused by the chase. In most cases, I'd think it could've been. After all, no one was dumb enough to venture into the heart of the forest. It was a death sentence, and the stories people told about it—well, they were often exaggerated, twisted to entertain or terrify. But there was truth in some of them. You could tell when the stories were real: when the storyteller's face grew pale, or they wore scars to prove the dangers were more than just words.

I snapped out of my thoughts when I heard the pained cry of an animal to my right. The sound of hooves thundering through the underbrush followed, a desperate scramble for survival. A deer, probably. But I didn't look. I couldn't afford to. There was no chance I could save it, and stopping for even a second would only give the creatures a chance to catch me. It pained me, deep in my gut, knowing I couldn't help. But the reality was that if I tried, I'd be another carcass for them to feast on.

The wind shifted, carrying the sharp stench of decay and rotting wood. The smell hit me like a physical blow, almost making me stop and vomit right there. But I couldn't. I couldn't stop—not now, not ever. Sweat stung my eyes, blurring my vision as it dripped down my face. Every breath felt like I was inhaling fire, my lungs burning from the effort, but there was no time to slow down.

I barely had time to focus again when a large boulder loomed ahead. My heart dropped, panic surging, but before I could crash into it, an arm shot out from the trees, grabbing me by the waist and yanking me to the side. My shriek echoed in the air, surprise and fear taking over my senses. The impact of the creatures crashing into the boulder was deafening behind me, but I didn't have time to process it. I was being pulled faster than I'd ever run, stumbling over tree roots, my legs giving out from exhaustion. Whoever was dragging me was moving at a pace I couldn't match, but they weren't stopping.

I didn't know where we were going, only that I had to trust whoever this was. My heart raced as we cut through the trees, faster and faster, the sound of the creatures fading behind us, but not enough to ease the terror that gripped my chest. Finally, we skidded to a halt, and I was thrust into what seemed like a hidden cave. Thick vines hung over the entrance, tangled with moss and flowers, almost making it invisible to anything or anyone passing by.

The guy who grabbed me shoved me roughly against the jagged wall of the cave, and before I could even think of protesting, his hand shot up to cover my mouth. His finger pressed against my lips, shushing me with a quiet, urgent command. Instinctively, I held my breath, forcing myself to stand as still as possible. My heart hammered in my chest, and I could feel the adrenaline surging, making it hard to stay quiet.

Outside, I saw shadows moving past the cave entrance, and I tensed, every muscle coiled with the instinct to flee. I squeezed my eyes shut, praying they wouldn't notice us, willing myself to remain silent. The sound of heavy footsteps grew faint as the shadows passed, and I could feel his hand lift from my mouth.

The moment he gave me the signal, I didn't wait another second. I doubled over, my hands bracing against my knees as I sucked in ragged breaths. My chest burned, and I couldn't stop shaking. My dress was a mess—torn in several places, the fabric torn at the hem and stained with dirt and blood. My hair was tangled, a mix of leaves, twigs, and sweat sticking to my skin. I couldn't remember the last time I'd felt so out of control, so raw.

"Come on, we need to keep going or they're going to find us." the guy said as he turned to look at the entrance of the cave seeing shadows and gurgles of the monsters from outside it. "If that happens, then we'll be even more fucked than we already are right now," he finished in a worried tone before turning and walking back towards me.

In all honesty, I didn't blame him. Nobody could. If I had gone out of my way to save someone from being crushed into a boulder and then torn apart by the creatures in this forest, I probably wouldn't have done it without fearing that they would then be coming after me, as well. But he did it, which not only confused me but also made me wonder why he would've bothered saving a stranger in the first place. I know I wouldn't have saved someone, especially without having an actual reason; I would have used them as bait to save my own ass at this point.

I nodded my head at him, while still trying to get my breathing under control and put my hand up, raising one finger in response to silently tell him that I needed a minute to breathe.

However, instead of giving me a minute to breathe, I heard him sigh before he decided to grip my arm. He then harshly pulled me forward to follow behind him. He took large steps forward walking in the direction opposite the entrance which caused me to move my head to look around him to see if there was anything ahead of us, but all I could see was darkness.

I looked up and noticed how much taller he was than me — probably a foot or so. I couldn't see any other features on him because of the dark cave. However, what I did know was that I didn't appreciate him gripping my arm. I quickly pulled my arm out of his grip, but once I did, he turned to face me, and he looked pissed. I didn't know why, though; he couldn't just grip my arm and expect me to be okay with it. He went to open his mouth — more than likely shout at me — but before he could, I shouted at him.

"Who the hell do you think you are!" I shouted while rubbing my hand on my wrist that he so harshly grabbed for no reason other than to be an ass.

If I had to guess, I would assume he raised his eyebrows at me and rolled his eyes, crossing his arms in front of him. He was probably shocked and annoyed that I chose to shout at him instead of thanking him for saving me. I was right, or at least, I thought I was because as soon as my eyes adjusted to the darkness, I could see that his arms were crossed over his chest and he was staring down at me. It was almost the same look my dad used to give me when I would do something wrong. It would've scared me if I were the same girl I used to be, but now, it was just a look to me.

"I like to think of myself as the guy who saved you from being killed by whatever the fuck those things are," he replied in a calm, collected tone.

I just rolled my eyes and looked over my shoulder to see the entrance of the cave.

"What the hell were you even doing this far out in the forest by yourself this time of night, anyways?" he asked.

I flicked my head back in his direction and looked him in the eyes before shrugging and walking past him. However, I froze when I heard the crackling of the creatures outside as if they were communicating with one another. I jumped in fright when I saw a large disfigured shadow run past the entrance of the cave. I stood frozen watching more of them run by before I heard the cry of another animal.

I heard the guy behind me curse quietly before he gripped my arm again, however this time it was gentle and he pulled softly instead of harshly.

"Come on we need to go before they catch our scent and tear us apart," he stated quietly

This time I turned towards him before going back to the entrance of the cave and nodded. I turned around and walked past him grazing his body with my shoulder.

"You still haven't answered my question about why you were out alone in this forest this late at night?" He asked me again while walking behind me.

I could've asked him the same question if I had wanted, but I chose not to, hoping he'd get the fact that I didn't talk to people I didn't know, or anyone, at that. Not unless I choose to talk to them, at least. He wouldn't be the first to try and talk to me and he most certainly won't be the last, but he is going to be like everyone else and not get a response.

Ignoring him, I decided to take a glance around the cave.

It smelled like wet stone and rotting vegetation, the stench making my nose wrinkle in disgust. I tried to push it away as I walked toward the walls. They were crumbling, small chunks of rock falling away, and dust stuck to my fingers as I touched the surface. I quickly wiped it off on my sleeve, grimacing. The floor was covered in dirt and leaves, likely blown in by the wind or dragged in by animals. As I looked around, I noticed claw marks gouged into the walls—deep, jagged scratches that could've been made by anything from wolves to griffins, or something worse lurking in these woods.

Water dripped down from cracks in the ceiling, landing on my forehead. I wiped it away quickly before it could slide into my eyes, but the cave still felt unsettling, as if it were holding onto more than just dust and memories.

As I continued to walk forward, the guy who dragged me into this cave followed silently behind me. The leaves crunched under our feet and I could hear the faint sounds of animal cries outside of the cave, hopefully somewhere far beyond it, but there was no room for sympathy in me. There never would be again.

Not for a while anyways.

As we continued to walk deeper into the cave, I spotted a small source of light up ahead. I squinted my eyes when the source of light became more noticeable, I began trying to figure out what it could be. I took a deep breath, noticing how the smell of the cave shifted from rotten vegetation to the smell of burnt wood and cooked animals. I turned my head to the guy behind me with a questioning look on my face, but he kept his emotionless front. So, I turned my head back and continued forward until we reached a small fire in the middle of the cave.

I stopped abruptly, as I wasn't sure what to do. I watched as the guy walked around me and sat on the opposite side of where I was standing in front of the fire. He sat down and reached his arms out in front of himself, probably attempting to warm himself up. He looked up at me for a short second before looking back into the fire but mumbled a soft, "Sit."

I took a seat in front of the fire hesitantly and brought my knees to my chest. Still sitting, I let myself drift off into my thoughts and stared directly into the fire, letting it warm my skin. I closed my eyes for a small moment and listened to the crackling sound as the fire continued to burn through the wood. Unfortunately, it didn't last long as the guy on the other side of the fire started to speak again.

"So, are you going to tell me why you're out here alone," he asked making me open my eyes and look towards him. "Or are we just going to sit here watching the fire in silence?" he asked after he noticed me looking at him before he looked up at me.

I looked up at him for a second or two before looking back into the fire, which brought back memories of my home being burned to the ground until it was all ash. Despite the fact that I didn't stay long enough to see all of that, I heard people talking and assumed that my home had been burned down to nothing.

I heard him sigh, which brought me out of those thoughts, but he didn't ask or talk about anything else after that. Instead, he stayed silent and allowed the silence to surround us completely, relaxing me slightly.

I shifted my gaze subtly, raising my eyes just enough to study him without seeming obvious. He was staring into the burning embers of the fire, his expression distant, lost in thought. Unlike me, though, he wasn't sitting on the floor but perched on a rounded piece of oak. His posture was relaxed, but there was something guarded about the way he held himself. He didn't seem to notice that I was watching him, giving me the chance to assess him without interruption.

Why, I wondered, would he bother helping me if he was just going to yell at me afterward? Granted, he had every right to be angry, but the shouting felt more like a reaction than a solution.

I closed my eyes for a moment, letting my thoughts drift away, then reopened them, this time taking in the details of him more carefully. His skin was fair, almost pale, and he carried an air of mystery—like someone who doesn't spend much time under the sun. I couldn't help but think that he was probably from the North, where the days are shorter and the light barely touches the land.

A mark caught my attention, drawing me in closer. A faint, almost imperceptible burn scar on the left side of his neck. I squinted, trying to make out its shape, but it was too subtle to be anything less than intentional, perhaps something he didn't want to talk about. It gave me a sense of who he was: secretive, guarded, and likely untrusting.

But who was I to judge? I certainly wasn't in a position to be handing out opinions. After all, I wasn't planning on discussing the giant scar that ran through my own eye anytime soon.

I squeezed my eyes shut for a moment, trying to shake off the thoughts, before opening them again. I noticed that he was still staring blankly into the fire, his gaze distant, as if his body was here but his mind had wandered far away.

This time, I let my eyes linger on his face. He had a lean, angular structure, with a pointed nose and narrow lips that were set in an unreadable line. His almost-black eyes were upturned, so subtle that they might have gone unnoticed if you weren't paying attention. His shoulder-length hair was straight, dark, and unstyled, hanging loosely behind him, falling off his shoulders. He looked like someone who had stopped caring about how he looked a long time ago.

His arms were toned, his hands large and resting in tight fists on his knees, a sign of his tension, even in stillness. His brown boots covered wide feet, pulled in close to his body as if he were trying to conserve warmth. His clothes were mostly black and loose, rumpled with wrinkles as though they hadn't been washed in days or had been hastily shoved into his bag and pulled out whenever he needed them. He wore a hood over his shirt, made from some rough straw material that seemed to be falling apart in spots, with small holes scattered across it.

It was odd—most people from the North would wear fur to keep themselves warm, but he didn't. That detail sparked an interest in me, and before I even realized it, my theory clicked into place. He wasn't wearing fur because he was likely a wolf. The Abolystic species were the only ones who didn't wear animal pelts—at least, not in the way others did. They saw it as immoral, as a sign of disrespect to the animals they were so connected to.

I barely had time to process this thought before he suddenly stood up, pulling me out of my contemplation. My relaxed state shifted into something more guarded as I watched him walk toward his bag. His movements were deliberate, and as if sensing my gaze on him, he turned his head, catching my eyes for a brief moment. A soft chuckle escaped his lips, and then he turned back to his bag, leaving me to wonder what he found so amusing.

"You know if I wanted to kill you I would have done so by now, you don't need to be so tense." He said as he pulled out what he seemed to be looking for before turning back towards me leaving his bag unzipped.

I watched cautiously as he turned and walked over to where I sat, slowly unwrapping something in his hand. When he was close enough, he held the open wrap out toward me. I glanced at the thing in his hand, then back to his face, but he simply shook his hand as if urging me to take it. Hesitant, I reached out and grabbed it, only to realize it was some type of dried meat, tough and leathery to the touch.

He didn't wait for me to respond. Instead, he turned and walked back to his spot, ripping into the meat with his teeth. I watched him chew through two pieces before he finally looked up at me, his eyes catching mine. He swallowed the last bite, his gaze steady on me, as though waiting for something.

I hadn't touched the meat. I wasn't sure if I should, or if I could stomach it just yet. His eyes lingered, as though he knew exactly what I was thinking.

"It's not gonna kill you ya' know," he said while nodding his head toward the meat in my hand.

He didn't say anything after that and instead turned his attention back to staring at the fire. I looked back and forth between him and the meat before feeling my stomach grumble in hunger as I realized I hadn't eaten since yesterday. I eventually let out a sigh of annoyance and gave in to the hunger and took a hesitant bite out of the dried meat.

Chapter 4

It's been a little over two hours and neither of us has spoken a word to each other. He's been staring into the fire, deep in thought, but every so often I could feel him staring at me, however, I never opened my eyes to stare back. I know he has questions to ask me, some of them being the same questions he's already asked, but he hasn't asked them which I'm grateful for.

After a while, I got tired of feeling his stare on me, so I opened my eyes and looked at him as well until he looked away from me and back into the fire. When he did move his stare back into the fire I let my own eyes drift to the burning embers as well before I eventually felt my eyes droop until they closed completely.

Before falling into complete darkness, I stood up and slowly moved myself away from the fire, and laid down in a more comfortable position. Once comfortable, I continued to watch the fire dance away while the crackling sound surrounded both me and the guy I'm with. When I could no longer keep my eyes open, I allowed them to stay closed until I felt myself drift into darkness and I could no longer hear the crackling sounds of the fire eating its way through the wood and leaves, turning them into ash.

I could only see darkness.

Only the darkness.

I'm finally in my own world, a world of silence. I don't have to try and find any solace. This is my safe place, even if it is only for a few moments. It's still my safe place. There is no smell, no sounds, nothing. Everywhere I look it's just pure blackness with no end.

Everything was fine. No dreams — or nightmares, I guess — about past events, death, or even just images of that room full of blood all over the place, on the walls, ground, windows, or on my hands. It's just quiet; peaceful almost, full of endless darkness that I could walk through for forever without anyone trying to harm me or take me from anyone.

It wasn't like this for a while, unfortunately.

Not even a few minutes into being in the darkness did I begin to hear the whispers, the dreams always start with whispers which would slowly begin to get louder and louder until the whispers became voices; loud, angry voices. I can remember hearing them as a child, but I can't place a face to them. They're always clamoring brutal and violent words at me until I'm begging for them to stop with tears sliding down my face. My eyes would become puffy and bloodshot, but I would continue begging them until the tears eventually dried out. Thankfully I would eventually wake up and once I did they would start to quiet down, but they never went silent, I would still be able to hear them in my head repeating the same words over and over again. Words I wouldn't want anyone to hear. Words that no one should ever have to endure hearing.

I tried to ignore the voices like usual, but it didn't work. The louder they got the harder it was to contain my tears. The words would break me down piece by piece until I was completely shattered. Unfortunately, when I wake up, I'm a new person, a person with the same problems as

I had the day before. The only difference is that I'll be going somewhere different.

I held my hands to my head and covered my ears trying to prevent myself from hearing the words. I'm not sure how much more of these nightmares I can take until I finally reach my breaking point. I just want them all to go away. I need them to go away even if it's only for one night. Only for a moment, that is all I asked, but I never got it. Unfortunately, the yelling continued to get louder, until I could no longer put enough pressure on my ears to keep them from entering my ears. So, I uncovered my ears, and sat down, cradling my legs to my chest with my head on my knees while rocking back and forth begging for them to stop. I start whispering apology after apology after everything they scream at me. Whispering how I agree with them. I want them to quit reminding me of my past. For once I didn't want to think about any of it.

You're a murderer!

"I'm sorry," I whispered in response.

Innocent people died when you should've just been given to the King to end all our suffering!

"I know," I whispered back once again, holding my knees tightly to my chest.

It's all your fault!

No one will ever care about you, not after what you've done!

Everyone you go near ends up dead, you should just kill yourself before anyone else dies!

You let your mother and father get killed only to end up a failure!

"I'm sorry," I whispered again in response with tears pouring down my face as sob after sob racked through my body.

You let innocent children die just so you can run for the rest of your life!

"I'm sorry," I whispered again in response, the tears finally starting to blur my vision and burn through my eyes.

Your mother must be glad she can't see you like this, a murderer, a fugitive running from the King and his guardsmen, a child who can't even outrun a beast without needing help, and a monster who blames people for her own problems!

You're a disappointment to your own people!

"I know!" I screamed out pain laced in my voice. However, it did nothing but make them shout back at me even louder causing me to sob while holding my head.

"Please just stop." I sobbed out while placing my hands back on my ears while rocking back and forth on the ground.

I don't know what the King could possibly want you for!

You should just kill yourself now!

The words they shouted echoed endlessly in my mind, growing louder with each passing second. My body trembled, and soon the tears started flowing uncontrollably, mingling with the frantic gasps of breath as I tried to hold it all in. My face was slick with tears and snot, the sting in my eyes barely registering as I blinked them away, letting the droplets slide down my cheeks, my chin, and drip onto the cold ground below. My chest rose and fell erratically, struggling to keep pace with the desperate sobs that wracked my body.

I screamed, a raw, anguished cry, begging for the voices to stop. But instead of fading, they only grew louder, their words now a relentless, screeching torrent that made my head throb with the intensity. I clamped my hands over my ears, but it was useless—the noise pressed in from all sides, suffocating me.

I collapsed onto my side, curling into myself, my knees drawn tightly to my chest as I sobbed uncontrollably into the suffocating blackness.

I could feel the wetness of my tears soaking into my skin, but it didn't matter. Nothing mattered anymore.

This was just the beginning.

Soon, the ground beneath me would shift, turning into a thick, viscous liquid that would latch onto me, its cold grip pulling me down into the depths. I knew what would come next—how the dark water would fill my lungs, how I would struggle in vain to find air, and how, only when I was fully submerged, gasping for breath in the suffocating darkness, would the voices finally stop. But by then, it would be too late.

And I would wake up, only to find myself right back here.

By this point, I could no longer understand what the voices were saying as it was all jumbled together. All I knew was that it was nothing good, and it never would be anything good.

The tears kept cascading down my cheeks, most likely leaving tear stains that wouldn't even show in the morning. They'd be another internal scar that no one would ever see. No one ever sees the emotional scars. If they did then I'd be able to tell that I'm more than likely not the only person who has issues going on with them, but if someone found out about the scars, I wouldn't hesitate to try and get them out of my life as soon as possible. Mainly because if they know me that much to know about my emotional scars then they'd be the next to die at the King's hands. And I won't allow that, never again.

Suddenly, the voices started to quiet down, not much but enough to where it caused me concern.

This wasn't supposed to happen.

I didn't know what was going on, so I uncovered my ears and wiped the tears from my face. I slowly stood up looking around for any clue on why they finally quieted down a little bit. However everywhere I looked all I saw was darkness. An infinite trail of darkness. The tears were somehow still falling, and I kept swiping them away every so often and sniffling, but that didn't stop me from searching for what caused the voices to go away.

I walked straight ahead of me to see if there was anything that could explain the sudden quietness, but there was nothing. Though even if there was something, I wouldn't have been able to see it anyways.

But then I heard it. A new voice. One that I've heard before, but not one that has ever really shouted at me and told me everything was my fault. No, this voice was soft, yet demanding. I just don't know how to explain it.

Don't listen to those voices Sephy. They're just lying to you and saying things in an attempt to break you down. They're not real. It's just in your head.

I fell back in shock at the voice as I had never heard it in my head before. I knew it was a voice I recognized from my lifetime, but I wasn't sure who it was as it could be anyone's voice.

I didn't understand what the voice meant when it said, 'It's just in my head,' because if that were true then the voice talking now would also be in my head and could be lying to me right now. Trying to make me smile or be even the slightest bit happy only to allow the other voices to rise again and break down my walls. If only I could just place the voice, I would know who it is and maybe trust them but I'm not sure who the voice is. And it's frustrating.

As I sat on the ground thinking about whose voice the voice belonged to, it spoke again.

You need to fight Sephy. Fight and never stop. Live your best life even if you get caught. But never, EVER listen to those voices.

I didn't know what to do here. So, I just decide to respond back to the voice in the only way I really can.

"Who are you and what do you want?" I shouted back to the new voice, my voice sounding raspy from all the crying.

The voice didn't answer right away, so I feared that it left and would allow the others to come back to hurt me again. But nothing happened. The voices didn't come back.

I'm no one you need to worry about, all I want is for you to wake up, fight, and release yourself from the past and all the pain it has caused.

I wanted to let go of everything the voice had said, but I couldn't. I couldn't just forget all of it, not now. I was the only one left who still remembered them—the people who had come before me, the ones I couldn't save. How could I leave them behind? How could I abandon their memories, their pain, their lives? Letting go would mean erasing everything I had fought for, everything I had suffered. It would be like erasing twelve years of my life, like the past didn't matter.

Without that pain, without the heartbreak and sorrow, I would be nothing. I would be no different from the King—the same as him. A monster who had caused destruction but felt nothing, not even remorse. I could never see myself as that kind of person, a hollow shell who didn't care. The weight of my memories, painful as they were, were still mine. I couldn't turn my back on them, even if it hurt.

After the voice's words echoed into silence, I sat alone, waiting for the flood of other voices to return, but they didn't. The silence stretched on, and with it, my thoughts began to spiral. I thought about everything that had led me here. About the guard I had crossed paths with only hours ago, and the dangers that awaited me if they found me. The thought of being caught terrified me, but I couldn't escape it. It was inevitable, wasn't it?

But there was one thing I never allowed myself to think about—freedom. Because deep down, I knew it was out of reach. I knew I would never get it. Not on my own. And I would never allow anyone else to help me either. So I resigned myself to the truth: freedom would always remain a distant dream, just beyond my grasp.

Still, I couldn't help but reflect on the voice's words. What would it be like if I did what it wanted? If I let go of everything and gave in? The thought of surrendering to the King crossed my mind. I could finally learn what it was he wanted from me—the thing I had been trying to understand for so long. But at what cost? Would I end up dead, just like I feared?

The more I thought about it, the more I realized that either way, the King had something planned. Maybe he was plotting against us all, maybe that's why the Lord in my village had been killed. Maybe it was all part of his plan to destroy us. But that didn't matter right now. What mattered was the choice I had to make.

Eventually, after sitting in the dark, alone and quiet, I knew what I had to do. I would listen to the voice. It was time to wake up. But even though I knew I had to wake up, I knew I would keep fighting. I couldn't stop running, couldn't stop surviving.

Still, something about the voice felt different. I wasn't sure if it was trying to lead me somewhere or if it was just my mind trying to pull me out of this void. Either way, I couldn't let them catch me, not like that. I would fight if they did, no matter what. If they came for me, I would fight back. I would make sure they couldn't take me without a fight.

With one last breath, I closed my eyes, and let myself fall back. Hoping that when I opened them again, I would be back in the cave. Wherever I woke up, I would fight. Because that's all I knew how to do.

Chapter 5

I woke up to the sound of shuffling and quickly sat up alert, looking around only to notice how I was still in the cave. I let out a breath and rubbed the sleep out of my eyes before standing up. I looked around and saw the guy from last night sleeping as comfortably as he could on the cave floor. I assume the shuffling sound was him shifting around to get more comfortable and sleep better.

His arm was draped over his face and his hair was a little tangled but not much considering he had tied it back before going to sleep. His breathing was evened out so I knew I didn't need to worry about having to sneak out with him being awake or about him following along with me. I looked over to the fire and saw that it had been put out. I don't recall it going out, but I guess he put it out after I had fallen asleep, or maybe he just continued to watch the wood burn in utter silence whilst listening to the faint sound of water droplets hitting the ground while I slept.

I shook my head from those thoughts and let out a silent breath, grateful that he was asleep and that I could leave before he woke up. I hurried over to where I had placed my bag and threw it over my shoulder, but not before checking it to make sure everything was inside of it. After

I did so I turned around only to let out a yelp in surprise as the guy was standing right in front of me with his arms crossed looking down at me blankly. Well, he looked at me like I was an idiot, which I guess in this case to him I probably am, but he doesn't know me or what my life is like so he can screw off for all I care.

I looked up at him with a blank look on my face as neither of us said anything. I thought about how he had snuck up behind me without me noticing, as I'm almost always on high alert. It made me think that I had let my guard down when I noticed he was sleeping knowing he wouldn't be able to hurt me or alert the castle guards of where I am if he was working with them. Which reminded me that I need to get to the other side of the forest before they do.

"You're not seriously going back out there alone, are you?" He asked in a tired yet stern tone.

It caused me to come out of my thoughts, but I didn't respond, instead, I looked over at him. I noticed how he had heavy bags under his eyes as if he hadn't slept in a while which made me wonder what time he fell asleep last night. I noticed how even the look in his eyes seemed exhausted and how his body language radiated off how tired he was, but he tried hard not to show it.

I rolled my eyes and pushed past him only being able to take a couple of steps before he gripped my arm once again which caused me to freeze. He has no right, not a single right to grab me. No right to stop me from leaving. It's my own choice and if he doesn't like it then that's his own problem. He doesn't know me and I sure as hell don't know him.

I took a deep breath to stay calm, but when I felt his grip tighten I lost control and turned around quickly. I kicked him with my right leg and pulled my arm out of his hold, as he grunted in pain while holding his chest where I kicked him at.

"Don't touch me again," I stated in a flat threatening tone.

I then turned the other way and continued to walk out of the cave so that I can hopefully make it out of this forest. I did not want to spend another night worrying about if I'll live or if the bloodthirsty creatures will eat me.

When I reached the exit of the cave I walked through the thick vines that were hiding the cave from the creatures, and looked to see what the outside of the cave looked like. On the outside, it's covered in bright green moss with tree vines going up and down both the left and right sides of the cave. The tree vines were twisting into each other causing knots to sprout like your hair after you've slept or when you don't brush it for a certain amount of time. The moss was everywhere, dangling off the tree vines, sticking to the sides and edges of the cave on both the inside and outside, and laying on the ground in front of the cave. The moss also went into the cave where all the leaves lay.

The wind was blowing, not harshly, but still enough to make it chilly enough to need a coat or shawl which thankfully I have. The wind blew my way, and I could faintly smell the stench of blood and rotting flesh, but I ignored it and walked to the right. I lifted my hood to avoid getting my hair in my face. I walked for a while in complete silence only being able to hear birds chirping back and forth as well as the sound of frogs croaking in the far distance before I heard leaves crunching behind me. I froze for a second knowing I was being followed.

Once I realized I was being followed I moved over to hide behind a tree and waited for the person to pass by so I could attack. I heard the crunching of leaves start to get louder and closer until it finally stopped. I held my breath hoping they would pass by. I heard the shuffle of leaves, and I knew that the person was turning in multiple directions, probably confused about my sudden disappearance, but I still didn't move from my spot. I heard the person let out a sigh before they finally started walking again, this time they did walk past me which gave me the upper hand.

I slowly moved from my spot behind the tree, making sure to avoid stepping on any of the leaves. When I went to lunge at them they swiftly turned around shocking me as they pinned me to the ground. One hand was wrapped around my throat whilst the other was holding them up. One of their knees was between my legs right at my knees and the other was on the outside of my right leg keeping themselves stable. My vision had gone blurry when my head hit the ground but thankfully it came back quickly. When I saw who had pinned me to the ground I couldn't help but feel enraged.

"What the hell is wrong with you!" I shouted at him as soon as I realized it was the same guy from the cave.

"What's wrong with me, you tried to attack me when I wasn't looking. Do you have any idea how rude that is?" He asked in a slightly angry tone, but I could hear a little amusement laced in his voice. I could also see a little mischief in his eyes when he spoke.

"Well sorry, I just wanted to make sure the person following me wasn't someone trying to kill me!" I replied in a snarky way while rolling my eyes.

"Believe me if I wanted to kill you I wouldn't have saved you when those creatures were chasing you." He replied in the same tone I used on him.

"Great, now do you mind getting off of me?" I asked in a demanding yet bored tone, so he knows that I wasn't messing around. I didn't want to be in this forest any longer than I need to be.

He stared at me for a few moments before rolling his eyes and standing up. Once he was up he stretched his hand out to help me, but I simply ignored it and stood up on my own. He scoffed at me doing so before lowering his hand and crossing his arms over his chest. Once up, I dusted myself off before walking past him to get to the next town faster.

I heard him sigh behind me but within seconds he was beside me, he kept quiet which I appreciate. Fortunately, we stayed like that for a while.

"So little traveler where are we headed?" He asked as he continued to walk in step with me. I chose to ignore him seeing as once I get to where I'm headed, I'll be able to lose him and find somewhere else to go.

Once he realized I wasn't going to respond to his questions, he tried a different approach. I'll admit it's a good one, but it still won't work on me.

"Well then, my name is Barric, I'm from Amiheathen." He said while turning around and walking backward while looking at me.

I glanced at him for a moment before looking straight again, I knew he was from somewhere up North but now that I know he is, he just gave me an even bigger reason to lose him.

"My parents kicked me out because I was, according to them, an 'unnatural beast'." He admitted with a sigh before turning back around and walking in step with me at my side.

What he said caught my attention, but then he continued when he noticed I wasn't going to say anything.

"Though I find that quite rude, I decided I wouldn't stay in town, so I left. I didn't look back because there was nothing to look back to. And now I'm here." He let out another breath before continuing again, "I stayed in Mavill for about a week before setting off somewhere else, and well here I am now walking in the one forest that I could quite possibly end up dead in, with a girl who I don't even know the name of." And with that, he finished the summary of his life.

I felt bad for him, but I don't understand why his parents would kick him out for being a wolf considering his parents themselves also had to be wolves. I could tell in his speech that he wasn't being completely truthful about why he left his home, however, I wasn't going to ask him about it. I could tell that he was hinting at the fact that he doesn't know my name in an attempt to get me to tell him my name, but I'm not giving up my name to someone who could quite frankly be part of the royal crew and fuck me over. I'm not sure why he told me his life story, it sure did pass the time, even if it all was a big fat lie anyways.

When he mentioned being an 'unnatural beast' I knew he was a wolf, but I don't understand why his parents would call him one especially if they're both wolves as well. Nevertheless, I know that since he's alone and in the middle of the forest, it would be safe to assume he's either rogue or a lone wolf. Either way, I don't care enough to pity him in any way. But I wonder why his parents would kick him out as the only way he could be a wolf would be if his parents are wolves, so it doesn't make sense to me. Regardless, it's not my business to know if he doesn't wish for me to know, just like I don't want him to know why I'm even out in this forest.

Every so often I could see him looking at me with curiosity, however, I wasn't sure if it was for me not telling him my name or if he could sense that I knew he was lying and I didn't ask him about it. Unfortunately for him, his next question gave me the answer that I needed.

"So, what's your name? You know since I told you mine and every-thing." He asked while trying to make it reasonable as to why he should know my name. But I ignored him once again.

It was reasonable for him to want to know my name, but he isn't the first person to come up with a good reason to want to know it and he won't be the last. Especially not if the guards end up catching me. The last person to say my true name was my dad on the night the massacre happened. Other than that, it was a short nickname I had given myself that everyone called me in my hometown and fake names I used when booking a room to stay in at cottages.

I decided after a while to give in because his staring is bothering the hell out of me, and it needs to stop.

"I'm sorry your family kicked you out Barric, but I'm not a person you would want to be around so as soon as we get to wherever we're headed we need to go separate ways," I responded with an emotionless voice, not bothering to even glance at him because quite frankly I don't need to look at him to know his face shows complete shock and utter confusion.

He stopped walking a few seconds after he registered what I said, but I didn't care. I'm used to being alone, so I continued walking onward. The sun was completely up in the sky shining brightly down on my fair skin so it gave me options on what the time could be now.

After a few moments, Barric came running back up to me and slowed down to match my walking pace again.

I'm not going to tell him to leave because one I told him what was going to happen, two I don't like repeating myself, and three he can make his own decisions just like I made my own decision to not make any new friends or stay in one spot for too long.

"I think I'll stick with you for the time being. Try and get to know as much as I can about you." He said while glancing at me before continuing, "Though that may be difficult from what I've already figured out within the few hours of being around you, I am up for the challenge." Barric admitted with excitement laced in his voice as we walked on.

I glanced over at him looking him up and down before rolling my eyes in response. If it wasn't for the fact that he's alone as well as the fact that I could almost smell the wolf radiating off of him, I would assume that he's a spy that the King sent out. Fortunately, I doubt that the King would send one of his guards out into this forest. Not unless he didn't care if they died or not.

"Whatever works for you bud." I sarcastically responded in a low voice hoping he wouldn't hear it.

Unfortunately, he did hear it, and he gave a low chuckle in response causing my cheeks to redden in response. It shocked me because usually when I whisper no one hears it, so it works when I need to talk to myself to think things out. Though I guess since he's half beast it makes more sense, I'm never usually around wolves. Although I do recall how my dad was always able to hear what I said too, sometimes he even used to laugh about the things I would mumble which always confused Mom and embarrassed me. So I assume it's a wolf thing and they can hear anything and everything which sucks for me right now.

He didn't respond or say anything about my blushed cheeks or about what I said. Instead, he stayed quiet and we walked onward hoping that we would both make it out of this forest alive.

Barric and I have been walking for a while, and all that could be heard was the sound of leaves being crushed from under our feet and the croaks of the frogs in a far-off distance. Once and a while I would turn my head to the left and see the fur of a deer sticking to logs or tree trunks with flies flying around it. It caused me to turn my head back so I wouldn't have to look at it as it made me feel sick.

I looked up at the sky and I could tell that the sun was starting to set but it wasn't too late so I assume that it was probably around mid-afternoon.

We continued walking but after a few steps, I could hear the faint sound of water flowing causing me to stop walking. Barric had also stopped walking with me and turned towards me while raising his eyebrows in question. I raised my hand to my ear in response as if to say 'listen' and I guess he did since he turned his head to the right nodding his head before walking in that direction. We walked for a while and as we walked the sounds became more noticeable. Before we knew it we came across a small stream of fast-moving water.

Figuring it was either following the stream to the closest town or taking the risk of staying another night in this forest, we chose to follow it hoping it would lead us to the source. Thankfully after a couple of minutes of following it, it led us straight to a waterfall surrounded by rocks, trees, and a small patch of grass.

The water was crystal clear, and I could see the different colored fish swimming around inside it. The waterfall created a large cloud of mist almost like fog as the water broke the surface of the pond. Lizards were crawling on some of the boulders as well as some fish jumping in and out of the water. At the bottom of the pond, I could see rocks with lots of bumps and sharp points which made me realize that they weren't rocks but they were Zaratans. However, considering that it's almost wintertime I would say they've more than likely gone into Hiberlory which is the time of year when the water creatures sleep for the entire winter season and wake up afterward. No one's sure how they survive that long without sleeping, but no one questions it either.

I let myself drift from those thoughts and continue to look around the area. As it's probably the most magnificent sight I've seen in a long while. It makes me wonder how the water can be so clear along with clean while also being in the middle of Bloodthorn forest where the creatures reside. Another thought that came to my mind is why this pond isn't frozen over yet, I know it isn't quite yet winter, but it sure is cold enough for the water to freeze over right about this time of year. When I went to investigate the water, I could see the different colored fish, the way they moved around in the small pond, and how they all avoided the Zaratans at the bottom of the pond. There wasn't much fish from what I could tell, and I could see the bright green seaweed at the bottom of the river and the coral as well. The coral was of many different colors and shapes, some bright pink and others dark blue. It almost looked peaceful, but I know to think otherwise if it were night.

I held back a gasp when Barric brushed past me and towards the pond bringing me out of my thoughts. He grabbed a bottle out of his bag and filled it up with water and turned back around. He twisted the lid on the bottle to keep the water inside of it as we continued to where we were going. But then I came up with a way to find the nearest town.

"I say if we continue following the stream, it will eventually lead us to one of the closest towns as it is a water source," I said as I turned and followed the stream.

"Or you know it could lead us to our deaths as it's almost night out and we still haven't found a place safe enough to spend the night." Barric retorted back to me in response.

I quit walking after that statement but didn't turn to look at him. I looked over my shoulder a little bit and then responded.

"If you don't want to come then be my guest and find another cave, but don't expect me to do the same," I said before turning back around and walking away from him while following the stream.

I figured Barric wasn't going to follow me and find another cave until I heard heavy breathing and quick steps headed toward me. And after a few moments, he was right back up and next to me.

Chapter 6

We followed the small stream toward wherever it was it went. We would change directions when it did as well as go straight when it did. I could tell Barric was getting progressively anxious as he kept looking up at the sun from time to time only to see that it is getting closer to completely setting every time he checked. I'm not worried though; I could tell we're getting close to some town. I'm not sure how I know, but I do. If I do end up being wrong, I'm still not too worried, it just means that if push comes to shove, I can trip Barric and save myself. So, I guess Barric does have a reason to be worried, I mean that's what I've been doing for a while, so I'll keep doing it. Plus, if I do it in the forest the guards won't find the body and go looking for who killed him. The only problem is that Barric is worrying about the wrong thing, but that doesn't bother me.

It'll work in my favor seeing as Barric was kicked out of his home. So, he won't have anyone looking for him. Lucky him, I guess. I assume that if someone was listening to my thoughts, they'd assume I'm heartless, which in a sense they could say I am, plus they wouldn't be completely wrong. The only problem with it is that I'm not as heartless as the King, I'm just being heartless so that I can kill the King.

There was this one time, in the beginning, when I wasn't as coldhearted and cruel as I am now. It was a time when I made this friend a couple of months after being on the run, his name was Shilo. He helped me hide when the guards came to his town searching for me, he taught me how to fight in any situation that I was put in, whether that be some guy kidnapping me or even the simplest thing like someone stealing from me, and I guess he was just there for me when I had no one left. He was a friend to me, the last friend I ever really had. He was also a Fae who took pride in being kind and helpful to others. I was there when he taught young kids about all the species as well as when he helped little pups learn how to go through the change of becoming a wolf. I remember how he would sit with them the whole time when nobody else would. But most importantly, he taught me everything I know today.

Unfortunately, with all those lessons also came the day when the guards found out which town I was staying in and came on back. That was one of the second worst things that could've happened to me, especially at the age of seven. They had already searched the town so I figured I would be safe, at least for a while anyways. I thought I could stay in town with Shilo for a while before they figured out that I was in fact in Ormore. And so, I did, I stayed with him for a little over two years. Unfortunately, someone in the town started a rumor about Shilo doing suspicious activities in town and the King ordered them to go back to search again. And within days the guards came back. But Shilo being Shilo, he didn't want to leave me alone again, so he came with me.

We had to cross a lot of land including the Bloodthorn forest. It was the first time either of us had ever even entered the forest so of course, neither of us knew what we were walking into. Of course, we had heard stories, but we couldn't have predicted what would happen.

What did happen.

It was the second night that we were staying in the forest when every-thing went to crap, unlike the first night when we found a cave to stay in and keep warm as well as stay away from outside threats. The second night we couldn't find a place in time, we didn't care much about it so we decided to set up camp in the spot we were in.

A mistake I will never make again.

Within moments we noticed how the forest had gotten quiet, too quiet. However, before we even had a chance to figure out what was happening, one of the beasts jumped out at us. I had frozen on the spot, not even able to let out a scream of fear but Shilo had yanked my arm to turn me around and when I came back to it I realized we were sprinting as quickly as we could. We were getting chased by the creatures or monsters as I called them back then for hours.

We ran and ran even when we could no longer breathe. The sweat was sliding down our foreheads, down our necks, as well as down our chests. All the while the bloodthirsty beasts sounded like they enjoyed hunting down their prey. I don't doubt even for a second that they didn't. We had eventually found an exit out of the forest, but that's when my worst fear happened, Shilo had tripped and before I could even slow down enough to turn around and help him, he had screamed at me telling me to go, to leave him, to survive and live my life no matter what. That was the first time I had cried after what had happened to my home. The second time my heart broke. But this time, this time I didn't want to listen, I didn't want to leave him, and I didn't want to run. I wanted to fight back and try to save someone I cared for.

So, I did. I fought with everything I could, but nothing worked. I tried to get the beasts to look in my direction, to go for me instead of Shilo, but all they cared about was their meal right in front of them. I watched with tears streaming down my face as the beasts tore into him like a wolf eating a deer. I watched as the blood started to coat the grass deep crimson red and as tears poured from his eyes as if he was in pain. I watched as he turned his eyes in my direction and I could see all the pain he was going through as well as all the things he wanted to say to me, but he didn't, he couldn't. So with his last breath, he begged for me to run and for me to live my life the best way I could. I remember his very last words as if they had only been said yesterday.

"I love you, and no matter what anyone says or does to you, you never forget that because I will always, always be with you." Of course, he coughed in between some of the words, and blood was spilling from his mouth, but I never forgot those words as it was the last time someone had told me that they loved me.

Once he finished his sentence I watched as he turned his head back and stared up to the sky as he choked on his blood. All my eyes could focus on was the blood coming out of his nose and mouth until finally, he went completely limp, and his head fell to the side, his eyes looking dull of life staring right into my soul, and I knew he was gone.

My hero, my best friend, my person was gone.

I was taken from my focus when I heard the monsters and remembered what Shilo had said, so I listened, and I ran. One of the monsters had heard me and decided to chase after me. When I went to look back to see how close it was, it had clawed my face where I now have the scar and after that I just passed out, only to wake up the next morning in a patch of flowers, alone once again, without any help.

The memories of what had happened that night came back to me only moments after I had woken up which caused tears to stream down my face, and I pulled my legs to my chest as I realized I was alone once again. My heart shattered all over again as I realized that another person had died, and it was because of me. Maybe if I hadn't frozen in shock in the beginning, Shilo could still be alive, he could still be here with me telling me that everything would be alright, that one day this would all be over, and I wouldn't need to fight anymore. I held on tightly to my knees as they were pulled to my chest and screamed into the sky cursing out every wrong thing the Gods had taken from me. How they would pay for it all even if it's the last thing I did I would make sure they paid for it.

That was the day I swore not to let anyone into my heart, to not trust anyone, and to fight like hell for the rest of my life. If not for me then for my parents, my home, my old friends, and Shilo. I have kept that promise for many years now and I will continue to keep that promise until the day I die.

I was taken out of my thoughts when I heard the screech of a crow. I looked up and saw three crows fly over my head and stopped walking to see them land on the branch of a tree squawking at the ground below us causing me to furrow my eyebrows in confusion. I heard Barric gasp next to me, so I quickly turned my head in his direction, where I saw him looking down. So, I did the same.

That's when fear struck me.

Fog was starting to cover the ground. I have no idea where it came from, all I know is that once it starts rising, there is no stopping it. I remember reading a book after Shilo had died that was written by someone who had experienced many things in this forest as he wanted to know everything he could find out about it in order to warn others. I remember how in the book he talked about the dangerous creatures, and not just the ones I got chased by last night. The book talked about the *Crawlers*, the Crashows – the ones I was chased by, and finally the Kreeshen, or the creatures that live in the fog to be exact. I myself have never come across them before, but now that I am, I know that there is no way I can get out until I escape the forest before the fog reaches my mid-thigh.

When the fog began to rise off the ground and up to my ankles. I chose to run hoping that I would make it to the next town before it reached my mid-thigh. I heard Barric curse behind me before I heard his feet hitting the ground telling me that he was running behind me as well. I know that If this fog keeps rising, then sacrificing Barric to save myself won't work. The Kreeshen, the creature that lives in the fog, is completely different from the other creatures that were chasing me yesterday. These creatures are unavoidable, and you never know when they will attack or where because of how thick the fog is. All I remember from the book is that if the fog reachers mid-thigh before you find a way to escape the fog, then you're basically dead because if the creature grips you and drags you under the fog, there is no way of escaping it.

I heard Barric curse next to me quietly as the fog continued to rise, it was about halfway to our knees now. But moments after he swore, I saw it. I saw the structure of a townhouse in the near distance. With this new motivation, I ran faster than before which caused Barric to do the same.

Once we reached the very edge of the forest, I felt something grip my leg causing me to trip and fall. I screamed out and struggled to get myself free as I could feel the claws of the creature digging their way into my skin causing me to screech in pain. I thought I was going to die at this moment, but what surprised me was that Barric gripped my hand and started pulling me out seeing as he was on the safe side of things. I could feel my skin tearing as he continued to try and pull me out causing me to let out a cry in pain.

He looked at me apologetically while silently asking me if I wanted him to continue.

I responded by nodding my head with tears dripping down the side of my face and so he continued pulling. Thankfully, it didn't take long for the thing holding me to give up and let go, causing Barric to fall backward pulling me along with him and landing on his ass. Tears were streaming down my face from the pain, and I didn't want to look at my leg. Knowing that the skin on my calf and front of my leg is completely torn with blood leaking out of the cuts made me shiver involuntarily. I knew I would have to look at it eventually, so I took in a shaky breath and turned my head slightly to see the damage.

What I saw made me want to gag on the spot. The entire bottom half of my right leg was completely torn up. My skin looked as if it had been peeled off and blood was leaking from all directions of the torn skin. I rolled over onto my back and slowly sat up so that I was able to lean forward to inspect it. As expected, when my finger made contact with the torn skin it stung painfully. I quickly retracted my hand away from the cuts. My eyes stung as tears were threatening to fall, but this time I quickly wiped them away before they had the chance to. I looked over towards Barric and saw him trying to catch his breath while lying on the ground with his arm covering his eyes. When I turned my head back, I closed my eyes and thought about what to do.

I know that if I don't clean the wound soon, it will get infected, and if that happens then I'll either die or I'll have to cut it off which won't help me escape the castle guards any faster than I am now. I'm hoping that when I do get up and find a place to stay that they'll have some type of disinfectant, otherwise I'll be screwed.

I decided that I wouldn't sit here any longer, so I took in a shaky breath and slowly but surely pushed myself off the ground. Once I stood up, I put most of my weight on my left leg as no damage had been done to it and fixed my dress as well as dusted myself off. I hissed when the bottom of my dress hit the wounds but took in a shaky breath telling myself that it wasn't the worst thing that could've happened. After I finished dusting off, I looked to see Barric resting on his elbows staring at me while sitting on the ground. He looked exhausted, as he was out of breath which told me he wasn't used to running that much, especially not in two days. When he looked down at my leg to make sure it was fine I could see a slight twitch in his eyes as he opened slightly more than normal. When that happened he quickly stood up and reached a hand out to help me walk.

I scoffed in response and limped past him to find a place I can stay for the night as well as find something to wrap around my leg to make sure it doesn't get infected. I lifted my hood over my head to hopefully cover up at least the top half of my head but still allow myself to see what was in front of me. Thankfully I still have my bag on me, so I didn't lose anything from my travels.

I heard a slight sigh come from Barric as I continued walking. I know he must think I need help walking, but I don't.

After a few seconds, Barric came running up next to me and not so casually kept glancing at me from time to time. I ignored him each time and continued to look for a place to stay in this town.

"I know you don't want my help little traveler, but I can tell you're in pain." He started before turning his head to look at me as he matched my slow pace as I limped along. "We could probably find a place to stay faster if you let me help you walk or at least let me carry you or something to get you off of your hurt leg." He finished as he looked at me with pleading eyes, almost as if he couldn't stand to see me in pain.

I felt bad and didn't want him to feel that way, however, my thoughts were taken from that when I saw a small sign blowing slowly back and forth in the distance. I limped towards it, and it read 'Isbrills hut.' I smiled at this and walked over to the door and opened it. The door let out a small creak as I did so, and I stepped inside.

As soon as I walked in, I was engulfed in the warmth of the fire burning in the far back of the sitting area. I could smell the burn of the wood and it smelt refreshing as well as safe. I let out a breath and walked over and up to the front desk trying my best to hide my limp. Once I reached the counter, I rang the small bell that was sitting at the check-in desk, and within a few moments, a petite woman with light chestnut hair walked out and smiled sweetly at me.

I couldn't tell what she was so I just assumed she was fae because I couldn't see her wrist to see if she had a tattoo of anything. She also still didn't show any characteristics of any other species.

"What can I help you with dearie?" She asked in a calm and collected tone.

I let out a sigh of relief as she didn't sound rude or pissed off. Usually, the people who work or own these buildings are rude and overly self-centered. Which confuses me because I'm the one giving them the money, while they need to keep their job and have enough money to buy themselves food or pay off their tolls to not get on the King's punishment list.

"I was wondering if you had a room that I could stay in for a couple of days. If not, I can go look elsewhere." I asked simply while looking around, checking my surroundings to see if anyone would jump out to attack me at any moment.

She looked at me for a moment before turning towards the book on the counter and flipping through the pages before stopping at one of them and humming. I looked at her confused before she turned and walked into the back room with a sign next to the door that read *employ-*

ees only. I waited a couple of moments before she came back out with a silver key in her hand.

"Yes, we have a single room left open. It has two queen beds, and a bathroom in it." She said while glancing towards Barric who was busy looking at one of the paintings hanging on the wall before looking back at me and continuing. "The cost will depend on how long you plan on staying here." She responded while placing the key on the counter and leaning over it to get a better look at me.

Before she could get a good look at me, I quickly responded by saying with a tight-lipped smile "Just a few days." Before I quickly grabbed the key out of her hands quickly which caused her to open her mouth in shock.

She continued to gape at me as I turned my back to her and walked away while trying once again to hide my limp before she could even get the tiniest peek at me.

I walked out of the room and towards the stairs. I'm not sure what the room number is, but I'm sure I'll figure it out.

"Your room number is 267" I heard her call out to me.

As I walked towards the stairs, I noticed the paintings on the walls and how some of them were of the country's national flower while others were paintings of the King with a sword in his hand or even just him sitting on his thrown with his crown on his head. To the right of the entrance was a sitting area with a table by the window with two chairs, there was a fireplace that had a sofa and four chairs for people to sit on in front of it, there was a wall to the left of the fireplace with an arch in the middle of it and I assumed it was the entrance to the dining room. To the left of the entrance was the check-in area and just in front of the entrance was the staircase leading up toward the rooms.

Once I was out of her eyesight, I still didn't relax as I knew anyone could pop out at any moment. I wouldn't relax until I reach my room, close the door, and lock it. Then and only then would I be able to relax. As I walked up the stairs, I made sure to count them to see if it would save me time to run down them if I were to get caught by the guards chasing me. I counted exactly seventeen steps, which wasn't particularly good or bad. Once I reached the top step, I looked back down the stairs to see the shadow from the fireplace lighting up the rooms downstairs. I turned back around and walked down the hallway making sure to keep an eye out for my room number.

When I was about to reach room 267, I bumped into someone. I didn't need to look up to know it was a guy so I tried to go around him but that didn't work. Instead, he gripped my shoulders and shoved me into the wall.

"Watch where you're going, kid." He said in an angry and threatening tone before walking past me.

I had to hold the wince back until I was sure he was gone so I looked up towards the ceiling with my eyes squeezed tightly and gritted my teeth together to not let out a sound.

I could tell almost as soon as he touched me that he had been a dragon. When he had done so, my shoulders became slightly warmer than they were before he had pushed me. Another thing that made it slightly obvious that he was a dragon without me even looking at him to be sure was how he handled the situation. Sure, some species may be the same, yes, but only to a specific other species. But dragons, no, they're just indifferent to everyone. However, I'm not complaining because it was a very quick and brief interaction, plus he didn't try to see my full face which I'm thankful for.

When I heard his footsteps get further away until I could no longer hear them I let out a sigh of relief and relaxed slightly against the wall. After a few moments of waiting there trying to let the pain calm down, I continued to walk to my room with a slight limp still in my step.

When I saw the room number in which I was staying, I immediately went and opened the door. Once I stepped inside the room, I let out a breath and tried to close the door, only for it to get stuck. I looked down and saw someone's shoe blocking me from closing the door completely. I was about to curse out the person for not letting me close the door but then Barric barged inside and closed the door behind him. I didn't even have time to take in the room before he decided to take up half the space which he was not even paying for.

"What the hell are you doing, get out!" I bellowed at him. But he just rolled his eyes and took off his jacket, set it down on one of the tables in the room, and then fell backward relaxing on one of the beds in the room.

That made me angrier because he didn't even bother to ask if it was okay to take over half the room, he just did it. I'm not even surprised his parents kicked him out at this point. Some things I've come to realize about Barric in just two days is that he's annoying, he doesn't ask before doing things, he just does them, and he's like a lost puppy who will do anything to try and become friends with anyone he meets as soon as he can, even if he knows they don't want to be friends with him in any way. I was about to lecture him on it, but before I could open my mouth, he beat me to it.

"If you haven't noticed yet, this room has two beds, and there are two people in this room," Barric said while throwing his hands up and gesturing toward the room. "So, I will not be leaving seeing as this is the only room left in this place as well as considering this is the only place I can stay in this town" he responded without getting up from his lying position on the bed. After a few seconds, he sat up on his elbows and asked, "What town are we in by the way?"

I looked at him like he was stupid, but I answered him. "We're in Direcrest I believe because of the short distance we had to travel through the forest," I answered back to him in a slightly annoyed, yet calm tone. "But if you have somewhere else to be you can leave," I added after a few seconds.

He nodded in response before relaxing back on his back letting his arms lay down by his side.

I released a sigh giving up knowing he won't leave, even though it annoys the hell out of me, even if I drag him out, he'd probably knock on the door until I let him back in. So, I let it go and took my shawl off as well as my boots. Then I quickly disappeared to the bathroom and closed the door behind me.

Once in the bathroom, I looked around for a towel and thankfully found one under the sink in the cabinet. I quickly pulled the rolled-up towel out and hung it on the hook next to the bathtub above the chair holding all the soaps. I turned the water on for the bath water and placed a few drops of soap in it to get bubbles. However, before I undressed I walked back out of the bathroom and got a change of clothes while ignoring Barric the entire way. When I reentered the bathroom, I sat on the edge of the tub and dipped my hand in to feel the water to see if it was warm enough for me. Once it was, I got undressed and sat in the tub slowly allowing my muscles to loosen and not be as tense as I had been all day. As soon as I was fully submerged in the water I took in a few deep breaths before letting them out as the pain from my leg was around a level eight. The color of the water immediately turned a brownish red as the blood from my leg and dirt seeped out into the water.

The water is cooler than I'm used to which means I'm getting further from the Northern Mountains where the Royal family resides. I'm relieved to know that the chances of the King getting his hands on me are slowly lessening each day. Although I still know I need to avoid the guards that'll be coming after me soon enough. I'm not sure when they'll show up, but I do know that I'll need to leave Direcrest sooner rather than later.

I'm not sure how much longer I can take this. The further I get away from the castle the colder the water will get seeing as the weather gets warmer the further away you get from the Lambridge Castle located in front of the Northern Mountains in the town of Newmore, also known as the Capital.

The King is known to be evil to the people who live within the town's borders. Even if the smallest law is broken, he'll punish them. Not with death but with a public punishment. If it's a capital crime he would publicly humiliate them as well as sentence them to a lifetime of living in the Northern Mountains. And nobody could ever possibly survive a day in those mountains. I've heard there could be other punishments such as being sentenced to serve the King for a certain amount of time, which to me seems to be the worst punishment of them all. You'd have to suffer endless torment and abuse from the King for as long as he wishes instead of dying in the mountains or even being humiliated in public. Regardless a punishment is a punishment depending on how you look at it.

If you are sentenced to live in the Northern Mountains for the rest of your life, you're most likely going to die considering the winds are too harsh, and the snow is too thick to see through when there is a snowstorm. Unfortunately, those two things are just additions to what would kill you, as the temperature alone would kill anyone within two hours at most. So, in a way, it's worse than death, but not servitude.

Either way, I'm going to do all that I can to stay far away from that castle until I have thought out my revenge plan repeatedly and until I was positive it would work. Consequences be damned.

When I finished washing in the bath, I got out and wrapped my towel around myself tightly, and went to the mirror to brush my hair out. When I finished brushing my hair, I changed into my night clothes which consisted of a long black silk dress that reached down to my knees. I went to drain the water out of the tub when I saw that it was a slight shade of pink from the blood which reminded me that I needed to find something to wrap around the wound. I walked out into the room after draining the tub only to not see Barric anywhere in sight.

I let out a hopeful sigh hoping that he changed his mind and decided to leave because that would be perfect for me. If he did that, he would be saving himself from death seeing as that's the only thing I can bring anyone at this point. I decided to look out the window for a little while before heading to bed because it was still too early to go to sleep. When I looked out all I saw were trees, and small cabins scattered around. The forest was out a little way from the cabins which was a little concerning. But it was a nice view considering I couldn't see much.

My mind drifted back to the morning before everything in my life went to crap when I went to sleep with a smile on my face from seeing all the bright colors of the Wisps and waking up to my mom's signature breakfast meal. The thoughts alone made me smile just a little bit.

I jumped slightly when I heard the doorknob twist and the door open slightly. I quickly turned and went to hide next to the wall so whoever it was couldn't see me. When the person passed the wall, I immediately punched them square in the nose. I heard a crunch and then a groan following right after, which I quickly matched to Barric.

"Fuck! What the hell were you thinking? You can't just leave and not tell me and then randomly show back up!" I yelled at him as he grabbed a piece of cloth to collect the blood coming out of his nose.

I'm positive that I broke it, but that's his damn problem, he shouldn't have left and then shown back up without giving me a warning or something beforehand. I didn't feel the slightest sense of pity or sympathy for him. Instead, I started walking toward my bed.

"I apologize for not informing you that I was leaving the room for a minute." He said as he pulled the cloth away from his nose before walking towards the bathroom and throwing it in the trash while saying "But I still don't get how you attacking me solved that." He replied in a throaty tone.

I rolled my eyes before turning and walking back towards my bag and stuffing my dirty clothes inside it and grabbing my book from inside it placing it down on the table next to the bed. When I turned around I saw Barric walking out of the bathroom with his nose looking better than it had before. However, I noticed he was holding something in his left hand causing my eyebrows to furrow in confusion before I walked up to him and snatched the bag from his hand.

In response, he let out a shout, but I ignored him and dumped all the contents of the bag onto the bed closest to me. Turns out it was a bag of food, a wrap, and a disinfectant bottle. I opened my mouth in surprise before picking up the disinfectant bottle as well as the wrap before turning my head toward Barric in question.

He grunted before responding. "I went out to get food, figured since we've been walking all day in the woods, you'd be hungry because I sure am. I wasn't sure what you liked so I just grabbed a bunch of things." He replied, before taking in a breath and pointing to the disinfectant and wrap and continuing. "The wrap is for your leg, I figured you might want to clean it with disinfectant before you wrap it, so it doesn't get infected or anything like that," he said before walking towards the bed.

I nodded my head up and down slowly in thanks before turning back towards all the snacks. Before I could grab anything he quickly grabbed what I think was a bowl of Blue Mahogish, which is one of my least favorite foods.

I looked at him in disgust which he didn't seem to pay any mind to before I looked for something else to eat.

There were a lot of options to choose from, but none of them called for me. They all just looked unappetizing to me, and I didn't want to eat them. I could hear Barric eating which annoyed the flippers out of me, so I disregarded him and focused on trying to find something to eat.

After digging through all the food on the bed for at least ten minutes, I came across a bag of Shellpest. Which are simply bowtie-shaped chips with a golden type color to them. They are salty with a little sour taste to them, and you can almost smell the saltiness of them as soon as you open the bag, I don't even know how to describe it. They just make my mouth water as soon as the bag opens. I placed the bag to the side and grabbed the wrap and disinfectant bottle so that I could clean and wrap my leg before eating. I slowly limped towards the bathroom with the wrap and disinfectant before sitting on the chair in the bathroom next to the bathtub.

I quietly opened the packaging of the wrap before placing it gently on my lap and slowly lifting the bottom of my night dress over my knees. I then grabbed the disinfectant being sure to clean every open wound and the rest of my leg to be sure that I wouldn't get an infection. I hissed each time the disinfectant hit the open skin but knew that I had to keep doing it to get the best results. Once I finished applying the disinfectant, I picked up the wrap from my lap and slowly wrapped it making sure to cover every piece of open skin so that not even a spec of dust can get into the wounds.

Once I finished wrapping my leg I washed my hand and walked out of the bathroom being sure to shut the door behind me. I walked towards my bed and quickly snatched the bag of chips off of the side table where I had placed them and opened them quickly making sure to take a quick inhale to smell the saltiness of them as well as a mixture of something else that I could never quite place.

Barric stared at me with a concerned look and a little bit of something else, but I gave him a blank look and he chose to look away.

Chapter 7

B arric and I decided after eating, that we would get some rest. Well, I decided. I turned off the light and when Barric complained about it I told him it was my room and that he could leave if he didn't like it.

Truthfully, I just want to be alone again. No more annoying company that I didn't ask for. Even if he did save my life, I still don't want him to stick around like honey stuck on the bottom of my shoe. He's like my shadow that won't go away. Although like a shadow, he'll eventually go away, just like everyone else does. Like a shadow, it stays with you and then at a certain point, it disappears and goes away. Only to have it show up again, but for me, it would be a different person. I never see the same person twice, not anymore. I can only hope that he'll leave me behind and not stick around long enough to get himself into trouble because of me. I can't deal with another death on my hands.

I was taken out of my thoughts when I heard Barric putting everything back inside the bag, before placing it on the desk in the room. After doing that he walked back to his bed quietly, but not quite enough. I could hear him pulling the covers to get under them before turning off his light to place us both in complete darkness.

"Goodnight little traveler." I heard him whisper.

I chose not to respond to try and convince him that I didn't hear him or that I'm already asleep. I didn't want him asking me questions about why I'm not going to sleep as I was the one to turn off the light. I didn't want him to pretend to care about me especially when I don't want him to care about me.

I heard him shuffling in his bed trying to get comfortable, but I didn't move. I remained still on my side staring at the wall in front of me.

Eventually, it was quiet and I knew he had found a comfortable position as after a few moments the room was filled with his light snores.

While staring at the wall in front of me, I couldn't help but want to let Barric in. I've only known him for a short amount of time and yet I feel like if we had met under different circumstances we probably could've been great friends. But I can't let that happen, he'd only end up hurt or killed. So, I'll have to find a way to escape him or lose him so that he won't get hurt. Even if it hurts me to do it, it's the right thing to do. So, with a soft sigh, I let my eyes flutter until they eventually closed and I fell into the nightmare inside of my head

I woke up early enough to see the bright mixed colors as the sun rose behind the trees the following morning. It was a beautiful sight that I wish I could admire every morning like I am right now. It's the little things such as the bright colors of the sunrise, the sound of humming-birds, or even just seeing the Wisps at night again, that brings a smile to my face. The simple things can do that for me better than people can, and I'll never take it for granted.

I could hear the light snores coming from Barric reminding me of where I am. So I decided to get dressed, brushed my hair styling it into two tight French braids, before putting my cloak on top of what I'm wearing, and putting the hood over my head. Before leaving I rewrapped my leg in the bathroom quietly and then walked out being sure to place the room key on the nightstand next to Barric. I then slipped my boots on before walking towards the door with my bag over my shoulder and looked towards Barric once more before slipping out of the room being sure to shut the door softly behind me.

When I walked out of the hut, I could feel the soft drops of rain hitting the point of my nose causing me to look up toward the sky to see dark clouds above me. It isn't pouring down rain, instead, it's only drizzling. I noticed that there aren't many people out, which isn't shocking considering it's still the early hour of the day and it's raining. I decided to walk into town to see if I could find a fruit stand or any place that was selling fruit, especially blueberries or raspberries. The blueberries remind me of my life in a sense, because I used to be a sweet kid always joyous and full of energy, and then I became sour, I didn't want people to be around me as I knew the consequences that it could cause, and now, now I'm bitter. I don't care about life anymore I'm simply just here and full of anger that I'm ready to unleash.

Raspberries on the other hand, I can remember how my mom would try and get me to eat all types of fruits, but raspberries were the only ones I would eat without a struggle or a fight. Looking back on it now makes me smile.

As I walked around, I kept looking over my shoulder not feeling comfortable enough in this town to relax even the slightest bit. It felt strange being in the middle of a town, with not a single person out and about. Luckily, I found a small fruit stand and there wasn't a line so I wouldn't need to be out here much longer. So, I hurriedly walked over to the stand and searched for the two fruits I wanted.

"Is there anything you're looking for in particular?" The old man who was running the stand asked me while looking at all the fruits he was selling.

I looked at him for a moment before looking behind me to see if there was anyone standing around, but I didn't see anyone, so I looked back at him and responded.

"Do you have any blueberries and raspberries by any chance?"

Instead of an exact answer, he hummed and grabbed a bag before looking around. I watched him with a confused face while looking behind me every so often as I began to get queasy as I felt like someone was watching me from a distance. When I turned back I saw the old man had finished filling the bag with blueberries, however before he could even look for the raspberries I grabbed the bag from his hand and quickly replaced it with three silver coins before I turned and left.

"Hey!" I heard the old man shout from behind me, probably wondering why I left without the raspberries.

I ignored him however and began walking away faster in fear that the person watching me was one of the guard's men.

I wasn't sure where the person watching me was, I just know that they were somewhere very close to me. I sped-walked back in the direction I came, making sure to keep my head down and not look around anywhere. If this person was smart, they'd wait to get me alone and not in the open. Although it's not really out in the open considering how early it is and no one is awake, plus it's raining so even if people are awake, it's unlikely that any of them would want to come outside right now.

As I continued walking I looked behind me for a moment and when I looked back a pair of arms quickly grabbed me causing me to drop the bag of blueberries from my hand in order to grip the arms that were around my body.

Before I could scream, one hand covered my mouth, and their other hand wrapped around my waist pulling me behind two buildings with me kicking and fighting to get free, but nothing worked. Their arms were locked around me tightly leaving me no room for a chance of escaping. As they dragged me behind the buildings, I continued to struggle and I scratched at the person's arm tearing the skin, feeling their blood coat my fingers. I heard them hiss in pain, however, they still didn't loosen their grip on me. Instead, they pulled me closer to their body, so much so that I could feel their body heat radiating off of them and onto me. In return, I let out strings of curses, but all that could be heard were mumbles as their hand covered my mouth.

I was pushed up against the wall of the building, my head hitting harshly against it causing me to groan in pain. When I opened my eyes all I saw was a blurry figure in front of me, I blinked a couple of times to get my eyes to adjust, and once they did I stared straight into the eyes of the person who grabbed me. That's when I froze. All my senses were shut down for a single second before I became paralyzed.

It's my luck that it was the same guard who caught me before I left for the woods three days ago. And since that's the case, that would mean...

Crap.

I need to get my stuff and leave this place. I need to head back West because they realized I was trying to get as far away from that castle as fast as I possibly could. However I would then be going in the direction that they want me to go in, so maybe I'll show them I'm going to go West and then head back to where I said I'd never go.

Home.

We continued to stare into each other's eyes except mine mostly held hatred and fear whilst his held curiosity as well as something else I couldn't quite place. It was like he was trying to read a story through my eyes, a very long story.

I took the time to examine his eyes as I didn't have the chance to in direct sunlight the first time we saw each other, and they were certainly something. They were a silver color, like the color of thick smoke during a large fire or like the clouds when it's about to rain. They looked almost soulless yet looked full of life at the same time. His eyes had small little brown freckle-like dots in different places, but they were mostly just silver. They're the only eyes I've ever seen that look like that. It made me shiver in fear from not knowing what it meant or if it even meant anything at all.

We continued staring into each other's eyes for a while, neither of us blinking. After a while, I looked behind him to see if anyone else was around. Thankfully I didn't see anyone, but because I moved my range of sight to behind him it seemed to knock him out of his examination of me as well. However, instead of moving his hand off my mouth, he waited for me to calm down.

When he was certain I wouldn't scream he took his hand away from my mouth, which caused me to turn back and look at him. Once his hand was off my mouth I took in a breath and all I could smell was cinnamon. He took his other arm and placed it on the wall behind me as if he were caging me in so I wouldn't run. When he did that, I took note of the tattoo on his arm of three dark circles going up his arm.

Fae? He's a Fae? I didn't see that coming. I could've sworn he was a Griffin shifter. Or maybe he just got a tattoo so he could hide the fact that he is a Griffin shifter, but who knows? What I do know is that it wouldn't make sense for him to be one of the Royal guards if he were a Fae especially one of high ranking. Usually, the King only gives that role to the Griffins or Dragons as they're the only Abolystics who are able to assert dominance among the other guards while staying calm. It made me think that he was pretending to be a Fae, but if he is, then I don't understand why. It makes no sense for someone like him to hide who they are, especially when there could be others like me who aren't even sure what species they even belong to.

For a while, we stood there in silence, with me looking at him and back to his tattoo trying to figure out what was going on. But after a few moments of thinking, I realized that I could easily escape him. Well, I hoped I could escape him as my only option is to punch him in order to escape his hold on me. So I fisted my knuckles slowly before raising my hand and punching him square in the nose.

Unfortunately, he reacted quickly by placing his hands on my shoulder gripping me tightly, but he didn't say a word. Hell, he didn't even move an inch back or flinch when I hit him.

His nose started bleeding, but he wiped it away with his arm which caused the blood to smear and get on his shirt sleeve. When he saw the blood, he smirked and chuckled slightly, before he looked back into my eyes. This man gave me a whole other reason to be terrified out of my mind. When I looked back into his eyes, my breath hitched for a second as the look in his eyes changed. They were still curious but now there was a hint of rage. He seemed to be holding it back for what I'm guessing is my benefit but I'm not entirely sure.

Both of us have yet to speak a single word, so I still have no idea why I'm here, and I don't plan to ask either. Unfortunately for me, before I could do anything else he spoke.

"You know it's quite rude to punch someone correct?" He asked in a gruff voice.

It reminded me of what Barric had said when I punched him, however when I punched him it wasn't really his fault. It's not like he dragged me behind a building and held me hostage. Instead, he went out and got things that we both needed.

I didn't want to respond to him, but for some reason, I felt the need to defend my actions seeing as he decided to grab me out of nowhere and expected me to be ok with it.

"Well, I also know that grabbing someone who has done nothing is also quite rude, don't you think?" I retorted back to him in anger.

I'm sure if I was looking at myself right now all I would see is rage as well as the burning fire in my eyes. I'm pretty sure that if I were a dragon, he would've been a melted corpse by now. Unfortunately, the dragons can't actually do that, not even the strongest ones of their species.

He smiled at that and shook his head a bit while laughing. I don't know why he's laughing, as nothing is funny at the moment. I just want to be left alone, but clearly, that can't happen.

Eventually, he stopped and looked back down at me noticing how I held up a blank face.

He sighed and loosened his grip on my shoulders which caused me to raise my eyebrows at him.

"Look, I'm not here to hassle you, I just wanted to ask why you ran into the forest the day before the town search?" He asked calmly and looked me straight in the eyes.

However, when I looked deeper into his eyes, I could also see a little bit of concern and wonder. The concern could mean anything, but the wonder definitely means that he wants to know how I survived in the forest for two days and came out without a single scratch, well one that he couldn't see.

I was shocked, to be honest. I figured he would've figured out why unless they were searching the town for something else. Something that isn't a person. Or maybe they were looking for someone, but it wasn't

me. On the other hand, this could be a trick. He could be playing me
right now to get me to let my guard down so he can strike me later. It's
more of a possibility that he's messing with me and he knows exactly who
I am and why I ran. Especially if they have some sort of idea about what
I look like.

"That depends, what was the town search for?" I asked back.

I didn't plan to answer his questions, instead, I planned to ask questions right after he asks his. Or at least repeat what he said, in different
words.

He squinted his eyes and pursed his lips only to then nod in response,
mumbling something inaudible under his breath before looking back
up at me. He seemed to be debating something with himself before he
turned his head to look behind him as if looking for someone and then
back at me. He stared into my eyes for a moment before deciding how
he was going to respond.

"We've been looking for someone, for a while, and recently the King
has been getting antsy about it." He said before he paused looking at the
building behind me before continuing. "The person keeps slipping from
our grips as soon as we find out where they are. They end up leaving no
trail or anything and just disappear. All we know is that they're heading
away from the castle." He spoke back quietly.

He looked to the side of us and then the other way checking to see if
anyone heard, though I doubt anyone could hear what he said considering it's still early out and we're basically behind two buildings.

The moment he admitted they were looking for someone my eyes
widened, but they quickly reverted to normal, and I hoped that he didn't
notice otherwise I'd be screwed. Right now, I need to find a way to get
them off my trail. Then again he also stated how they knew the person
was heading away from the castle so that would mean my only chance of

surviving would be to head back up towards the castle, in order to throw them off.

I thought about questions I could ask that would make me sound curious, but not so curious that it makes it seem like I'm the person they're after. However, I'm almost certain that he knows it's me and that he's just messing with me so any question I ask will be useless either way. Although I will get to find out how little they know about me.

"So, this person, do you have any idea what they look like, or why they're running?" I asked back.

He quickly turned back to me at the question and looked at me like I wasn't already going to get him killed for telling me that he was even looking for someone in the first place. Although when he flicked his head, I was also able to spot a small speck of mischief in his eyes, but it quickly disappeared and all I could see was how unsure he was about telling me anything.

I mean it's not like I made him tell me anything to begin with. That was his own choice that he made and will continue to make if he gives me more information. But I guess I could cross loyalty out of the running by trying to figure out what kind of Fae he is, that is if he even is one. If he were one I'd assume he's a trickster, but he doesn't have a tattoo that matches that of a trickster, so I'm unsure.

He stared for a long moment, probably trying to decide if I could be trusted with this information. Quite honestly I'm probably the last person he'd want to tell this information to. But then, he decided to answer.

"No, we don't have a name, no details or anything that could help us find them. All we know is that it's a girl, and she's very important to the King. No one knows why though." He whispered back to me.

I nodded in response.

Luckily, they have nothing on me, that is if he's telling me the truth which isn't likely. However, if it is the truth, then it's an advantage for me, and the longer it stays like that the better. Before I could open my mouth to say something else, he started talking again.

"As for why she's running, I would presume it's because she doesn't want to be caught. I believe she knows why the King wants her and wants to get as far away from the castle as possible." He said while looking me straight in the eyes.

He's not wrong, I do want to get far, very far away from here, but so far, it's only ended with me almost getting caught, killed, or getting grabbed and snatched like right now. I looked to my side as he continued to stare at me and then I looked down and sighed. With his arms still holding me against the wall, it made me assume that he knew it was me and that he wanted to see how far he could take this 'joke' going for. So to hopefully get me out of this situation, I decided to ask him to let me go, hoping he would do it.

"If you don't mind, I'd like to be let go so I can go back to my room and eat something after you so graciously caused me to drop my blueberries all over the ground," I said to him with an annoyed sigh as I looked towards the blueberries that were covering the ground.

He looked over to where I was looking before he looked back at me with an apologetic look.

"I didn't mean for you to drop those." He said quietly as he looked at me.

I scoffed in response as I waited for him to let me go.

He looked to where his hands were resting gently against my shoulder and stepped back while letting go of me in the process. I sighed in relief and rolled my shoulders feeling them pop as I did so. I then dusted myself down, being careful not to hit my leg in the process.

"Thank you, and I hope you find who you're looking for," I said before turning to walk away.

Hopefully, by now Barric has woken up and thinks I ditched him. So hopefully he decided to venture off to look for me, but I doubt it.

Before I could walk far enough though, my arm was gripped once again, and I was turned around to face him again. He quickly pulled my hood down which caused me to let out a gasp and look down. But that only caused him to grip my chin in a tight hold and force me to look him in the eyes. He looked at me with amusement and there was also another look in his eyes that I couldn't place. But all I know for sure is that the smirk on his face isn't the 'thank you and I'm sorry about your blueberries look,' it's more of the 'you really think I'm an idiot don't you,' look. And that's when my face fell into a look of terror.

I knew he was messing with me, I just thought he'd give me time to walk away before shackling my wrists.

Chapter 8

I don't know why I did it, but I'm most definitely screwed now unless I somehow manage to escape. I mean what the hell was even going through my mind, this could seriously get me killed. I wasn't even thinking at that specific moment obviously, but what kind of excuse is that? My life is so messed up. And I mean that on a multitude of levels.

When my hood was pulled down, instincts kicked in and I punched him in the face, again, and then I ran like hell when he loosened his grip on my arm. It was my flight or fight kicking in except I did both, and when I started running it was like I completely forgot about the pain in my leg as I was too focused on him catching me. I heard him shout out at me after a short moment of shock and then I heard him start chasing after me afterward.

Currently, I'm not entirely sure how far behind me he is, but I can still hear him shouting at me to stop. All I know is that I need to get away and lose him as quickly as I can. But thanks to the weather, the wind isn't helping much. Fortunately, I know that talking will only make chasing after me much more difficult because the longer he tries getting me to stop the more he runs out of breath, and he will have to eventually stop running.

As I ran I looked back for a moment to see if he was still behind, but when I saw he wasn't there I looked ahead of me only to trip over a rock and hit the ground face-first. I let out a grunt as I hit the ground, but when my leg hit the ground I had to suppress a scream as well as the tears that were threatening to spill from my eyes. I took in a few breaths before slowly standing up to check my leg.

Once I was up, I lifted my dress to check my leg, and what I saw made me hiss just by looking at it. The wrap around my leg was crimson red and seemed to be getting darker and darker as blood continued to cover it. Soon, the blood would start to seep down my leg toward my foot, I knew that if I didn't rewrap my leg soon, I would fall unconscious from blood loss. Plus if I don't clean it with the disinfectant it will more than likely get infected. Which wouldn't be the best thing right now.

I looked around to see if I saw anyone around, and thankfully there wasn't. Therefore, I closed my eyes and let out a soft sigh. I went to start running again, but before I could get my foot off the ground, I was tackled to the floor. I let out a small yelp of surprise and pain as my leg was already in bad shape, and running didn't help. The person and I rolled over each other until we came to a stop with him on top of me and me under him with my hands being held in a tight grip at my sides.

I struggled to get out of his arms, but nothing worked so I gave up in order to save energy to fight later. Until then I won't speak, I won't move, hell I won't even give him the satisfaction of seeing any emotions that may or may not be showing through my eyes. I looked him in the eyes with a blank look and he responded by tilting his head and giving me a fake look of sympathy before looking down and across my face analyzing the scar on it.

He lifted my hands above my head and switched his grip so that he was able to hold them with one hand alone, before dropping his other hand down towards my scar. He dragged one of his fingers across the scar feeling the jagged lines and bumps that came with it. I wanted to flinch when he touched me, but I didn't want to give him that satisfaction so I stayed as still as I possibly could.

"This scar is old, when did you get it?" He asked as he continued to drag his finger along it going over the dip of my nose and down to my cheek.

I refused to answer him and instead looked away from him before turning my attention back to him when I calmed myself down a tiny bit.

He soon looked back into my eyes and gave me a soft smile, but still didn't loosen his grip on me or move. At this point, I wanted to kill him, get on with my life, and be on the run for the next three weeks from not only the King and his guards but from this dude's friends and family. From the type of uniform he wears I'm assuming he's one of the more dominant guards, maybe the commander of them, and if that is the case, then this is not good. I don't even know how I didn't realize it until now.

"This scar is in an odd place too is it not?" He asked after realizing that I wasn't going to answer his first question.

He held onto my arms with one hand tightly as if afraid of what I would do if he loosened his hold ever so slightly. When I tried to get my hands free he tightened his hold causing me to whimper in pain. He looked at me and turned his head sideways with a sad smile on his face before he smirked and tightened his hold again before loosening it just a smidge.

I looked at him with anger and confusion in my eyes, but he didn't seem to be affected by it. As we lay on the floor I prayed that he would let me go, I prayed that he wouldn't take me back to the castle and that he only wanted to scare me, but I knew none of that was going to happen.

I knew he was going to take me to the castle, and I knew that it was all my fault for getting caught so easily.

I knew it was my fault.

He hummed in response to my angry eyes before shaking his head and looking down. He chuckled softly, yet darkly before looking back up at me looking a lot more serious than before. He leaned down close to my face causing my breathing to become uneven, but then he moved over to the side of my head near my ear.

"You know, I think I'm remembering a few things about this girl we're looking for," he whispered in my ear softly.

My breath hitched at that, and I could feel him smile against the skin of my ear before continuing.

"I know where she was born, how she has these eyes that could have anyone's attention in seconds, you wanna know why?" He asked but paused for a second and I felt his finger move my hair behind my ear which in turn caused me to shiver slightly at the feeling. "Because she had one brown eye and one green eye." He breathed into my ear softly.

My eyes grew large at that statement.

Fear and melancholy are what I felt at that moment. Fear of being found, fear of disappointing my home, friends, and the ones who saved me. Fear that I've broken my promise to keep fighting and running for as long as I could no matter what. Melancholy because I feel as though I've just fucked up everything, I've tried so hard not to do it, all the sorrow and grief are climbing out of me from the inside out, and the only thing I've been fighting for years just went down the drain. Melancholy is the worst of the two things I'm feeling right now, and I don't know how to deal with it. I've never felt like this before, sure I've felt pain, grief, sorrow, and sadness, but this feeling tops all of that completely. I'm not sure if I want to burn cities down, scream my whole heart out, let go and become numb and mute, or if I should cry and let it all out for once in my life. I don't know what to do. And I can feel all of those things I kept deep down coming up and out of me.

The voices ran through my head over and over from the people who raised me at my worst, saved me when I needed it, and sacrificed themselves only to tell me to keep going, that I deserved life and all things it had to offer. despite that fact, right now I don't feel like I deserve anything. They just keep reminding me over and over about what I am and what I've done, and they won't go away no matter how hard I try to push them back deep within my mind.

You're a liar...

A murderer...

A destroyer...

I've become all those things in just twelve years. I left, I ran, and I let all those people die when I could have saved them. I allowed people to help me only to let them die in the end anyways. I'm a destroyer, a murderer, and above all, I am a liar.

I started to struggle in his grip, wanting to be let go, wanting to continue to fight until I couldn't anymore. I wanted to hurt him the way he hurt me by bringing up memories I fought so hard to push back. He laughed at my struggle and lifted his head back up to see the fear and pain in my eyes. This brought a spark to his eyes, like a verification that the girl is me and he wasn't mistaken the first time. That's when I knew I had fucked up, and that I had given him the reaction he wanted. He was bluffing and I had given myself away to him, when he found the realization in my eyes he laughed throwing his head back before calming down and looking at me.

"Well, I'll be damned. How is it after years, you get caught by accidentally running into me?" He asked dumbfounded and then let out a chuckle.

I understand his surprise I mean I'm surprised and upset at myself for being so stupid.

Due to his laughing, he let me go just enough for me to roll over and attempt to crawl away and escape. Unfortunately, before I could get the chance to stand up on both my feet, I got pulled back down and he climbed onto my back. However before I could do anything, he dug his hand into my hair and gripped a handful of it, and pulled my head up causing me to cry out in pain. His grip is anything but soft and it felt as if he squeezed any harder, he could pull out a bunch of hair from my scalp. I went to open my mouth to say something, but before I could even open my mouth he pulled my head back by gripping my hair tighter causing me to let out a whimper in pain as I could feel him lean down towards my right ear.

"Tsk, Tsk, Tsk." He whispered and I could barely hear him before he said, "The King will be pleased to know you've been found. But for now, we best get headed back towards the castle." He uttered as he stood up pulling me by the hair along with him.

I cried out in pain as he did so as not only did my leg hurt, but now my scalp does too. He pushed me in front of him so that he could keep an eye on me as we walked, but I could still feel the lingering pain from where he gripped my hair on the back of my head. I turned to look at him, but all I saw was a blank face as I lifted my hand to massage the pain away.

This can't be the way I go to the castle. This can't be the way that they all finally get what they want. I need to make up a plan to escape or quickly come up with a plan to take out my revenge on the King before we get to Newmore.

"Please, please don't take me back. I'll do anything. Please just let me go." I begged him as I suddenly stopped walking.

This caused him to let out a feral growl before he gripped my hair and pulled me closer to him while tilting my head back. I whimpered in response to his action as I could see the frustration in his eyes growing.

"Please." I whimpered as I lifted my hands to the hand that he had gripped in my hair. I was putting all my weight onto my left leg as I could already feel blood beginning to seep down my leg.

Instead of responding to me he ignored me and continued to walk with his hand still tightly holding onto my hair causing tears to build up in my eyes. My begs continued to go unheard as he kept dragging me harshly behind him. Tears have begun to fall from my eyes no matter how hard I tried to keep them in. I tried pulling his grip from my hair, but that only caused him to grip harder causing me to hiss and whimper in pain. I turned my head slightly to try and get the pain to hurt slightly less, but when I did I saw the trail of blood coming from my leg. I gasped in surprise causing him to stop and turn around to face me while loosening his grip on my hair. When he saw where I was looking he looked as well and his eyes opened wide as he saw the blood before moving his focus to my leg.

"I guess we're going to be needing a doctor now." He said as he quickly lifted me off of my feet and continued walking towards wherever it is we were supposed to be going.

Not soon enough, we got to a spot surrounded by several carriages. My eyes widened when I saw multiple castle guards walking around up ahead, and I started to struggle much more ignoring the pain as he gripped me more harshly pulling me closer to him. The action made me turn and glare at him, but he didn't seem to care. I let out a huff in defeat which in turn made him turn his head towards me and lighten his grip just ever so slightly.

I tried turning my body in his grip to get comfortable, but there wasn't much of a way to do that. When I saw more guards show up, I freaked out and struggled a lot more which caused him to drop me on the ground and I could hear him let out a curse before calling the other guards over for help. When the guards reached us he lifted me up and one of the guards held my arms allowing two others to restrain me completely before they led me to one of the carriages and pushed me in. Fortunately, before they closed the door I could see the guard who 'kidnapped' me talking to someone else who didn't have one of the guard uniforms on.

As if he could feel my staring he turned to look at me and winked with a smirk before turning away. However, my view of him was completely taken away when the carriage door was slammed shut in my face.

I sat for a while waiting for someone to enter the carriage and eventually, someone did.

The carriage door opened again after about five or ten minutes and in front of me stood a skinny guy in a white outfit, with a pair of glasses resting gently on his pointed nose. In his hand, he is carrying a briefcase of some sort that he placed in the carriage next to my feet. He looked behind him before nodding his head and looking back at me for a moment. After looking at my face for a couple of seconds he lifted the skirt of my dress above my knee before he got to work on inspecting my leg. We didn't speak to each other as he started working, instead, we sat in silence.

When he was finished inspecting the wound, he opened his briefcase and began to address the wound making sure to clean it first. I hissed when he went over the wound with some anti-infection spray before he began stitching the wound. Once he finished he put everything back into his briefcase before glancing at me with a stink-eye and pulling out a needle causing me to freak out before I told him to stop. Unfortunately, nothing seemed to work as he stood up slowly and jammed the needle into my neck causing me to hiss in pain.

While the needle was still in my neck with the doctor leaning over me, I looked behind him and I was able to see the guard who had made me drop my blueberries. When he noticed my looking he made sure to smile at me sadistically before waving mouthing *goodnight* before turning around to talk to the other guards who had approached him.

When the needle was taken out, the medic left making sure to close and lock the carriage door behind him. I felt my eyes droop after a couple of minutes before blackness started to consume me. The last thing I remember before falling into complete darkness was the talking of the guards outside the carriage and the sound of shouting and punches following.

And to think all I wanted was to eat my blueberries and leave before Barric woke up and noticed I was gone.

I woke up drowsy and my eyes fluttered open for a few seconds before I squeezed my eyes tightly again. I opened them again after a few moments and started blinking them quickly to get used to the light showing through the small window of the carriage. I couldn't see much out the window as the curtain was covering most of the outside, but I could still see out of it. I don't have any idea how long I've been sitting here alone and unconscious, but it's been a while as I can now see the sun shining over the top of the forest.

When my eyes finished adjusting to the light coming in from outside the carriage, I took the time to look around the carriage.

The seats seemed to be made from wood and have a drawer you can open to put things in such as a map or weapons like daggers or arrows. On top of the seat is a blue cushion most likely filled with cotton or feathers from birds. The art design is beautiful but expected. In front of me, on the opposite seat from me, is a beautiful painting of the Northern Mountains with leaves blowing and snow covering the floor and mountains. On the two walls next to me are the colors blue and gray, the same as our kingdom's flag. The blue symbolizes ice and how tough it can be, yet it can be easily broken depending on how thin or weak it is, or it can be thick or strong making it more difficult to break. The gray symbolizes the kingdom itself to show that there is no room for emotion if you want to be the strongest kingdom. The flag symbolizes an awful feeling, but it's been the flag for centuries and I doubt it will change.

Behind me is the same as what was in front of me, a painting of the Northern Mountains and its many beauties yet ignoring its many flaws. The mountains have more blood covering them than I do, but no one ever seems to mention it. On the sides of the painting, though, are pine trees to symbolize the forest surrounding the kingdom. After I analyzed the painting, I looked down at the floor to see that it was made from some type of thicker wood, which I would assume to be from the village of Amiheathen.

Unfortunately, before I could analyze the carriage any further, the door opened, and in climbed the same guy who dragged me into this mess. He pulled himself up into the carriage before closing the door behind him and turning back to sit down in his seat.

"What the hell do you want?" I sneered as I looked him up and down watching as he sat down in the seat in front of me.

My comment caused him to snort out a laugh, not that I was joking or trying to be funny. It annoyed me more that he thought this situation was funny.

He wiggled and adjusted himself on the seat and once he got comfortable, he looked at me and stared over me for a few moments before leaning back against the wall.

"Just wondering how you got the scar is all." He responded in a monotone voice, but he still didn't answer my question which annoyed me even more.

He crossed his arms over his chest and continued to stare me directly in the eyes waiting for a response in which he will be getting, just not the one he wants.

"Well, you wouldn't be the first to wonder about it, and you're not the first to not get an answer to it either," I said in response and rolled my eyes as he raised an eyebrow at me.

Then after a few moments, he hummed which caused me to raise my eyebrow at him. He smirked however and turned his head so that he could stare out the window.

I rolled my eyes and followed his action of staring out the window once more. A few moments later I felt the carriage jerk letting me know that we were now moving. I figured we were headed towards Newmore castle, or at least the closest next town to get rest for the rest of the journey.

"Just know the King will want an answer and if you plan on giving him the same response you just gave me," He said as he leaned forward placing his hands on his knees before continuing "Well I'll just say you won't like the consequences." He spoke out of nowhere but continued to stare out the window and not even spare me a glance.

That confused me and made me wonder why the King would want to know why I have a scar going through one of my eyes and across my nose. Even if he does ask about it, it's not like I plan on telling him how it happened. That memory is my memory and I refuse to bring it up again to anyone. But I chose to let the thought pass through me and forget about it for now.

After the small conversation, if you can even call it that, and the thoughts rolling through my head. We rode in well I guess the most comfortable silence we could have considering he kidnapped me.

Within the next few moments, I started to get tired, I fought the urge to sleep, but soon enough I couldn't fight anymore and gave into my tired eyes letting them close. I knew I wouldn't die with him in here with me, as the King would have his head. But that doesn't mean I'm any more comfortable falling asleep with him in here anyways. He's a stranger, and guard, possibly one of the guards who ambushed my home and killed my parents. However, I doubt it as he seems about the same age as me if not older. I can assume that since he's a higher-ranking guard, his father was one of the guards who ambushed and killed my family in cold blood. Yet I couldn't help the darkness that was slowly starting to fall over me.

The last thing I remember before falling into complete darkness was the feeling of soft fabric being placed over me as I leaned my head against the wall as well as the soft words that he spoke.

"Goodnight *princess*."

Chapter 9

I'm suddenly woken up when I feel someone throw me over their shoulder and I'm brought into the chilly weather of the outside air.

I gasp and start to struggle but that only made the person grip tighter around me. After a few moments of struggling, I realized I wouldn't get free, so I stopped and let out a sigh of defeat. Which in turn caused the person holding me to loosen his grip on me the tiniest bit.

When I finally managed to wake myself up more, I looked up to see my surroundings. I didn't see anything I recognized, which concerned me a lot. What I did see were bushes and lots of trees surrounding us which made me question what forest we were in now. I couldn't smell anything like food or smoke, all I could smell was the earthy scent of the wilderness. If I had to assume which forest we're in, I would assume it to be the Bloodthorn forest, but that also didn't seem right. There was no blood or smell that gave off that we were in that forest, but at the same time, it was the only forest we could've been in. It made me think that we were in a different part of the forest or that we had already gone through it while I had been asleep which made me believe that we were in a forest not too far from Bonemire.

Fortunately if were are near Bonemire, then that would mean that we are also close to the Sylph Mountains which gives me an opportunity to escape. Although my escape plan relies on how well-healed my leg is. I knew I had to come up with a plan soon as I could tell we were going to get to the castle as fast as possible.

I was taken from my thoughts when I heard a door open ahead of the guy who was holding me in a tight grip and when we entered the unknown building, I could feel my body warm up at the sudden warmth that the building gave but when I looked up, I felt my breath hitch at what I saw.

Animal heads along the walls ranging from all sorts of animals which told me that this building had been here since the very beginning, it may have even been here before the fall of the human race. There were also paintings of towns I'd yet to run to or visit. Among those paintings was the castle with the King and Queen in front of it. The Northern Mountains were barely showing in the background as if they didn't want that to be shown in the picture I assume. Almost like the artist wanted to keep the secrets of the mountains hidden, but I know, I know how much blood is hidden underneath all the snow, how many lies are buried within the castle and the mountains. I just don't want to figure them out, because that would mean going back.

Back to where it all started

Some of the paintings seemed older than others as the paint seemed to be fading away or the frame was outdated, which would make sense if they were painted before the fall of the humans.

As the guard holding me continued walking, we passed a couple of the guards talking to what I'm assuming are the owners of this building. We walked up the stairs before we came to a sudden halt. That is until I heard another door open, and we walked through it. I heard whispering but I couldn't quite figure out what was being said or who was saying what.

I looked around the room we had walked into and it looked like a bedroom of some sort. There were two windows in front of me before I was turned around where I then saw a bed. The bed seemed like it could fit no more than two people and it looked slightly comfortable. I questioned why I was brought into the room when we could still be in the carriage traveling, but before I could ask anything I was thrown rather harshly onto the bed.

Once I landed on the bed I turned around and glared at the guard who threw me, but he only smirked in response before looking at something to my right. Before I could react though, I felt a stabbing pain in my neck causing my hands to reach up and grab the hand that was by my neck. When I turned my head I saw the same guard who 'kidnapped' me and then the doctor who was holding a syringe. I went to open my mouth but I saw the guard who 'kidnapped' me shaking his head while shooshing me and I could feel myself being gently laid back and before my head even hit the pillow I had passed out.

"Please," I whispered before everything went completely black.

I awoke slowly, fluttering my eyes open and once they were adjusted, I realized that I was in a dark room. The room smelled like vanilla which made me sigh with a sense of calmness, but then I came to realize that that wasn't even close to being true.

When I realized that, everything came rushing back to me.

I remember how I was forced into this room. Forced onto this very comfortable bed and drugged to sleep for who knows how long. I might not even be in the same room I was thrown into. Hell, this might be a whole different building in a different town, if we're even in a town that is. For all I know we could be in one of those suspicious huts in the middle of nowhere surrounded by nothing but forest, and I honestly wouldn't be surprised if that were the case.

I sat up on the bed quickly looking around for any place to escape knowing that there more than likely won't be anywhere to escape from too easily. There is of course the door that I could open and walk out of, but they've probably already thought about that and locked it or put a guard outside of it. I looked to my left and spotted a window with a latch. I quickly looked to the door and back towards the window before jumping out of the bed quickly but quietly and rushing to the window.

I took a quick note of the fact that the room was about two floors up which wasn't that bad. I have a twenty-five percent chance of breaking a bone and a seventy-five percent chance of getting off without breaking anything and I'll take that chance. Then again I have a one hundred percent chance of being in pain and bleeding as my leg is still very much injured, but I'll still be taking the chance.

I looked back towards the door and attempted to lift the window. When I heard a click and the window moved up, I couldn't be happier. The idiots probably didn't think I would be stupid enough to jump, but when you've been on the run from the King for years you don't have many things to be afraid of.

Idiots.

The window wasn't exactly large, which seemed to be the only thing I'll have difficulty with, but I'll find a way to squeeze my way through it. I looked out the window again to see if there was anything that would make my landing soft or painful and I took note of the rose bush right below it. I cursed mentally knowing that if I landed on that I'd be picking thorns for a while, maybe even from places where thorns shouldn't be. But it's worth getting away from these monsters.

I heard footsteps outside the door and quickly shut the window, making sure to lock it again before jumping onto the bed. Nobody walked into the room right away which gave me enough time to get into a comfortable yet normal position on the bed. I heard two people whispering to each other which made me assume that I guessed correctly and that they had placed a guard outside of my room. Unfortunately, I couldn't quite hear what they were saying as their words sounded like mumbles to me.

I heard the jiggle of the doorknob, but the door didn't open right away as the two guards were still talking. It took roughly a minute longer before the door was finally pushed open causing my body to stiffen for a second before going back to normal. I attempted to relax as much as I could in this situation and I hoped that the person who walked in hadn't noticed or that they didn't pay close enough attention to my body language. When I didn't hear anything I assumed that they didn't. However, I was proven correct when I heard them walk in except they continued speaking to the guard outside the room.

"I'll call for a meeting later tonight about what'll happen when we arrive at the castle, be sure to inform the others." The guard said which I recognized as the one who had 'kidnapped' me and told the medic to knock me out.

Once the door closed, the scent of cinnamon started invading my nose once again, letting me know that I was right and that it was in fact him. I wished I could sit up and punch him straight in the face over and over again and hopefully break more than his nose. I wish I could watch as his blood covers my hands until he passed out. Unfortunately, I couldn't do that, I needed to stick to the plan and get out of this room and as far away from here as possible.

So, I repeated it in my head.

Lay still and breathe evenly.

Wait for him to leave and listen to the footsteps before getting up.

Unlock the window and jump out.

And then run like hell and don't look back.

That's the plan.

I felt him walk closer to me, but I still refused to move an inch. Moving would more than likely get me drugged again and I would sooner jump out of an eight-story building window on the top floor before letting that happen again.

I heard the screech of a chair next to the bed being dragged next to me, and I fought hard to not flinch. Which I didn't so I let out an internal sigh of gratitude.

It was quiet for a while. Only the soft sounds of my breathing and the heavy breathing coming from him could be heard in the room. I heard him shuffle around in the chair trying to find a comfortable way to sit, but he eventually gave up on that. Which made me wonder why he is still here. I mean there is a slight chance of him knowing I'm awake, but I doubt that. I may be many things but getting caught easily isn't one of them, except for when I stupidly got myself caught. Hell, I could probably fake being dead and they would believe it, well they would believe it until they checked my pulse.

I suddenly felt him move a strand of my hair out of my face and to the side of my head to give him a better look at me. Not creepy at all. Though that wasn't what got my attention the most, it's what he said after.

"I am sorry about this." He whispered in a calm and sad tone.

I wasn't sure if he meant it or what he was saying sorry about, but I wasn't going to stick around to find out what it is he is sorry for.

Soon enough the chair was pushed back into place, and I heard him walk towards the door. I would've opened my eyes, but I heard him stop walking for a moment. I'm assuming to look back at me or look around the room just in case something was out of place. I peeked my eyes open to see what he was doing and I saw him turn before opening the door and walking out.

Once out he shut the door quietly, I felt like I could open my eyes and move, but instead, I kept my eyes closed until I heard the click of the lock. When I heard the loud footsteps that reminded me of stomping going away from the door and down the hall, I jumped from the bed and rushed back towards the window.

I quickly opened the window as quietly as possible, and lifted myself, sticking my legs out of it. I let out a breath and did a silent prayer in my head hoping to not die in this moment of poor decisions before I slowly pushed myself out. I made sure to push myself as far out as I could hoping to avoid the prickly bush below me. Thankfully I landed on both feet in a crouch just inches away from the bush. I quickly let out a breath of relief as well as a hiss in pain from my leg before standing up. I wiped my forehead with the back of my hand while looking back up towards the window and smirking at it.

"Thank you Shilo," I huffed out quietly before turning around and sprinting for the thick, branchy trees that were calling out to me.

If I could get far enough into them, I could make a turn and then another and eventually lose this place as well as end up somewhere else. The key word being 'if'. I have no idea how long it'll take for them to realize that I'm no longer in that room, but hopefully, it'll be long.

Unfortunately, no longer than three minutes after escaping and finally reaching the edge of the forest did I hear shouts from guards saying I had escaped. That caused me to run faster and deeper into the woods.

I'm not entirely certain if this forest is Bloodthorn or if we had passed the forest considering I've been knocked out for most of the 'trip' if you want to call it that. Either way, I'll figure out if it's a normal forest or not tonight.

I heard the snap of twigs and the crunch of leaves telling me that they'd made it to the forest and aren't far from me. I cursed at the realization that I wasn't fast enough. I made a stupid decision and looked behind me for a split second and when I turned back, I had no time to stop before I tripped over a root coming off the ground. My head hit hard against the ground causing my vision to go blurry and yet all I could think about was how I was never going to look behind me while running again. I heard a shout from a guard claiming he had found me, and the sound of footsteps getting closer to me.

I moaned as I began to lift myself up into a crawling position before opening my eyes and wincing at the light. I brought my hand to my head as I could feel a headache forming causing a whine to escape my throat. When I pulled my hand away, I looked down at it and saw blood coating my fingers. Unfortunately, before I could try and stand to leave, I was shoved back into the ground by a boot hitting my back. From the lack of warning my head hit the ground once again, this time causing me to pass out.

Before passing out completely, I felt myself being picked up off the ground but before I gave way to complete darkness once again I whispered in a desperate voice, "Just let me go."

Chapter 10

I *tried* to open my eyes, but the darkness pressed in from every side, thick and suffocating. No matter how hard I strained, it was as if my eyelids were glued shut, refusing to let me see anything but the void around me. It was like a nightmare, but the usual chaos and voices were missing. Just silence.

I opened my mouth, desperate for a scream, but my throat was dry—nothing came out. No sound, no breath, only the hollow sensation of emptiness filling my chest. Panic rose as I twisted and turned, my gaze searching frantically for any sign of light, any shred of something real. But there was nothing.

The cold sank deep into my bones. It wasn't the sharp bite of winter, but a pervasive, numbing chill that seemed to seep from the very air. I hugged my arms around myself, but it didn't help, not even a little.

Turning again, I tried to find something, anything, that might offer an escape from the all-consuming blackness, but it stretched on, unbroken and endless. My heartbeat quickened as unease crawled through me—this was no comfort, no safety.

Without thinking, I ran. My legs moved, but no matter how hard I pushed forward, the distance never seemed to change. It felt like I wasn't even moving at all, like I was stuck in place, my body betraying me, trapped in this waking nightmare.

There were only two possibilities that came to mind. Either I was asleep—lost in a dream that wouldn't let me wake up, or... this was it. My time was up, and this was where I would be judged, suspended between realms, alone in the dark. The thought made my stomach twist.

I couldn't remember *why* I was here—couldn't remember what had led me to this place. And that scared me more than anything else.

At least that's what I thought.

The Gods decide our fates. They're the ones who weigh us, measure us, and choose who earns peace beyond death and who suffers. They cast judgment, tormenting those who deserve it, dragging them through pain worse than anything they could ever imagine.

I could blame them, I suppose, for the hell my life has been. But that wouldn't be fair. The Gods don't control what happens to the living—they don't choose our actions. They only decide what comes after. They decide whether we find peace on Spirit Island, with the others who have passed, or whether we are left to rot in agony forever.

And now, I think, this is it. This is my end. I've failed, not just others, but myself. All the promises I made—they're gone, meaningless now. I'm free, at least, in some way. Free from running, free from the lies, free from the pain that has never stopped. Free from the King—he'll never have what he wanted from me. I won't even have to know why he wanted me at all.

And that's okay. I can die without knowing. I'll go without the answers, and maybe, just maybe, that's enough. I can face that, even though I know I've failed everyone.

What's the point of promises now? The ones I swore to never break? They mean nothing in the end. There was no reason for them, no reason to hold on for a future that never came. I'm left here, in this never-ending abyss, to meet the end I've always feared. It's not fair, but it's not unexpected either. Life never was kind to me, so why should death be any different?

I can't shake the thought that maybe I deserve this. Maybe the Gods think I'm nothing but a monster. Maybe they see me as weak, as a coward who only fought for herself and hurt others in the process. Maybe they believe I should be alone, left to suffer in isolation for all the people I didn't save, for all the times I turned my back on those who needed me.

I have no say in this. The Gods hold all the power. They've made their decision for me, and there's nothing I can do to change it. I don't even know why they chose this for me—why they made my life such a cruel, endless cycle of grief, of loneliness, of pain. But I can't question them. I have no choice but to endure.

And really, what else could I expect from the Gods?

But this... this has to be better than whatever the King had planned for me. All the lies, all the punishments he surely had lined up. At least I managed to escape those, even if it's through the coward's way again. Maybe the Gods decided to grace me with one small mercy, even if it's this.

Not like anyone would care. I'm a nobody. The few who might've cared are dead. Then again, the King might care—he's wanted me for years, and now, the one time his guards manage to get their hands on me... I die. Oh, how I'd love to see his face. Too bad, or maybe fortunately, I don't have the time for that now.

Seraphina...

I jolted, a silent shriek escaping my lips as the voice whispered my name. I whirled around, but there was nothing—just the endless, suffocating darkness.

A soft breeze brushed past my right side, raising goosebumps all over my skin. My body stiffened as the air around me grew colder. Instinctively, I wrapped my arms around myself, looking frantically around for any sign of something or someone. It can't be wind. There's nothing here that could create it, no visible opening or vent, no source at all. Maybe it's just my mind playing tricks, making me imagine a cold draft. But somehow, I didn't buy that.

Seraphina...

Sephy...

My heart clenched, racing wildly in my chest as I heard the voice again. That name. My name. I hadn't heard it in over a decade. My breath hitched as panic surged. Whoever this was, they knew me—and I didn't know whether to be terrified or curious. But fear was starting to take over. My flight-or-fight instinct was kicking in, and I had no idea what to do.

I scanned the darkness again, squinting, trying to catch any movement, anything out of place. But it all remained the same—endless black. The stillness felt suffocating. My eyes had adjusted to the dark, but it didn't help. I wasn't going to waste time searching anymore. I needed answers.

"Who's there?" I called out, my voice thin in the oppressive silence.

Nothing. The silence stretched, thick and unbearable, making my anxiety spiral higher.

"Whoever you are, you're messing with the wrong person!" I shouted, my patience snapping.

Still, no response.

The silence deepened, so complete that even if there were insects, I should've been able to hear them skittering across the ground. Instead, the temperature around me began to rise, the warmth spreading like a slow burn, but still—nothing. No light, no answers, just the empty, suffocating void of silence.

I waited. I waited for something—anything—to happen. A sound, a shift in temperature, a flicker of light in the distance. But there was nothing.

The stillness stretched on, suffocating, unyielding. A sigh slipped past my lips, one that carried the weight of defeat. Maybe this was it. Maybe this endless, oppressive silence would be my eternity. My suffering. My punishment. It had never stopped before, so why would it now?

After a long while, I curled in on myself, drawing my knees up to my chest, wrapping my arms around them. My head sank into the crook of my arms. If I had to be abandoned in silence, I figured I may as well do it in some semblance of comfort.

You know who I am, Sephy...

The words slithered into my mind like a whisper, and before I could think, my head shot up, confusion etched across my face. It took me a moment, a long one, for those words to sink in. Despite the chill of dread creeping through me, I forced myself to focus.

Who had spoken? The voice was unfamiliar, yet... it had called me by my nickname. *Sephy.* Many had used that name, people from my past, people I hadn't seen in years. People I had lost. But none of them sounded like this.

What does this mean?

A flicker of panic crept up my spine. Was it someone from my village? Someone I couldn't even remember? Or was it my mind playing cruel tricks on me, dragging up forgotten faces and memories just to torment me further?

I didn't know anymore. I didn't know what to believe.

"What do you mean?" I spat, my voice sharp despite the crushing silence. "I need a name. I need answers! Why am I here?!" My words echoed, but there was no response, only the deafening void pressing in around me.

My heart hammered in my chest. I *needed* to know. What had I done wrong? What sin had condemned me to this place? And why—why did this voice think I should recognize it?

The silence was almost suffocating now, so thick that I could almost hear the beat of my own pulse in my ears. If a single drop of water had fallen to the ground, I would've heard it. The silence was absolute, a void so complete it felt like a trap.

I stood there, waiting. Waiting for a response, for any sound, but nothing came.

Only silence. Endless, suffocating silence. A silence that would drive anyone to madness.

A silence that gnawed at the edges of my sanity.

A silence that would make even the King, in all his power, falter with unease.

I squeezed my eyes shut, pressing my forehead into the crook of my arms, trying to focus on anything other than the suffocating stillness. My mind raced, grasping for reasons, trying to make sense of why I was here.

Then, the voice spoke again.

You need to wake up, Sephy...

Wake up?

I blinked, confusion swirling in my chest. *Wake up?* I was awake. Wasn't I? Darkness pressed in from all sides, and I could barely breathe, but I was awake—alive, even if trapped in this void. Certainly, this was better than the endless running I'd done for so long, always looking over my shoulder, never finding rest. But still...

What do you mean, I am awake? I asked, my voice cracking as I spoke into the dark, a mixture of confusion and unease creeping through me.

I expected silence, another endless stretch of waiting. But instead, the response came *immediately*—louder, more insistent.

WAKE UP SERAPHINA!

The command was so sharp, so forceful, that I stumbled backward, my feet tangling in some unseen obstacle. I hit the ground with a thud, the impact rattling my bones. My heart thudded against my ribs as confusion twisted tighter, making my head spin.

What was happening? What did it mean?

A cold, biting chill washed over me, and I shivered uncontrollably. The temperature plummeted so suddenly that my breath caught in my chest, visible in front of me in misty plumes. The darkness around me deepened, becoming thicker, almost suffocating.

I tried to speak again, my throat dry, but my words were swallowed by the air around me. There was nothing—just that voice, echoing in my mind, sharp and unyielding.

WAKE UP! YOU'RE RUNNING OUT OF TIME!

Each repetition of the voice twisted inside my skull, sharp and relentless. The words were a hammer, pounding against my temples. A dizzying wave of lightheadedness washed over me. My limbs felt heavy, too heavy, and I crumbled to the floor, my hands and knees scraping against the cold, unseen surface beneath me.

My vision blurred, flickering in and out of focus, as if my body were slipping away from me. I couldn't breathe. My chest tightened, a vice clamping down on my ribcage, and yet there was nothing there—nothing I could see, no physical obstruction, just the relentless pressure. I couldn't move. My arms, my legs, they were useless, numb. Every part of me felt as though it had gone completely still, frozen in place.

I gasped, but the air wouldn't come. Panic surged through me, my body stiffened, but it was as if I was trapped in someone else's skin. I couldn't move. I couldn't fight against the invisible force squeezing the air from my lungs. I sank to my back, eyes wide, staring into the black void above me.

WAKE UP!

The voice repeated, each time sharper, closer, drowning me in its command. I could hear my own breaths, shallow and strained, but they seemed so distant, so disconnected from my body. Tears burned my eyes, streaming down my face, cold against my skin, a mix of fear and confusion choking me from the inside out.

The world, the darkness, the voice—everything seemed to be closing in, tightening around me. I couldn't tell if I was slipping into unconsciousness or if I was truly awake. But the fear—oh, the fear—was real.

It was all real.

The voice grew fainter, distant, as if slipping away into the darkness itself. With every passing second, it seemed further, more out of reach. Yet the suffocating grip around my chest remained, unrelenting. My lungs burned, a weight pressing down on them, making it impossible to draw even a single breath.

I tried to fight it, tried to push back against whatever invisible force had a hold of me, but my limbs wouldn't respond. My body felt as though it had turned to stone, frozen in place, tethered to the nothingness that surrounded me.

Panic crept in, clawing at my throat, and I gasped for air, but there was nothing. My chest ached, tightening, desperate for release, but no matter how hard I tried to suck in a breath, it wouldn't come. The air refused to fill my lungs.

My vision began to blur at the edges, and I could feel the weight of unconsciousness pulling at me. My heart hammered in my chest, each beat louder than the last, each one echoing in the oppressive silence. The void felt like it was closing in on me, and my mind screamed for relief.

But nothing happened.

The last thing I heard before my body succumbed to the darkness was the voice—its words faint but still laced with urgency.

Don't stop fighting, we're always watching over you. Now go, wake up...

And then, the world faded completely. My body went limp, my mind drowning in an endless abyss, and I was swallowed whole by the dark.

Chapter 11

My eyes were closed, but something felt... different this time. The darkness around me wasn't as suffocating as before; it felt almost alive—like it was pressing in on me, but theres was still space for my mind to move. I could feel the whirlwind of thoughts crashing against each other, tumbling one over the other. I could hear every single one of them, the frantic planning, the constant self-blame, a flood of regrets and fears battling for dominance. I could feel my body, but it didn't respond. It was like every part of me was locked in place, frozen. Not a single muscle obeyed my will. My fingers, my toes, all felt as if they'd turned to stone, trapped in some unseen cage.

I tried to move, tried to break free of this suffocating paralysis, but nothing happened. The more I tried, the more the weight of my stillness settled over me, and I felt like I was sinking deeper into a void, not quite asleep but not fully awake either. It was the worst feeling I've ever known.

The voice—whoever it was—screaming at me to wake up, made sense now. *I'm awake. I know I am.* But what's the point if I can't move? If I can't even open my eyes? What good was being awake if it felt like my body had betrayed me, locked in some kind of cruel trap?

I didn't want to be stuck. I couldn't afford to be. I *won't* be. I could feel the familiar pull of desperation tightening its grip, like a noose around my throat. The panic starting to rise again—my heart pounding in my chest like it was trying to break free.

Stuck.

I couldn't let myself be stuck, not again. Not when I still had a chance to escape, to outrun whatever's closing in on me. There was no time to waste. If I stay like this, the prison walls will close in on me, and when they do, my life will be over. All the promises I'd made, all the lies I told myself, will turn to dust. I'll be lost in this darkness forever, my hope swallowed whole by the void.

The thought of that fe worse than anything I've faced before.

The King will win.

The realization hits me like a punch to the gut. Everything I've fought for, everything I've run from—none of it will matter. The King will finally get what he's wanted, whatever that is. I won't be able to stop him, not when I'm stuck like this. Not when I can't even move.

But at least... at least no one else will suffer. At least, in the end, there won't be any more blood on my hands. My failure will be my own, and I'll carry it alone in this endless dark. I'll be nothing but a shadow, forgotten, just like everyone else who's ever been cast aside by fate.

I try again, forcing my eyelids to flutter, desperate to see something, anything. I pour all my energy into it, but still, they don't open. I can't see. Not a crack of light, not even a hint of where I am. It's like I'm locked in a void with no way out, and the longer I stay like this, the more it feels like it's winning.

If I stay here long enough, if I can't get out of this prison, I'll be back at the castle. The King will find me, unconscious and vulnerable, and I'll be nothing more than a prisoner again. The guards will be interrogated, but they'll have no answers. And when the King doesn't get what he wants, I know what'll happen. I'll suffer for it. Worse than I've ever suffered before.

I can't let that happen.

I *have* to wake up.

But the more I think about it, the less I understand. How can I wake up if I can't even move? I *am* awake. I can feel it, deep down. But it's like my body has shut down, trapped in a nightmare of its own making.

I try to force my eyes open again, this time with everything I've got, but the effort feels like it's draining the last of my strength. My head grows heavier, my limbs more sluggish. It's like the more I try to fight, the deeper I sink into this void.

I don't know how long I've been here. It could have been minutes, or hours, or days—it all blurs together in the endless darkness. I'm exhausted, but I can't give in. Not now. I won't. I refuse to.

I try one last time to open my eyes, to pull myself out of this paralyzing grip, but nothing happens. The darkness is too thick, too suffocating. It's as if it's wrapping around me, refusing to let go. It's like gum stuck to the bottom of your shoe, following you no matter where you go, impossible to shake off.

I can't take it anymore. I feel my consciousness slipping again, the pull of unconsciousness stronger than before. There's no point in fighting it. My body is too weak, my mind too tired.

And so, I give in. Slowly, I sink back into the darkness, too drained to care about anything else. Maybe it's better this way. Maybe I can find peace here.

But even as my mind fades, I know one thing for sure: I will fight until the very end.

I woke up again, but I still felt frozen in place and my eyes still wouldn't budge. No matter how much force I attempted to put into getting them to open. It was starting to frustrate me to the point where I wanted to cry or punch something. I was taken from my frustration, when I heard something, making me put my focus on trying to hear rather than trying to open my eyes.

I let out an internal sigh when I heard footsteps from somewhere in the room, or outside the room, or who even knows where they were coming from at this point. I'm not even entirely sure if I'm even in a room. I could hear the footsteps get closer and closer with each passing second. The closer they stepped, the more dread started to fill me. I mean here I am immobilized, free for anyone to take. This thought alone made my heartbeat increase and I can guarantee that If I could, my breathing would have hitched.

I mean on the bright side I'm able to hear things around me, just not move, look, or touch anything.

I'm vulnerable to anyone and anything. They might as well drag me back to the castle now since I won't have a chance to get away. It'll be an easy mission for them. Granted I doubt whatever the King wants with me, that he wants to do it to me while I'm unconscious. But you never know.

I'm taken away from those thoughts when I hear the footsteps get louder. I assume the person is getting closer to wherever I am. In response, I try to force myself to wake up, but it doesn't work. I keep trying anyways, that is until I hear the door open and a chair close by me being dragged out. I try to listen for any more noise but all I could hear is the shallow but rough breathing of whoever is near me. I wondered if they were going to say anything until I finally heard them let out a rough sigh.

"Three days it's been since the day you idiotically ran into the damn forest, and you tripped over a tree root which ended in you hitting your head pretty hard." He said in a low voice before pausing briefly.

All I could hear when he spoke were the words *three days*, they repeated over and over in my head confusing and scaring me all at once. If I've been unconscious for three days, then that gives them the ability to do almost anything to me without me fighting back.

"We didn't do anything but bring you back to the cabin and have one of the doctors we have look at you and make sure you didn't kill yourself,"

It calmed me slightly knowing that they hadn't done anything to me except bring me back to the cabin. I'm glad they had someone check over me, although if it was the same doctor from before when he caught me in Direcrest, I'm shocked that I'm even able to hear him considering he seemed to enjoy keeping me passed out unable to fight.

he paused for a short moment to take in a breath before continuing, "he said you were fine other than the huge gash on your leg which he cleaned up again and used one of the King's healing mixtures this time. Now there is just a scar in its place." He said sadly.

I'm glad the gash on my leg is gone now, although it made me wonder why he didn't use the healing mixture the first time. Then again I assume they'd prefer me injured considering it would make it easier for them to catch me if I were to run.

"Unfortunately, he's not exactly sure when you'll wake up. Not that it matters, we waited until the next day before moving forward." He paused again.

It confused me when he said *moving forward,* however, I didn't get time to dwell on it as he began speaking again drawing my attention once again towards his voice.

"Right now, we're about a town away from Newmore. We should be there in about two to three days. Hopefully, you're awake by then, I don't think the King would appreciate us delivering something he's been waiting for for years to be unconscious." He let out a small but sarcastic chuckle when he finished saying that which confused me more.

The one thing that did seem to tick me off was how he was comparing me to an object or a thing and not a person. As if I'm some type of thing that the King has wanted or a fresh piece of meat that he's been waiting to get for dinner that he's finally getting.

"Anyways the doc said you might be able to hear us so here I am talking to someone who might listen and can't leave. Though technically speaking you could try to leave but you'd have to be awake for that." He said in a kind of glum tone.

No really, I thought I could do that by being unconscious I thought to myself sarcastically.

It was quiet after he said that, almost too quiet. I know he hasn't left the room yet because well I haven't heard the door and the chair hasn't been put back yet. So, I know he's just sitting there watching me. Or he could be staring up at the ceiling, but I doubt it.

I heard him mumble something before he spoke up again to me, or I guess to me at least, "You need to wake up soon, if not for any of us then for yourself." He paused shortly and he let out a rough sigh.

I heard him push the chair back to where it goes roughly and his rough steps as I assume he was walking towards the door. When I heard the door open, I thought he was going to leave however I was proved wrong when I heard him whisper, "You need to be able to fight and you can't do that like this." And with that, the door closed and I was once again alone.

Left alone in a room to think, to let all my thoughts wander around in my brain mindlessly.

I'm not sure why he would want me to wake up considering that would only be hell for him and every other guard here. More important-ly, why would he want me to fight back? If he didn't want the King to get his hands on me then why even take me to him in the first place?

Maybe, he wasn't the only guard that day when I ran into him. Maybe there was another guard, another guard who saw everything, heard everything. Another guard who doesn't care if the King gets his hands on me. Or maybe there wasn't another guard, and he just wants me to fight so that I'll waste my energy by the time we do get to the castle. That would be the only logical reason. But I'm not so sure anymore.

I'm not entirely sure if I'll even wake up, I mean if I don't, am I breaking all the promises I've given to so many people? I'm still alive, just not awake. I mean if I don't wake up, is the King even getting what he wants? I mean sure he'll have me, but would he? If I were looking for someone and I finally got them, I'd want them to be awake, not unconscious or half dead. Then again, it won't be my problem.

It'll be the guards' problem, but just thinking about that doesn't sit right with me. I mean sure they kidnapped me, they're holding me hostage, and they're taking me to the sadistic King of the Northern Mountains. And Although I have a lot of blood on my hands, lost myself within these years, and become a completely different person. I refuse to get any more blood on my hands even if I am unconscious and can't control it.

I have to fight like hell to wake up.

So once again, I began trying to force my eyes open, unfortunately, I realized that I was too exhausted to actually do it, and I ended up falling back into never-ending darkness. This time knowing that I'm alone and defenseless surrounded by an unknown number of castle guards.

Chapter 12

When I woke up again, I felt different, I felt more awake compared to before when I couldn't feel myself. I don't feel paralyzed, instead, I feel as if I could run a marathon and not be tired afterward. I feel alive. Though I'm not sure if I want to be alive.

With that thought in mind, I started thinking up ideas of what I would do once I started to wake up. Like where I would go to escape, what town to head towards first, and the quickest way to get there. I thought of a plan on how to get revenge on the King if I couldn't escape the guards in time before we made it to the castle. I kept conjuring up ideas that would keep me alive for a bit longer and to keep my mind focused on something other than the fact that I'm only half-conscious.

With all the thinking and planning I'm putting into coming up with ways of escape, I didn't realize that my eyes were slowly fluttering open. When my eyes opened just the tiniest bit, I quickly closed them again while letting out a hiss when the light hit them. I know I have to let my eyes adjust, but I don't want to. I know the light will only make the headache I'm beginning to feel get worse. But oh well.

I decided to open my eyes again and did so quickly whilst blinking them rapidly trying to get them to adjust to the light slipping into the room through the window.

When I finally got them to adjust, I just lay there, quietly on the bed. I didn't move, I didn't blink, I didn't do anything but lay still while staring up at the ceiling wondering about how my life got so fucked up. I mean my life went from hearing bedtime stories and getting hugs from my mom and dad to being on the run with bloody ripped clothes whilst crying my eyes out until I somehow managed to pass out. And now I'm here laying in a bed that isn't mine with a growing headache, and I'm not sure if that's a good or bad thing.

I'm here laying on a bed waiting for someone to come tell me that my life is over. Waiting for the King to either kill me or for me to kill him. I'm here thinking of a plan to help me get my revenge on someone who has an entire army behind him while I have nothing and no one. So, I don't know if I should kill myself and make it easy for him, or if I should try to get my revenge for myself and everyone he's wronged.

I was taken out of my thoughts when I suddenly heard footsteps walk past the room going one way or the other, but no one had entered the room. It's almost peaceful knowing that I'm not locked up in a room, surrounded by people who want to hurt me and yet they have not come in here to kill me.

After a few more moments I realized that I didn't want to stare up at the ceiling anymore, so I carefully and silently got up. Once I was up I went to stretch my arms, only to feel a sting of pain in my right arm. I looked down toward my arm and saw an IV and quickly pulled it out. I opened my mouth in pain and realized my mouth was dry, however, when I looked at where the IV bag was, I saw a small glass of water sitting on the small table beside the bed. I quickly grabbed the glass as quickly as I could and began to drink it to get rid of the dryness in my mouth, and hopefully the headache as well. Once I finished, I put the glass back down before I turned to look around the room. To say I was shocked would be an understatement.

I realized that I was no longer in the same room I had been in before. Instead, I was in a different one. The walls were made from a darker wood and had a different pattern, and the paintings on the wall were in a different style as if painted by a different artist. I looked at the bed I was laying on and realized that even the blankets had been different. They were rougher, unlike the soft fluffy blankets at the last cottage we had been at. The smell of the room was also different, I wasn't exactly sure what the smell was, but I knew it was different.

For a moment I allowed myself to think about where we were and how far away it was from the castle, but then I remembered the guard who I had first run into saying that we were maybe two or three days away. Before I could linger on that though I heard more footsteps walking throughout the hallway which reminded me that I needed to find a way out. I slowly and quietly stood up from the bed before I began searching for a pair of clothes or shoes. I looked down at myself and noticed how I was still wearing the same black dress that I put on before leaving the room back in Direcrest to get blueberries, so that made me feel a little bit better about this whole situation, but not much. I didn't have any shoes on though, so I figure that'll be what I look for before planning my escape.

I quietly walked over to the closet in the room and cracked it open just enough to be able to see inside but not enough to where it made a loud creaking noise. From what I could see inside I can tell there aren't any shoes or boots inside so I closed the door and looked around for any other place where a pair of shoes could be. I looked towards the bed again and decided that I might as well check underneath it just in case. I walked over to the bed and got down so that I was able to see under it. But to my dismay, there was nothing, not even a speck of dust underneath it. Having said that, I stood back up and let out a distressed sigh, and continued to look around the room.

However, after a few moments of searching and not being able to find any shoes, I concluded that they had probably made sure to keep all the shoes out of my reach until they deemed that I needed them or so that I wouldn't run off again. But jokes on them, because I can easily escape without shoes. Granted my feet will freeze and get thorns stuck in them, but it's better than going to Newmore in my opinion.

To be quite frank, anything is better than going to Newmore, especially in the winter.

I looked towards the door and noted how I could no longer hear anyone walking outside of it. So, I knew that I could quickly, but quietly shuffle towards the window. When I got to the window, I looked out and noticed how it was much higher than the last time, which sucks. Thankfully, it was nothing I couldn't handle. I quickly tried to lift the window to open it, but it didn't budge.

I looked down at it and saw that it had been locked so that if I attempted to open it, it wouldn't. I rolled my eyes at that and proceeded to try and unlock it, but that unfortunately also didn't work. It was as if they had frozen it or melted it so that it wouldn't open without the correct amount of force that I couldn't produce.

I guess they were prepared for me to escape and so they made sure to keep everything locked up tight. I rolled my eyes at their petty attempt to keep me locked up. It's almost like they don't think I'll find another way of escaping.

I let out a sigh after a few more moments of struggling with the window before I turned around to face the door. I looked down for a second to think but then decided to walk over to the door, but before I could open it, I saw the doorknob twist which caused my heartbeat to pick up. So, as quickly as I could, I moved back a couple of steps from the door but didn't do anything else. I stood frozen in my spot and stared directly in front of me waiting for the person to walk inside the room.

I heard talking outside of the room and when I looked down I could see one set of feet walking away from the door. I was going to let out a sigh, but then I saw the other set of feet turn toward the door and then the doorknob slowly began to twist, and the door was pushed open slowly.

I didn't get a good look at the person because the door wasn't opened completely, but when they did enter the room, I could finally see them. They entered the room quickly, closing the door behind them before stopping and looking straight up at me.

When we both looked at each other I could see how his body became stiff as he had frozen in place, clearly not expecting to see me out of bed and moving. I also froze in place as I didn't expect him to come into the room, at least not right then. I figured I would have more time to come up with an escape plan before he showed up.

After a moment I came out of my shocked state and I began to feel my anger rising within me. It was almost as if I could feel the smoke coming out of my ears and nose. The anger continued to build up as I felt like the control in my life had been taken away from me and I wanted to let all the pent-up anger out. I decided in a small moment that I was going to let it out so before he could even react, I moved forward and attacked him.

As quickly as I could, I ran straight at him, and seconds before he came out of his shock and realized what I was doing I jumped on him and started throwing punch after punch at him.

He attempted to get me off of him, but it proved to be difficult since we both landed on the floor with me on top of him throwing punch after punch. I got a couple of hits on his face before he flipped us over so that he was the one straddling me, but instead of punching me, he was holding my arms above my head keeping me still so that I wouldn't be able to land another hit on him. Which only caused the anger to build up to rage.

"Let go of me you bastard," I shouted at him as I struggled in his hold.

Unfortunately, he didn't respond instead he stared at me and squeezed his legs around the sides of my body as if trying to get me to stay still.

I continued to struggle to get out of his hold, but that only caused him to tighten his grip until I calmed down. It took only a few moments longer, of me struggling and twisting trying to change our positions, for me to finally calm down. When I did calm down, I took a few breaths, and then I took the time to get a good look at him.

From what I could tell he had a busted lip, and a cut just above his left eyebrow, and if I punched him in the right spot hard enough, he'll most definitely have a black eye in the foreseeable future. Though it probably won't last long as he could just get one of the doctors to heal it for him later today.

Eventually, he loosened his grip once he realized I was calmed down enough, but he still didn't get off of me. I look at him confused, wanting an answer as to why he hasn't gotten off of me yet, but he just smirked.

"It's rude, you know, to attack the person who saved you when you were defenseless and unconscious right?" He asked, lifting his eyebrow.

I scoffed and rolled my eyes before responding to him, "And you know it's rude to kidnap people and take them somewhere they don't want to go, right?" I said quickly before trying to find a way to get out of his hold.

I looked slightly behind him to see if there was anything I could grab, but I made it look as though I was uninterested in him.

While looking behind him, I noticed how he loosened his grip enough for me to move my arms a little bit but not enough. Fortunately, there was enough space for me to knee him where the sun didn't shine. So that's exactly what I did. I moved my eyes back to focus on him and stared him straight in the eye. I smiled sweetly at him and when he looked confused, I brought my knee back and kicked him causing him to shout as well as fall off of me, his grip going with him.

It didn't last long because as soon as he shouted a bunch of other guards hurried inside the room and once they saw what was going on four of them rushed over and tore me off him harshly whilst trying to restrain my arms behind me. Eventually, they did succeed in tying my hands behind my back. The other few guards that were left in the room that weren't helping to restrain me, were helping the idiot who thought he could hold me down and not get hurt.

I struggled to be let go as I didn't want to feel the consequences of my actions. I wasn't sure if they'd call the doctor in again to stick a needle in my neck or if they'd beat me to a pulp. All I knew was that I wanted to be let go.

When he finally got up, he still looked like he was in a load of pain which was a win for me. He looked at me like he no longer cared about what would happen to me, but I doubt he cared to begin with. I mean if he did care I wouldn't be in this position now, and I most definitely wouldn't have bruises showing up on my skin right now.

After a few moments of staring at each other, he simply turned around and started talking to the other guards. I couldn't hear what they were saying. So instead, I struggled to try to get free of the hands holding me hostage but that only caused them to tighten their grip on me more.

Eventually, I stopped struggling and the asshole finally turned back around to face us. He didn't spare me a glance before speaking the words that had my heart racing as well as causing my blood to run cold in utter terror.

"We're heading out now, and we won't stop to rest until we've reached the castle." He spoke to all the guards before looking at the one holding me specifically. "Put her in the carriage and make sure she is secured and unable to escape. Then pack your things. I don't want to be out here longer than I need to be." He spoke in a strong and determined manner but held no emotion in his voice, and it shook me to the core.

Once he had finished speaking, he walked out of the room leaving me trembling in fear and worried about what my future will look like in the next few days.

The guard holding me didn't waste any time before harshly turning both of us around and pushing me through the door of the room.

"Let's go," he said once he realized I wasn't moving.

When I still refused to move the guard let out a huff before gripping my hair harshly causing me to wince at how sore my head still is from a while ago. The guard ignored me however and began pulling me out of the room towards the carriage outside of the building.

Chapter 13

I sat waiting in one of the carriages tied down, unable to move. This carriage is different from the first one I remember riding in the first time. There's no painting of the Northern Mountains at all. It's just plain. There's nothing special about it. I mean sure the wood was pretty, but that's all it was, wood. There was of course the drawer in each of the seats so I guess that stays the same for each carriage, and the curtains were black instead of navy blue.

My feet were chained to the ground and my arms are still tied behind my back so even if I tried to get comfortable it still wouldn't be the most comfortable I could get. The chains were attached to a small circular piece of metal that lay between my feet. I tried pulling at them to see if I could get them to detach, but it seemed to be no use. The only way these chains were coming off was if they were unlocked from around my ankles and I don't see that happening anytime soon. On the bright side though, the chains weren't short so I was able to lift my legs up onto the chair.

For a while, I attempted to get myself out of the chains, but I soon realized that the only way I was getting out of them was if I broke my ankles in the process, and if that were to happen then I wouldn't be able to run away anyway. So instead I sat waiting in the seat with the chains wrapped around my ankles and the rope that kept a tight hold on my wrists.

The chains that are binding me to my end.

The chains that are holding me against my will, leave me unable to even stretch my legs.

The chains that are deciding my fate for me.

It felt like I'd been caged like an animal and I was about to be butchered. I felt like my life was no longer my life. Even though my life consisted of running and hiding, it was still mine.

Mine to control.

Mine to make the decisions that I did.

But now, it feels like I've lost all of that. I feel like I've lost all the control I had left. Now I feel empty. But I'm not allowed to feel that way. I'm not allowed to give up. I'm not allowed to let them win. No matter how I feel I must fight. I must fight for whatever I have left. I need to salvage the little things I can still control. And I need to keep them locked up tight.

I don't know how long it's been since I've been caged in this carriage, all I know is that I am completely and utterly uncomfortable. My shoulders are becoming sore from my arms being secured behind my back and my legs are uncomfortable from being in the same place for too long. But it's nothing I can't handle.

I felt like screaming and I was about to, but before I could the door opened and the asshole who ordered me to be chained like an animal sat across from me and slammed the door closed.

I stared at him quietly for a while as he rested his head against the wall with his eyes closed and his legs stretched out in front of him. His breathing is steady and calm but not to the point where it is even, so I know he's not asleep.

After a few more moments of staring at him, I got bored so I laid my head back against the wall and closed my eyes hoping to go into the land of sleep, but right before I could the carriage jerked forwards and we were moving.

I sighed and turned my head to the right and stared out the window looking at all the scenery beyond this cage that I'm chained to.

I took notice of how the leaves of the trees have all changed colors from green to red, yellow, and orange. Most of the trees we passed no longer had left on them. Some leaves are barely hanging on by a thread. It made me wonder what the forest would be like if it were lit up by the Wisps during the night, but I don't think I'll have time to figure that out.

I noticed how dull and sad the environment was starting to get the more we headed west. How the trees started to appear dead as they would never restore the leaves that were once holding onto them. How the clouds in the sky got darker, but no rain would fall. How the wind started to pick up and dust and dirt started to fly everywhere.

I noticed how there were no longer birds flying in the sky and how the paths got worse and worse as we continued forward on them. The bumps and small pits on the paths seemed to make the ride more uncomfortable and harsh. I'm almost surprised that a wheel hasn't fallen off yet.

I took notice of how sometimes we'd start to slow down only to pick back up again signaling how tired the horses were, and yet they were not given a single break. I could hear the person controlling the horses shouting at them to keep going.

I couldn't help but think that this is seriously what my life will become of, just taking notice of simple things that no one else will. Or will these simple things be the last thing I'll ever have a chance to take notice of before being beheaded or publicly killed by the King himself?

However, the one thing I didn't seem to notice when I started to drift off was the guard staring at me with a curious look.

I was once again surrounded by pure darkness, not a single strand of light in sight. I didn't mind it though, as it was quiet. For some strange, odd reason it was quiet. It concerned me a bit because I'm used to the voices yelling at me for everything, but now I enjoyed the silence. I didn't usually get it, and now that I am I'm taking advantage of it and letting it sink in.

Once I entered the dark room, I decided to sit down and stare into the endless, dark oblivion.

After a few moments, I closed my eyes and let the silence sink in, but that's not what I got. Instead, I heard something, something that caused me to open my eyes and looked around in the dark, completely confused by what I heard but couldn't see.

"Seraph-"

I couldn't make out anything other than the fact that the person or the voice is trying to tell me something. But every time they tried, their voice got quieter and quieter, almost as if they were walking away from me.

In response to the voice getting further and further away, I decided to follow after the unknown voice calling out to me hoping the voice would get louder and I'd find out what they wanted.

"Seraphina!"

I heard the voice again but louder, I tried to respond but nothing came out. I couldn't speak. How could I respond to a voice calling for me if I couldn't respond?

"Listen to me-"

The voice got cut off once more, so I started running forward again and I took notice of how the farther I ran to get to the voice the colder and darker it seemed to get, but it didn't stop me.

"You'll soon find out something you don't want to know, but you-"

Once again, the voice was cut off, it was as if someone didn't want me to know what the voice wanted to tell me. Regardless, I ran faster, but that only seemed to make the air get thicker and colder making it difficult to breathe. But I still didn't stop, I needed to know what they wanted to say to me.

"You need to listen, listen to everything no matter what. Don't fight back, don't try to run. Everything will make sense soon"

After that, the voice went away entirely and I was left with no air in the cold. When I went to turn around, I felt something pulling me back into the cold. I tried to fight it but the more I did the stronger of a grip they seemed to get on me. I felt more things pull at me causing me to scream, only this time I could.

As soon as my scream came out the grips on me vanished and I sprinted out of there back into the warmth before turning around to check to see if the thing was still there, but there was nothing. I continued to stare into the darkness, I felt like someone was calling out to me and I could almost feel myself moving back into it.

However before I had any time to stop myself from moving forward, my arm was gripped harshly once again by cold hands, and the next thing I knew I was being pulled down. It felt as if I was being pulled under frozen water, I tried to breathe, but it was as if my body wasn't getting any air. When I raised my hands up to my neck, I could feel several hands wrapped around it, as if choking me. I tried screaming and shaking them off, but nothing seemed to work, I continued to fight until I slowly felt myself getting lightheaded, and then everything stopped and I felt like I could finally breathe.

I turned around in a 360 while rubbing my wrists and my neck. My breathing was coming out in harsh breaths. I went to walk forward and find the voice again even if I knew it wouldn't end well, unfortunately before I could make it two steps, I was pushed to the ground and knocked out cold.

I woke up with a jump, which caused the chains attached to my ankles to rattle. I rolled my eyes and shook my head to wake myself up before tilting my head towards the window of the carriage and noticing it was dark outside. It shocked me that we were still traveling even in the dark. The horses must be exhausted at this point unless they got a small amount of rest while I was asleep, which I doubt. I focused on the forest outside and could see all the colors of the rainbow flying around openly. I saw the purple and red Wisps and I saw the white and orange wisps. I only saw a few blue ones and I couldn't see a single black wisp, but I blame that on it being dark outside.

I smiled at the colors that lit up the forest, as it's been a while since I had seen them. I recall how I used to ignore my dad and hang around the Wisps even with the warnings he gave me. They were my friends, the only friends I could rely on as not many of the other children in my village liked to hang around me. I never knew why that was, but I guess it makes sense if all I bring around is bad luck and what bad luck I brought.

I looked over and noticed how - well whatever his name is - was still sitting where he was when he got in this damn thing, except right now he seemed to be sleeping, peacefully at that. His right leg was bent at an angle as it couldn't quite fit completely on the seat, while his left leg was dangling off of the seat. His hair was covering his eyes and his right arm was behind his head almost in a relaxed position. If I could get free and tear the chains out of the carriage, I could imagine myself wrapping them around his neck and strangling him to death. Unfortunately, that's all it was, an imagination, I knew I could never get these chains off of me, which meant I could never get close enough to him to make the imagination a reality.

I switched my focus to my arms after trying to stretch and I remembered that they were still bound with rope. So, I decided now would be the best time to try and get my arms free, seeing as my shoulders are killing me from being in the position for hours behind my back. I began wiggling my hands around trying to find any place that might be loose, but I couldn't seem to find one. I struggled for a couple of moments with it before finally managing to find a weak spot. I twisted in an attempt to unknot and loosen it and thankfully managed to pull one arm out.

I slowly lifted my arms in front of me hissing at how sore they felt. When my arms were in front of me, I was shocked at what I saw. My arms were covered in purple and blue bruises that looked like they had been caused by someone gripped onto them. It made me question back to the dream I had moments ago, but I shook it off as the possibility of my dream causing it wasn't likely, it's never even been heard of. I thought about it for a while before I concluded that it had to be caused by the guards who had tied my arms behind my back as well as the guard who brought me to this carriage.

After concluding that it was the guards and not my dream, I continued trying to get the chains that were irritating my skin around my ankles
off now that I had both my hands. I tried to be as quiet as I could as to
not wake the guard sitting in front of me, but apparently, I wasn't being
quiet enough because after a few moments of trying to get myself out of
the chains - whatever his name is - woke up. I didn't notice that he had
though as I was so focused on getting free, I did, however, know he was
awake when he spoke.

"What are you doing?" Was the first thing he asked me, not how I got
out of the ropes, or even if I'm hungry, just what I'm doing.

I looked up at him for a short minute with a look that said 'Are you
stupid what does it look like I'm doing' before continuing with trying to
get out of the chains. That caused him to sit up and rest his elbows on
his knees, and his chin on his fists.

He didn't say anything for a while as he watched me struggle with the
chains, but as he stared at me, I could feel his eyes raking over my body
as if looking for something. When his eyes began to go up towards my
neck again, he froze for a moment and lifted his eyes to look directly into
mine which caused me to stop struggling for a moment.

"What?" I asked in a calm voice while trying to keep my nerves under
control as I felt like he was going to say what I already know.

"What happened to your neck?" he asked as he lifted his hand slightly
and leaned his body forward as if to check the damage on my neck.

I took in a sharp breath as he asked the question and leaned back
away from him and shifted my body slightly as if to try and put as much
distance between us as I could. I wasn't exactly sure how to respond to
him as I knew I couldn't just say that someone or something in my dream
was choking me and it somehow managed to leave a bruise on my actual
body. So, I made up a lie.

"Why don't you ask the guard who you told to drag me into this damn carriage," I stated in an angry tone.

After saying that, he sat back in thought probably thinking about how to punish the guard or if I'm even telling the truth. I could almost see the thoughts flowing through his eyes. I wasn't exactly sure what he would do about it or if he would do anything at all, but instead of dwelling on those thoughts, I went back to messing with the chains.

"You're not going to get out of those chains without a key so you might as well quit trying now." He said again without any sort of emotion at all.

I looked up at him for a moment wondering if he was telling the truth or not. I knew there wasn't much of a chance of me getting out of the chains, but I still wanted to try. However, after a few more minutes, I responded with a sigh and sat back up resting my head back against the wall of the carriage.

I realized now that he's talking to me, I have a chance to get answers to some questions like one important question that should have been asked a while ago but wasn't.

I looked up at him and asked, "What's your name?"

He looked at me curiously for a minute before replying without my answer.

"If I answer that then you're going to have to answer some of my questions as well." He asked

I thought about it for a while before nodding back to him silently saying that I would answer his questions as well if he answered mine. I watched him squint his eyes at me before leaning back and crossing his arms over his chest thinking about whether or not to trust me and give me his name or not trust me and still give me his name.

"Well" he sighed before pausing and looking at me and shaking his head, "My name is Aleksandr, I'm twenty-two years old and I've been working with the King since I was eighteen when my dad retired. Guess it's a good thing though because I found you faster than he did" he laughed at his not-so-funny joke before returning his face to an emotionless front.

It's good to finally know his name as it'll help when I need to talk or yell at him about something.

"My turn to ask a question now, and it's the same question you asked but mine is more important seeing as no one has known your name or at least no one alive knows what your name is." He stated in a gruff tone.

Instead of giving him the answer he was promised, I sat in silence smirking because I had no more questions to ask him and he would never get the answer to his. I smirked at him when he realized I wasn't planning on telling him anything since he had already answered my question. Plus, the fact that he brought up how there is no one left alive that knows my name so it's not like he deserves to know it.

He crossed his arms and sat back looking pissed off which doesn't bug me considering he can't do anything to me without the King killing him in return. He mumbled to himself probably questioning why he was stupid enough to fall for my trick. I mean I haven't told him a single thing about me since we met and all of a sudden he thinks I'll give him my name. I mean I knew he was stupid but not that stupid.

I tried to hold in a laugh, but I ended up letting out a snort which caused him to flick his head toward me.

"What's so funny?" He asked in a serious voice.

I didn't answer, instead, I turned my head and looked out the window again noticing how there weren't any more wisps floating around. It saddened me that they were gone, but I was the one who had been ignoring them for so many years. I always wondered if the forest near my village had been burned down as well, and if that were the case then that meant that all the Wisps living in it had lost their home. They all more than likely passed away if that had happened, meaning that even if I did ever go back, then they would be gone as well.

I sighed at those thoughts before I fell quiet leaving us both in a comfortable silence, except for Aleksandrs mumbling that I hear every few moments.

"If you give me your name, I'll let you free of the chains," Aleksandr said out of nowhere causing me to turn and look at him with a raised eyebrow.

He drove a hard bargain, but I'm not stupid. I knew he wouldn't let me out, and I also knew that my name holds more value to him than it does me. If I tell him my name, then he'll tell the King. Meaning if I do get the chance to escape and I will, it'll be better for me in the long run if they don't know my name rather than them knowing my name.

Granted I could probably lie and say my name is something else such as Gwendolyn or Samarra, but that would be stupid since I hold the power of giving him my name or not.

So, I looked at him, staring him in the eyes with no emotion before turning my head back towards the window and closing my eyes to let myself think for the quiet moment I have.

Chapter 14

We had stopped moments ago to, I think, give the horses a short break, which I think is well deserved. When I asked Aleksandr why we had stopped he ignored me and instead stood up and left the carriage being sure to shut the door behind him. He did however mention that he was going to go relieve himself and get a drink before shutting the door, but that was all the information I was given. He didn't bother asking me if I needed anything, I guess he figured I didn't matter. Which is quite rude in my opinion.

I'm currently trying to get myself out of the chains once again even though I know I can't get out of them without the damn key, but I have nothing better to do so I might as well try. I tried pulling and twisting to get them off, but nothing worked. I should know by now that it wouldn't work, but that meant nothing.

I turned my head to look out the window as I could hear footsteps walking by the carriage, but I couldn't see anyone. All I saw were shadows, that barely showed through the crack in the door. I watched and waited as multiple shadows passed by hoping that one of them would let me out, but I knew it wasn't likely to happen. Especially not after I had tried to escape the last time they let me out of the chains and rope.

I jumped back and sat like I haven't been messing with the chains when the door to the carriage was thrown open.

I looked to see who it was thinking it was Aleksandr, but it was just another one of the guards that I didn't know the name of. He stepped inside the carriage which made me lift an eyebrow at him, but he didn't seem to care at all. He took something out of the pocket of his wolfskin jacket, the jacket instantly let me know he was a Rytian because only they would wear something like that to piss off the wolves. I looked to see what it was he pulled out of the pocket, and I notice it was a key.

The key!

The key was shaped strangely, it wasn't like a regular key you would stick in a door to lock and unlock it. No, this key was different, very different, at the top of the key had a skull at the top and then went down shaped like a spine. It creeped me out, to say the least.

I looked up at him skeptically and looked back down towards the key in his hand only to notice how he started to undo the chains.

"Wh-what are you doing?" I stuttered a bit which is new to me, but seriously I need to know if he plans on kidnapping me to get something or if he was simply just freeing me from the restraints.

He looked up at me for a quick second before continuing to undo the other chain from around my left ankle. Once finished he placed the key back in his pocket and gripped my arm not so gently as he opened the door. He stepped out of the carriage and waited for me to do the same, though once he noticed that I wasn't going to move he rolled his eyes, let go of my arm, and left. I waited for a moment questioning why I was being unchained, but I couldn't come up with any reason except for one. Maybe it was a test, a stupid test, but a test. Or maybe it wasn't a test and they just thought I wasn't dumb enough to run away again.

After a couple of moments of thinking, I decided to test the waters and jumped out of the carriage. I waited for a moment, but nothing happened. I looked left and then right and noticed all the guards talking and some of them sitting on logs drinking what I thought could have been water or some type of alcohol. When I went to walk forward nothing happened either so I released a sigh and took a few more steps forward. Before I could run, the same guard who freed me grabbed onto my arm and dragged me towards a log. I didn't struggle as he dragged me as I figured he was taking me somewhere where I could be closely monitored. He roughly pushed me down to sit before staring at me with a serious face as if to say 'Don't move,' before he turned and walked away.

I watched as he walked further and further away from me, not even bothering to look back to see if I was even still sitting where he had left me. It was kind of weird how he had unchained me, roughly placed me here, and then just left. I mean why go through the trouble of even chaining me if they were going to leave me here in the open? All I know is that I'm exactly where I wanted to be, put in the open, away from anyone's sight, and with nothing keeping me here. I could easily sneak away, and no one would notice for a couple of hours. But then the voice from my dream came back to me. There was something important I needed to know, but was it worth giving up and going to Newmore?

I don't know.

I'm not sure how long I sat here arguing in my head if I should stay here or if I should run back into the woods until I get to the next town over. Every time I came up with an idea to leave, the voice from my dream would interrupt me until I just decided to stay put. I was taken out of thought when I felt a hand grip my right shoulder causing me to jump and look up to see who it was.

Surprisingly yet not surprisingly enough, it was Aleksandr. He smirked down at me before sitting down on the log next to me. Once he sat down, he let go of my shoulder and stared straight ahead into the woods. I watched him for a couple of minutes before I turned my head and did the same as him.

The trees in front of us were a mix of dead and fully living. Some of them were covered in leaves with bright colors while others had tree branches barely hanging on by a thread. Some were large enough to hide behind while others were so thin they could be an arm. The forest ranged from many different colors such as green to yellow as the trees were very different. I could smell pine so I knew there were pine trees somewhere in the forest. Moss was hanging from some trees and the forest looked almost peaceful, the almost coming from all the dead trees making it look like something no one would survive in. I could hear the croaks from frogs and a few bugs inside the forest.

"Took you long enough to leave the carriage." He said softly without even turning to look at me while bringing me out of my thoughts. "I figured you'd leave as soon as you got released, but to my surprise, you waited, Why?" He asked as he finally turned to look at me.

To be quite honest, I thought that too. I mean I had plenty of time to run away and escape, but I knew it wasn't worth it. I knew that even if I tried they would catch me. And I was going to try, but before I could really get into the whole running thing I was grabbed.

Though I'm sure if I didn't get grabbed, I would be running right about now, where to? I have no idea. This wasn't my turf anymore, I don't know these woods as much as I wish I did. I've never been this close to Newmore as I feared it would get me caught too soon. Though I guess maybe if I had stayed right under their noses then maybe I'd still be free, but who knows.

I didn't answer him and instead, I stared into the woods flowing the Wisps as they flew side to side and up and down. It was nice and almost made me forget about all the bad things in my life. It almost made me think that all of this was a dream, and I am still lying in bed at home slowly falling asleep and waking up the next morning to my mom's famous breakfast. But almost isn't real, and it never will be real.

We sat in silence for a while with me drowning in past memories before he started speaking again.

"My mom was killed when I was almost six years old, my dad had done everything he could to make sure the same thing never happened to me. He started my training about two years after his death and he trained me up until I took over his spot on the royal guard." He paused for a minute looking down and then looking back up towards the woods. "Growing up he was almost always gone, always out looking for a girl. Nobody knew what she looked like or what her name was, he was basically out looking for a ghost." He let out a short laugh and that caused me to look at him and then turn back and look down. "He was gone for years looking in every damn town for you. And all it took was you running into me for me to find you. It took me less than a year to find you when my father couldn't do it in twelve years. I was only ten when he first left. He came back every so often, but he spent more time looking for you than taking care of his son." He sounded angry at the end, but he tried to hide it.

He brushed his hand through his hair in anger and looked towards the ground taking a few deep breaths before looking up and towards me. I stared into his eyes for a moment before turning to face the woods once again and responding to him.

"If you're expecting a sorry, you're not going to get it, I didn't ask to be chased after for twelve years. And if you're expecting a life story in return for yours, you're not getting that either." I paused for a minute and looked over at him before continuing, "I don't do trades unless it gives me my freedom."

With that, I looked back into the endless horizon of trees, and we sat in silence with him looking at me every now and again. Finally, after looking at me for about ten minutes, he asked what I assume he's been waiting to ask me.

"I'm sure there is someone out there who knows your name, so why don't you just tell me?" When he said that it made my blood boil, but I didn't let it show.

How dare he assume that there is a single person left who knows my name? His family, his guards, his King! They all killed my family, my only friends! They killed the only people who I have given more than two fucks about to give my name up to them. So, for him to say or even assume that there is anyone else is just beyond fucking believable.

I didn't bother to look at him when I answered, I just simply stood up and started to walk away before stopping and answering quietly, not caring if he heard or not.

"If there is someone who knows it, I'm sure you'll kill them soon enough anyways." And with that, I walked back to the carriage and sat back in my seat, just without the chains this time.

I stared out the window until the sun slowly started to set off into the trees. It was peaceful and no one bothered to check on me since I had gotten in this stupid carriage. I found it strange as I could have slipped through the window and escaped, but then I remembered that they'd probably hear me fall out or hear me running in the forest. I didn't see any more Wisps, which made me sad but I understood why they weren't out anymore as it was getting colder as the sunset.

I looked over towards the door when it started to open but just turned back before I even got the chance to see the person and continued to investigate the woods, leaving all my problems in the back of my head for the moment.

When the carriage started to move, I assumed we were going back to nonstop traveling until we got to the castle where my life would soon become a nightmare in hell.

I could feel Aleksandr staring at me, but I refused to give him even the slightest satisfaction of looking back at him, so I just blatantly continued to stare out into the endless night.

I could barely hear the frogs croaking or the leaves falling from trees when the wind forced them down because of the noise the carriages are making every time we hit a bump in the road. I could hear the horses galloping along the trail and the sound of the coachman occasionally shouting at the horses to keep going saying that there was no time for unnecessary breaks. Especially when we had just had one.

I made sure to focus my attention on everything else surrounding the carriage and nothing inside it. I let memories swarm around inside my head of when I used to walk around the woods aimlessly for hours on end before going home to dinner, and when Shilo was teaching me how to navigate the woods when I can't see the stars to get directions when I look up towards them.

At some point between the thoughts and focusing on the outside world surrounding me I feel my cheeks get wet. I raise my hand to my cheeks and that's when I realize that after so many years of continuous buildup of pressure and keeping everything inside me, I finally let some of it out. Tears were falling from my eyes freely causing my cheeks to dampen and most likely become an almost rose color. Before any more tears could fall, I lifted my hand quickly and wiped the tears away.

I turned my head toward Aleksandr but noticed he was passed out cold with one arm hanging behind his head and the other arm laying limply at his side. One of his legs was bent up and on the bench of the carriage and the other leg was hanging off the ledge almost completely off but not quite.

I closed my eyes, sighing in gratitude that he wasn't awake to see me in a weak state. I kept my eyes closed as I rested my head against the wall, hoping that the voice in my head would come back and tell me what the hell I am doing at this point.

Chapter 15

I have overheard the guards talking outside the carriage every time we would stop for breaks, which wasn't often. However, the conversations gave me clarification on how close we were getting to the castle, which I'm both terrified and thankful for.

They spoke about women and some even talked about their wives and how they were ready to go home to their kids and family. Some of them spoke about how they were ready for their well-deserved break so they could get drunk and forget about everything that's happened for one night. While others spoke about how they were ready for their next job, whether it be kidnapping another child or burning down an entire village because the Lord and their family don't visit Newmore as often as other towns do. The last thing they spoke about - which caught my attention the most and caused goosebumps to go all over my arms and make me shiver in fear - was that according to them, we're only about a few hours or so away from the castle.

I tried not to let that thought get to me, but it did. I couldn't stop thinking about what would happen to me once we arrived. I couldn't stop thinking that maybe my end is coming. Or maybe I'd be lucky enough to survive.

Although I highly doubt it.

I mean maybe I'll be the lucky species and not be killed because of how special I am. The King may or may not ask me what species of Abolystic I am and when I don't answer he'll probably kill me. On one hand, I could lie and say I'm a wolf, but I don't act or smell like one so that wouldn't really be believable. On the other hand, I could also say I'm a Phoenix, but that wouldn't work because I'm not nice enough to be that either. I have no idea what I am. I'm basically almost human. Regardless of that fact, I am a human who hasn't been caught by the King in like twelve years, so I count that as a win. I could call myself a vampire, but they've been extinct for the longest time.

All I know is that I need to figure out what to say before the King asks me himself, because if I'm not prepared then I might as well pull the trigger myself because I know he'll kill me right away.

We're currently in the middle of nowhere, not a single town is in sight. The ground is covered in snow as it continued to build up and up growing a few inches every hour. If it weren't for the blanket in the carriage that I had wrapped around myself I'd be on the right track for hypothermia. If I could see myself now my nose would probably be red, and my cheeks would be a rose color. Aleksandr had fallen asleep a few moments ago and is currently wrapped in his blanket with his cheeks as red as a rose. The tips of his ears were almost as bright as his cheeks, but not quite there yet. I knew that if I touched my own ears they would hurt as I'm not used to the cold weather.

The closer we seemed to get to Newmore, the colder it got. Pretty soon we'll get to a point where the snow is almost completely ice but not quite there yet. I guess that could explain why no one ever seemed to survive the Northern mountains as the mountains are as deadly, if not more deadly than the Bloodthorn forest is at night. Although only the dead know what vicious creatures wander through the mountains at night.

I couldn't sleep with my body shivering from the cold, my body isn't as used to this weather as it had been in the past. My body had gotten used to the warm weather, and I was so close, so close to my escape through the Southern Sea. It's a deadly sea, yes, but not as deadly as the Northern Sea, and I was willing to risk it if it meant escaping the King.

The Northern Sea consists of icebergs and large rocks with sharp points. Those could be easily avoided during the day, but during the night, storms build up and cause the waves to overthrow ships sending them under the water within moments. The crew members would probably try and swim back to shore but even if they did make it to land on time, they'd freeze to death.

The Southern Sea on the other hand is filled with creatures who would sink boats on purpose to get a food source. Everyone had assumed that's why they sunk the ships, because when they came they ate everything in the ocean leaving it deserted with only species attacking species for food. The waves aren't as rough and there is nothing in the path of freedom stopping you. Except for all the underwater creatures. Of course, the Northern sea also had deadly creatures in it, but nobody's ever died because of them as they quickly discover that no matter what they do their boat would sink within only moments of sailing in it.

I sat here, wondering if I would have even survived out in the sea. If there was, anyway, I could've prevented being caught. But all that I could think about was that I would've only made it so far. The Southern Sea would be a dead end, and I would have been surrounded by the castle guards in only a few days. So that only lead me to think that I've always known I would have gotten caught eventually, I was just delaying it by always running. But now that I'm caught. I'm locked in a cage and there is no fight left to give. At least not yet.

Not yet.

Running would be stupid. If it weren't for the harsh winter weather I would have a chance, but running through the snow, and having to go through the Bloodthorn forest again just to get back to where I was, doesn't seem like the best idea. I'd rather take my chances in the castle where it's probably warmer in the dungeons than risk my life in the freezing winter and the Bloodthorn forest.

I'll suffer through whatever happens to me. Even if that means punishment or being forced into labor. I will live for all those I've killed, for those the King killed, and for those that died by trying to escape the King as well. I will live for them, and eventually, I'll kill the King for them as well.

I've been sitting here for about half an hour now since the last time we had stopped, just watching the snowfall outside. Occasionally I would look over toward Aleksandr to see if he was starting to wake up from his slumber. He's been out for a while now which is concerning because usually, he's only out for about an hour and a half, but he's been out for almost two hours now.

I thought that maybe he died of hypothermia, but that couldn't be true as I saw his chest rising and falling with every breath he took. Another giveaway that told me he wasn't dead was how he would continuously try and wrap the blanket around himself tighter to get warmer.

After a while, I had gotten bored of sitting and waiting in the carriage listening to the same shouts that the coachman would yell at the horses. I knew that if I were cold then the horses had to be cold as well. They probably weren't as cold as me considering all the hair that coated their bodies. Granted I have tiny hairs covering my body as well, but it still doesn't do much to keep me warm.

I turned my head back over to the window to see that the leaves are completely gone and you can see endlessly into the forest. The bushes are covered in snow, and I think I saw a bunny with white fur hop out of them and shake its little head to get the snow off. I wasn't exactly sure if I had truly seen it tough as the lanterns on the side of the carriage only gave up so much light.

Through the corner of my eye, I saw Aleksandr start to stir so I quickly looked over at him only to see him struggling to find a more comfortable position than what he was in right now. Eventually, he gave up and opened his eyes with a tired sigh and stretched his arms up and over his head, or at least tried to.

Once he stopped stretching, he sat up and looked around probably thinking I tried to escape. His eyes soon landed on me and only then did he stop stressing and relax. He rested his head on the back wall and let out a breath creating a puff of fog to come out. It took a few seconds before he lifted his head and noticed my freezing state. I didn't care to stare back at him and again turned my head to look out the window once again as it seems to be my only source of entertainment.

I didn't think it'd be possible considering he has been an asshole ever since we ran into each other the first day we met, but he ever so thoughtfully, got up and placed the blanket he had on top of the blanket I'm already using.

I looked over at him confused but he stared at me with a look I couldn't quite decipher. I chose to smile at him and close my eyes and turn my head to rest it against the side of the seat on my right. I tried to block out the cold to get some well-needed sleep, but it wouldn't come so easily. I felt bad that I now had two blankets while he had none, but then again I'm not entirely sure how to feel since he's lived in the North longer than I had. I lifted my head to say something but before I could, he beat me to it.

"Rest, we should be at the castle soon, and I don't need you freezing to death before we reach." He stated before resting his head against the wall thoroughly ending the conversation that hadn't even started.

I didn't feel bad anymore about him not having one, and instead, I pulled both blankets tightly around my body before laying in a somewhat comfortable position and closing my eyes to sleep. It was difficult to get any sleep though as his words rang through my mind, *We should be at the castle soon.'* Those few words would mean everything to someone if this had been a fairytale story, but to me, it felt like acid had been poured over my entire body.

On the other hand those words came something I hadn't thought of before, I had to have been knocked out when we traveled through the Sylph Mountains. I mean there is a possibility that we traveled around them making the trip longer, but it made sense if the guards were unsure about how the Sylphs would react to us. The other possibility is that I was still in my coma and they wanted to give me more time to wake up so they wouldn't get punished by the King, but who knows?

If it were the first option and the guards weren't sure how the Sylphs would respond then that would make sense. I mean I had always wanted to visit the Sylph Mountains to see the Sylphs, but the stories I had heard from other people were not that great.

For instance, I heard they all resemble what people assume to be a Goddess because of their white wings and their sweet nature. But some act sweet and kind to lure you in similar to a White Wisp would do and then they'd end up either one killing you or two keeping you to torture just because you decided to pass into their land at the wrong time.

I've only ever heard of one person ever being held as their captive there, but the ruler of the Sylphs released them and killed the one responsible for holding them for so long. Nobody has ever seen the person who was held hostage that I've heard of, so most parents would just tell their kids stories about it to scare them. Or some parents wouldn't even tell their kids about it because they only believe in things that they see and not a rumor that was passed around. Either way, I avoid going through any mountainous region, fearing any creature that lives in them.

While thinking about the Sylphs, I didn't realize that I had ended up drifting off and succumbing to darkness. I didn't try to fight it as I was exhausted, and I am finally getting the chance for a little bit of rest.

Chapter 16

D reams are something one would hope for. Dreams are a series of thoughts or even images that appear in one's mind when one sleeps. A dream could also be your subconscious trying to tell you something important. Or it could even be something you don't want to hear. It could be tragic, painful, or even so emotional that you wake up crying.

I for one wish I was one of the many few who didn't have to go through having dreams. If dreams didn't occur, then my life would be a little bit easier. I would be able to get to sleep at night. I wouldn't have to close my eyes and see the image of a room covered in blood or hear the screams of all who had died. But more importantly, my sleep wouldn't be disrupted by the voices in my head telling me that their deaths were my fault. I wouldn't be dreaming of past memories only to wake up to a life of nightmares. It would be easier.

Right now, as soon as my eyes shut, it's peaceful. As if I'm surrounded by nothing and no one. As if there is nothing that could bother me right now. I almost feel safe. But I also feel cold. I feel as if I'm frozen inside of an iceberg or like I'm standing out in the middle of a snowstorm with nothing on except for a pair of loose pants and a shirt. I felt like if I didn't find a source of warmth I'd freeze to death in only moments.

Something I want and don't want at the same time.

I woke up in a warm room that was lit up with a single candle hanging from the ceiling. I'm lying on a soft, and probably the most comfortable bed I've ever laid on, tucked under a wool blanket with a pattern of black in gray in various places. When I let my eyes adjust to the room I slowly lifted the blanket off me, and noticed how it wasn't as soft as I had originally thought it to be. It was rough almost, but the part that was covering me was quite soft.

I found that I liked the blanket though I found it unsettling that it was made from wolf's skin. I wasn't sure if it was an actual wolf fur blanket from years ago, or if it had recently been made from a werewolf's death. Either way, I found it to be slightly unsettling.

I stared at the blanket for a while before I jumped out of the bed when I had come to realize that I have no idea where I am or how I got here. The last thing I remembered was falling asleep in the carriage after almost freezing to death and Aleksandr placing his blanket over mine. I tried to think back to anything, and then I remembered Aleksandr saying *'We should be at the castle soon,'* before I had fallen asleep.

I looked around the room taking in how dark it was and how the light from the one candle and the moon coming in through the window barely lit up the room. I could see that the walls of the room were black and the curtains by the window were dark red with black swirls going up and down them in a type of pattern scheme. There were four paintings on the walls, two by the bed on each side, and two by the door which I assume leads out to a hallway. I couldn't tell what they were exactly because of how dark it is, but as I moved towards the painting closest to the window light, I heard the jingle sound of metal chains dragging against the floor.

I looked over to where the sound came from and saw that there was a chain dragging behind me. I looked down to see where it was attached and noticed how it was connected to an ankle lock that was wrapped around my ankle.

My anger suddenly came back to me within seconds, and I bent down and began trying to get the ankle lock off my leg, but no matter how hard I tried it wouldn't come off. After twelve or so minutes of trying and failing to get it off, I went to find the source of the chain to see if that would work. Once I found it, I saw it was connected to the bottom bed post which was drilled into the ground meaning I couldn't lift the bed to get it off. The only way I could get it off was if I had the key, which I'm willing to bet is the same skeleton key they used to unchain me within the carriage. I decided to give up with a heavy sigh before going back to what I was doing beforehand. I stood up and walked over to analyze the only painting that I'm able to see even a little bit.

When I was standing right in front of it, my first thought was to rip this lock off my ankle or cut off my leg and bolt to the nearest town as fast as I could. But then I remembered how I wouldn't be able to get the lock off and it would be quite difficult to run without a second leg. So, I sucked up whatever I had left of myself and stared at the painting before me.

In the painting, the King was standing alone in front of the castle with a sword in his hand covered in blood from the bottom up to the edge of it. He wore his crown on top of his head and his face had specks of blood on his cheeks and chin. But the look, damn the look in his eyes shows pain, almost as if he couldn't bear standing there as if he might have something else to be doing but couldn't. I'm sure he killed the artist for showing the emotion, that is if he even noticed it himself.

It was weird to see so much emotion in a painting as most portraits of the Kings don't have their emotions shown. By looking at the painting in front of me, I knew exactly where I was, I was in the castle. It didn't take a genius to figure it out, I mean the bed, the candle, and now the painting it was obvious.

When I did realize that, I could slightly hear the voices in my head all over again.

'You're in the same building as the King, the man who killed us?'

'He's going to burn you alive and then you're going to see just how we suffered'

'I hope he kills you slowly and painfully'

It hurt when hearing some of the things the voices said, but I began to question if what they had said was true. I mean if the King were going to kill me, why bother placing me in what seems to be a guest's room? Why wouldn't he lock me in the dungeon? Then I remembered who exactly I was taken to.

I was taken to a bloodthirsty monster who thinks he can do anything he wants with no consequences.

A person who believes he can do no wrong and everyone will follow his lead because he thinks they all like the way he rules.

A person who loves to create pain amongst others with a smile on his face and doesn't care if he's taking people from their families and friends.

But I guess none of that matters. I guess most people only see the good in him. How he takes in kids and trains them up to be part of the royal guard. Or how he punishes those who try to take advantage of the power they hold over others. They will never see the real side, and if they have I don't understand why no one does anything. Sure you're terrified, I am too but I'm done watching the people I love as well as others die because of something no one can control.

I will never see the good in a man who burned my home down. I will never feel any forgiveness towards him for killing my family and all the people I've ever cared about. I can't do it. I can't see it. And I never will. I will never forgive him for being part of the reason why Shilo died that night, I won't.

I stared at the painting for a few more moments before I turned around towards the window and walked towards it standing straight in front of it staring straight ahead of me. When looking out, I was able to see the garden covered in nothing but snow and how the forest nearby had no colors coming out of it because it was too cold up north for the Wisps to survive. I could see how even though the ground was already packed in snow it continued to snow and build up anyways. I saw snowflakes land softly against the glass of the window before they slowly melted away turning into water and slid down the window to the brick wall below it.

The windows were slowly starting to freeze over as the ice grew along the edges and began to move slowly towards the center of the window until the entire window was covered in a thin layer of ice and then I could no longer see the outside of the castle.

I let out a breath and touch the window and to no surprise, it was ice cold. Even though I could barely see out the window, it didn't stop me from continuing to look at the sky. As I looked towards the sky I was hoping to see the stars twinkling and I did, I saw many of them. It confused me as there was somehow not a single cloud in the sky making me wonder where exactly the snow was falling from. I didn't put too much thought into it as I didn't want to give myself a headache. Instead,

I continued to stare up at the stars and avoided the glare of light coming from the moon.

But then, I saw a star, I'm not sure if it was the time or a coincidence, but when it twinkled brightly it caused my attention to go straight to it and completely forget about the other stars in the sky.

While staring at it I could only think about two things; my mom and Shilo.

I thought about all the things I wish I could say to her or even ask her. If she were here with me right now maybe my life would be better and I wouldn't have to worry about who I trust and who I don't trust. Maybe, just maybe I would be able to help those who've helped me, instead of running away only to let them face the problems I created.

"I wish you were here with me now Mom. All the things I would ask you if I was doing right. Or even ask if I am being stupid for not trying to escape right at this moment." I whispered before pausing and mumbling to myself. "I mean I'm locked up in a castle against my will and yet here I am staring up at the stars thinking of all the things I wish I could say to your face right now." I knew she wasn't really there and couldn't hear me, but it still felt good to be able to 'talk' to her.

I sighed before I continued talking, "I think the first thing I would do before anything else if I could see you right now would be to run up and hug you as if my life depended on it. I would hug and not let go. I wish you were here to tell me everything will be okay. And that I won't die in pain, but I'll die happy with everyone I love around me. But I won't get that." I paused with a sniffle while trying to keep my tears in. "Mainly because everyone I love is dead. I have no one left. The only person left to comfort me anymore is myself. Even so, it's not enough, not anymore. So please, please give me something, anything to let me know I'm doing the right thing. Tell me or show me that I'm not making a mistake by not fighting back right now. I need you to tell me because I don't think I can do this anymore. I don't want to have to do this anymore. I'm just tired." I whispered while looking out the window at the star.

With all those words running through my head, I wished I could see my mom again. I wish I could see her smile and hear her laugh or even listen to her talk about how her day was. I want to hear it all. And it hurts, it still and always will hurt.

I wasn't entirely sure if I saw it to make myself feel better, but once I finished talking, I saw the star shine just a little brighter as if my mom were telling me that she had heard me and would always be with me when I need her most.

I also thought about Shilo, and when I did I thought about the last words he had said to me and how he'd promised to always be with me no matter what. It made me smile slightly as the tears slipped down my cheeks. I wasn't sure if the star was a sign that he was still here and always would be, or if I happened to look at it as it was twinkling. When I turned my head back to stare at the same star I didn't see it twinkle as it had the first time. It seemed to be frozen in the sky as if it were staring at me trying to say something.

I ignored it and chose to wipe the tears that spilled from my eyes as I thought of everything, I would say to both my mother and Shilo. I thought about how if I saw them again I would hug them and never let go, I thought about everything. With one last wipe of a tear, I turned around, walked towards the bed, laid down covering myself with the wolf skin blanket, and closed my eyes hoping that this was all a dream and that it would be gone when I opened my eyes the following morning.

Chapter 17

I woke to the sound of a door opening slowly and I could feel someone staring at me as they entered the room. I could hear their soft
footsteps heading toward me after they had softly closed the door behind
them. It is almost as if the person was trying not to wake me, but they
did a poor job at it.

I rolled over on the bed onto my back and stretched my arms above
my head, yawning before sitting up and rubbing my eyes. I then let them
adjust to my surroundings, which was when I realized that I'm still in the
room that I had woken up in only a few hours ago. I let out a soft sigh
and closed my eyes letting myself listen to the soft breathing of the other
person in the room.

"I'm sorry to wake you so early madam, but the King has requested me
to get you ready for breakfast in the dining hall." A soft timid voice spoke
out finally.

Before I could reply on the topic of breakfast with the King the voice
continued.

"I have an outfit already picked out and ready for you. I also filled the
tub with hot water so you can get washed before getting ready." When
I heard that she had already got an outfit decided for me I sat up on my

elbows and looked to where the voice had come from on the right side of the room.

When I turned my head I saw a young female with bright blue eyes and brunette hair which was tied back into a bun. She's a little on the short side and she also has a soft voice which makes me think that she could be a young Fae or even a Phoenix. But I'm leaning toward the Fae side for some reason. It could be because she's quiet and timid or maybe it was just a feeling but she doesn't seem like a Phoenix to me. I feel as if there is another side to her that she's hiding that would make her Fae, almost like a darkness that is sitting at bay waiting for its chance to come out. This was different from a Phoenix's, as they don't have to pretend to be nice to people, they are and if they don't like you then they'll tell you they don't like you.

We stared at each other for a long moment until she looked down towards the ground while twiddling her fingers. The action made me roll my eyes and turn my head back toward the ceiling.

As I stared up at the ceiling, I could feel myself slowly starting to zone out and not focus on anything around me. I wanted to let myself free of my situation for at least a small moment. But I couldn't do that. Even with the voices gone, I couldn't do that. I closed my eyes, took a breath, and then I got up and walked to the bathroom, but not before stopping and looking down at my leg, which surprisingly wasn't attached to a lock anymore. When I saw that, I looked towards the girl, and she instantly looked towards the floor again making me lift an eyebrow in confusion but I ignored it and continued to the bathroom. Once in the bathroom, I shut the door softly and leaned my back against it letting out a soft breath, and close my eyes. While my eyes were closed I could slightly smell a hint of lavender and I could hear slight shuffling in the bedroom outside of the bathroom which is probably the girl getting the outfit ready for this ridiculous breakfast I'm supposed to attend.

Nonetheless, I stood leaning against the door for a moment to let my leg rest as it was still a bit sore from the attack in the Bloodthorn Forest. But after a few more seconds I got up and slowly walked over to the counter and mirror and looked at myself carefully. I noticed how my eyes had a dull look and how there was no longer a spark in them like there used to be. My hair was a little tangled no thanks to all the escaping I was attempting on the way here, but I could fix that easily with a simple brushing. But thankfully, I'm not on the pale side, so I didn't need to worry about getting much more sunlight. Assuming I'm not locked inside this castle for the rest of my life.

While looking in the mirror I moved my focus to my surroundings and suddenly saw the tub's reflection. I turned around towards the tub and noticed how it was completely made out of a dark type of stone. I slowly walk over to the tub and slightly drag my hand across the edge of it and take in how it feels smooth but a little rough, which was to be expected since it's made out of stone. I could see the steam coming from the water, so I dip my hand in and drag it across the water feeling how the warmth from the water creates goosebumps up my arm. When I pulled my hand out I noticed how my pale skin is now bright red from the temperature of the water. I walk backward slightly so that I'm a few inches away from the tub and start to undress, starting with my dress. I place my shawl on a hook that was connected to the wall on the left side of the tub and that's when I notice a small wooden bench right next to the tub just below the hook. On the bench, there were two white neatly folded towels sitting on top of each other, as well as some flowers laying to the right of them. I stared at them for a couple of moments before turning and continuing to undress.

Once I finished undressing, I entered the tub letting out a low sigh as I sat down allowing the warmth of the water to cover my body and relax my muscles. I laid back in the tub causing the water to rise to my shoulders and I closed my eyes titling my head back a little bit so that the water was covering all of my hair up to my scalp.

I sat there for a while just letting myself think of everything that could go wrong when I exit this room. How the King could kill me at breakfast or tell me fake stories about why he's been looking for me. While thinking about that, I also thought about how easy it could be if I were to drown myself right here and allow myself the liberty of dying before the King gets what he truly wants from me. Unfortunately, I was taken out of those thoughts when I heard a slight knock on the door causing me to open my eyes and sit up, turning my attention to the door.

"Madam I do want to inform you that the King gets a little irritated as well as annoyed when people are late. So if you could go a little faster it would be much appreciated." The same timid voice of the lady from before called out.

Although I would love to be as late as I possibly could, I sighed in annoyance and decided it would be best to just comply and get myself washed quickly so that I wouldn't cost the poor girl her life before it even started. So I unenthusiastically lifted my hand and grabbed the bar of soap beside me before I began to lather myself in it and rinse it off. Afterward, I washed my hair being sure to massage the soap into my scalp, not knowing when I would get the opportunity to bathe myself again.

As I stood in front of a mirror in the room looking at myself after the girl — who I learned whose name was Mabel — had gotten me an outfit and did my hair. I wonder why I'm allowing myself to do this. Why am I not fighting back as I should be? And why am I dressed in this stupid outfit just to go to breakfast?

Nevertheless, here I am, wearing a flowy emerald green dress with a corset tightly wrapped around my waist making it almost impossible to breathe. If it weren't for the fact that I had been given this dress by the King and it wasn't meant for breakfast, I would've loved it. Unfortunately, I see no reason to be dressing this nicely for breakfast, especially with the King. The sleeves are the length of my arms and wrap around my arms nicely as they were not too loose or too tight. I'm honestly not sure why the King would want to have breakfast with me to begin with, if I were him, which I'm thankfully not, I would've thrown myself into the dungeon with nothing but rags on to keep myself warm, but here I am standing in a beautiful gown for breakfast.

After I analyzed the dress, I moved on to my hair which was designed into one thick Dutch braid that began on the left side of my head ending on the right side and over my right shoulder. There wasn't a single stray hair sticking out or any wrinkle on the dress, everything was perfect, almost too perfect.

The outfit and the hair went together perfectly, and for once, I felt nice. I felt as if I never left home and that my mom was still here doing my hair and picking out my outfits each day. It put a slight smile on my face as I stared at myself in the mirror from head to toe. But it was quickly diminished when Mabel started talking again.

"Alrighty, since you're dressed and ready to go, we must quickly get to the dining hall for breakfast. So, let's go." She said quickly and gripped my hand lightly dragging me towards the door.

As soon as we exited the room and the door closed, the first thing I notice is the musty smell of the hallway, but when I looked around, I was awed by what I saw.

Paintings upon paintings cover the walls each being different from the other but all of them either being of the royal families from before to the King now. There were several paintings of the Northern Mountains, all of them being different from the others. Some of them were during the summer and others during the winter or even during autumn. But the one thing that stays consistent in all the paintings was that there was always snow covering the mountains at least somewhere. It was almost strange how there was no snow covering the mountains, but what's even more strange was how Kings always had the idea that if they needed to they could banish someone to live in the mountains. Although their life would only last about a couple of hours at most. My best guess as to why they would send people up there as punishment when they know the snow never melts is because they want them to die, but they want to keep their hands clean when doing it. But for all I know, that could be completely wrong

As we walked down the hallway I noticed how there were guards posted between each painting. They were all standing and staring straight ahead as if they were statues. Some of them could quite possibly be statues. It was honestly just creepy how still they were all standing.

I shook off that creepy feeling as we continued walking toward what I assumed was the dining hall. While walking we passed a painting that for some odd reason caught my attention, and it caused me to stop walking almost instantly. When I stopped walking, I heard Mabel continue walking without me but was pulled back by my sudden stop of movement. I could see out of the corner of my eye how she slowly turned around with a look of confusion on her face whilst I stared up at the painting in awe and confusion.

"What are you doing?" She almost hissed at me as she knew the King would punish her if we were late.

I didn't care to answer her question as to why I stopped walking. Instead, I continued staring up at the painting questioning why the people in the picture look vaguely familiar and yet look like total strangers at the same time. It only took me a few moments to speak out the question I probably shouldn't have asked, considering it would make us much later to the dining hall than we already are.

"Who are they?" I asked flatly, as I continue to analyze every detail of the painting trying to pinpoint where I'd seen these people before.

I could feel Mabel walking closer to me until she was directly beside me. I looked over to see that she was staring up at the painting as well waiting a few moments before answering my question.

"That's the King and his wife the Queen. No one knows what happened to her. But if you know her from somewhere you probably just saw another painting of them somewhere else but that could be doubtful." She said calmly and continued staring at it with me a little longer.

I looked back up at the painting for a moment before looking back toward Mable and asking, "What do you mean it could be doubtful?"

She sighed and shook her head before pulling me along with her once again towards the dining hall. I looked back toward the painting and waited for her to answer me. Eventually, she sighed and stopped but didn't look back as she answered me.

"I mean, the King and Queen didn't have many paintings of them together before she up and vanished. No one knows where she is or if she's even still alive at this point." Then she dragged me along basically stating that she wouldn't answer any more of my questions.

I wanted to ask more questions such as 'What do you mean up and vanished' or 'Why would she just leave,' but I chose against it seeing as we approached a large double door. Mable stopped briefly in front of the door before looking over towards me looking me up and down to make sure everything was alright with my hair and outfit. But then she spoke words that I wished could be true.

"I hope you're ready," Mabel said quickly.

However, before I had the chance to respond she moved forward and opened the double doors, and walked ahead of me into the room before introducing me.

"Seraphina, your highness," Mabel said, bowing down as we enter the room.

I looked at her confused as to why she bowed, but when I looked ahead I realized why she did it. This caused me to roll my eyes before looking back down and then looking back up after taking a small breath in. When I looked up I spotted the one person who has made my life a living hell.

The King.

We stared straight into each other's eyes as if there was nothing more we wanted to do other than make the other look away first. Neither of us said anything and neither of us backed down. We did this for a while until he suddenly stood up and walked towards us. Even as he walked my way I still didn't back down or do anything other than stare him straight in the eyes.

I could almost feel the atmosphere fill with tension and worry almost as I could feel it coming from everyone else inside the room. But no one said anything, not even their breathing could be heard. Probably scared to get killed or punished by the King himself. But not me. No, I didn't care what he did to me. Not anymore.

Never again.

"Thank you, Mabel, you may go." His gruff and deep voice sounds as he reached us.

He was now standing in front of me, staring me in the eyes not even glancing the slightest bit at Mabel before dismissing her.

Without any hesitation, I felt Mabel leave and the door closed with a soft bang behind her leaving me alone in the room with the King and his guards.

Unfortunately, it didn't last that long as after a few minutes, the King dismissed all the guards in the room and it was just us in the room with nothing other than tension filling it. And still, neither of us said a word.

Chapter 18

W e stared into each other's eyes for a while, neither of us daring to look anywhere else in the room fearing that it would make us seem weak. I didn't look away, not even when I could feel the heart-wrenching power radiating off of him. It was almost so painful that my body was begging me to look away as if I had nothing to go against it. But still, I refused to look away.

His eyes are chartreuse green with tints of amber around the pupil. They're almost hypnotizing, but I didn't let them take control of me, I couldn't. I continued to stare straight back at him with all the rage and hatred I felt toward him. So much of it has been bottled up and now I'm able to let it go. I could feel myself wanting to shout at him, scream at him for all the pain he's caused me. But for some reason, I couldn't.

I couldn't move.

I couldn't speak.

I just wanted him to see it all through my eyes. I needed him to see what he's done to me. I needed him to watch the horror scene through my eyes. And I wanted him to feel everything that I've felt.

When I stared into his eyes, I thought I would see nothing. I thought that I would see a monster behind everything. I thought I would see a cold soul who hasn't a single chance of redemption. But what I saw wasn't any of those things.

I saw nothing except for how desolate his eyes looked. If anything, I would have assumed he would be happy to have captured me. I would assume that he would have had me wake up in a cell hanging from the ceiling with my arms attached to chains. But right now, now I'm standing in the dining hall in the same room as the King, who looks almost full of guilt, misery, and grief. I saw no happiness, not even a small evil tint could be seen in his eyes, I saw none of it. And that made me worry more, more worried than I already am.

Soon enough he broke the staring contest by turning his body around and walking back to where he was seated beforehand. But not before pulling out a chair and gesturing for me to sit. I looked at the chair skeptically and then back up at him before choosing to ignore the chair completely and go to the opposite side of the table. Sitting two seats away from him to keep the distance good enough for me to feel even the least bit comfortable.

He sighed when I did that and looked down for a second before shaking his head and looking back up at me. He went to speak to me but before he could get a word out one of the servants entered the room with three trays of food on the table in front of each of us, fortunately cutting off whatever he wanted to say to me.

"Is there anything else you would like my King, juice maybe?" One of the servants asked him with a soft voice while looking towards the ground.

I could tell she was afraid just by the way she was shaking slightly and avoiding all eye contact with absolutely anyone in the room.

"No Naomi, that will be all." The King replied in a flat rude tone, not even bothering to spare her a glance.

As soon as he said the word no I could see how the servant or I guess Naomi relaxed her shoulders before quickly nodding her head and hurriedly exiting the room shutting the door behind her.

The King then picked up a cloth from the table next to his tray and fixed it over his lap before looking over to me once again and gesturing his hand toward the food.

"You must be hungry from your long travels, I had the servants make this dish, especially for you. I hope you enjoy it as much as I do." The King said before eating the meats and fruits that were placed beautifully on his plate.

I stared at all of it wondering how he could even eat all of this without wanting to throw it all up because of what he's done to so many families and other people. I don't understand how he can sit here and eat while there are people out there without a home who are struggling to even find any animals while hunting. But on top of it all, they're probably out there worrying about how they're going to pay taxes to the King on time, so their families don't have to suffer more than they already have this year.

Instead of eating and stuffing my face with the food in front of me, I chose to sit there and stare at my plate not feeling the least bit hungry. It felt wrong of me to eat the food when I've done nothing but run my entire life. Whilst others are out there busting their asses off and can barely get this much food to feed their family for a month.

I watched as he ate his food for a while before he realized that I hadn't even bothered to touch the food on my plate. So, he stopped eating and pushed his plate back before wiping his mouth with the cloth that he had placed on his lap beforehand. When he looked up at me I looked back towards my plate as I didn't want to have another staring contest with him.

He coughed to get my attention back I think but he could also be clearing his throat. I looked over toward him and waited for whatever he had to say. I'm guessing he had to take a few minutes to come up with the words he wanted to say which doesn't make any sense, but I waited.

Then after a couple of moments, he spoke.

"You haven't touched any food. Why?" He asked quietly and calmly compared to how he dismissed the servant earlier.

In my head, all I could think about was why he would even care or even bring it up considering he doesn't even care about his people. I mean he's been chasing me for years, and all he has to say is why I'm not eating the food he has so 'graciously' given to me.

I didn't answer him, simply because I didn't want to waste any of my breath on him. It was also because that was a stupid question, and he should know the answer to it. I did blink at him a couple of times and we stared at each other for a moment before he shook his head realizing I wasn't going to answer him.

In response, he stood up and pushed his chair in. Which in turn caused me to do the same wanting to be on an even playing field if he were going to pull any tricks on me.

"Right well if you're not going to answer any questions we'll just go to my office, and you'll answer everything I ask there." He said confidently with a gruff tone and started walking towards the door before I even had the chance to object. He stopped near the door though and without turning his head he said "And I would answer the questions otherwise there will be consequences."

I sighed before turning and following him out of the room and towards his office. I made sure to keep at least eight feet of space between us so he couldn't do anything to me while we walked.

We walked through endless hallways, all of which had pictures on the walls and guards stationed between each painting. It was almost beautiful.

Almost.

All the paintings were different, and the walls were all black or dark red like the room I had woken up in. The floors were made of a light gray stone. There were very few windows in the castle, but when we occasionally passed by them I could either see the Northern Mountains or I could see the city of Newmore covered in snow as well as smoke coming from very few of the houses indicating they had a fire to at least keep them warm.

I continued looking around every hall that we entered and noticed little differences from each hall until we had made it to the King's office. Or I guess the room he makes decisions in when he is making a new law or something. I assume he decides to execute or punish someone in the throne room so he can get the reaction of said person when he makes his decision. It's awful really, but I doubt any King before him would do it any differently.

When we entered his office, I looked around while he went behind his desk and took a seat. He sat quietly in his chair and observed me as I looked around his office in an attempt to remember every small detail about it.

It was a dark room, with a couch on the far right of the room, and on both sides of it are bookshelves both full of books, organized in chronological order. Some date back to when the first King ruled up until recent times with King Taeg. On his desk are four candles, two on each side in the top corners making sure there is enough light to see the person he's talking to. Behind him are two windows with a view of Newmore and beyond that into the woods. On the left side of the room is a chest full of who knows what and above it is another painting of the King and the Queen only they look younger in this painting. I tilt my head and continue to look at the painting for a moment before the King coughed drawing my attention away from the painting and back to him.

"Please sit, we have a lot to discuss and not a lot of time." He gestured to the two chairs in front of his desk.

I quickly looked back toward the painting before turning back and resting gently in the chair to the left of the desk closest to the painting.

I stared at him, and he stared back for a while before looking towards his desk and reading what looked like a piece of paper. When he did this, I narrowed my eyes for a second before ignoring it and looking back toward the painting hanging on the wall.

"It says on the report I got from Aleksandr that he's yet to get your name. But that's fine seeing as I already know who you are, Seraphina." He said and as soon as he mentioned my name I flicked my head back towards him with shocked eyes and in response, he smirked slightly.

When he did that I stood up quickly and backed away while keeping a close eye on him.

Meanwhile, he just sat in his chair looking relaxed as if he had nothing to worry about. While I on the other hand was in the process of having a panic attack.

"How do you know my name?" I asked him quickly without stuttering trying to calm myself down a little.

He turned his head slightly looking at something for a short moment before he closed his eyes. I followed where his eyes went and saw a picture frame in front of him, however before I could grab it he opened his eyes causing me to avert my attention back to him and note the frame.

"I know a lot of things about Seraphina, but that's not the important part." He said in a snide tone while raising his hand and picking up the picture frame before continuing "What's important is for you to know what happened twelve years ago." He said calmly while looking directly at me.

As soon as he mentioned that he wanted to discuss what happened years ago I couldn't stand it. No matter how badly I wanted to see what picture was in the frame, I didn't want to hear what he had to say about the past so without saying anything I stood up and exited the room quickly not giving him a single chance to respond to me.

I've been wandering through the halls of the castle and none of the guards have even moved an inch to even try to stop me. So, I assume the King didn't tell them to, not unless I am trying to escape at least. While walking I discovered that each hall was slightly different from the other if you were to pay close enough attention. Or if you were me and trying to find an escape route, then you would more than likely notice the small differences. For instance, I noticed how some halls had many paintings, while others had none. I noticed how some of the halls smelt like lavender whilst others smelt of cinnamon. I noticed that each of the halls has a specific number of guards in each hall. For example, one hallway would have nine guards whereas the next hall would have twelve or even eight. My first thought was that that was the hallway number, but then I thought that there could be something that needs to be kept secret and so the hallway has more guards. I'm not entirely sure.

I didn't even realize it until I had stopped and taken a breath and when I opened my eyes, I saw that I was back in front of the painting I had stopped and analyzed when I was walking with Mabel earlier. I'm not sure if it's coincidental or if I just happened to come across it by accident, but I'm glad I did. I stopped and stared at it trying to figure out what it was about this painting that was drawing me in to look at it. I mean it was just a painting hanging on the wall. Nothing special about it. Well, except for the people in the painting.

The King looks younger than he does now, and the Queen, well I don't know, I've not seen her and since she vanished, I guess I won't get to see her. But for some strange reason, this painting and the one in the King's office kept drawing my attention and I don't know why. But while I am here I guess I could find time to figure it out. Even if I have to do it on my own.

I heard footsteps coming up from behind me but didn't bother to turn around as I'm still trying to figure out what it is about this painting. I could see the colors which brought out certain parts of it such as the Queen's eyes and the King's crown. And I could see the shadow hiding the dress that the Queen is wearing.

"Seraphina." I heard a familiar voice call behind me.

I didn't acknowledge him, instead, I continued to stare at the painting before I was forcefully turned around.

I gasped in response to being turned around as the first thing I could see was his clothed chest making me realize how close we are to each other. I tilted my head up to see Aleksandr standing there with his arms crossed over his chest looking concerned but glad that he had found me. I backed up to put some space between us but stopped once my back hit the frame of the painting. We stared at each other for a moment before I remembered that he had called me by name causing me to furrow my eyebrows in confusion and him to smirk as if he realized what I was thinking.

"How do you know my name?" I asked in a rude tone, but it was important to know how he knew it, especially when he didn't know my name before now.

He stared at me for a moment, neither of us moving or averting our stares before he finally let out a sigh in response before walking forwards a few steps and grabbing my arm dragging me along with him to wherever it is we were going.

"The King told me and he also asked me to come to find you and bring you to the throne hall to discuss something important with everyone in the castle as well as the council members from every town in the country." He responded in a calm and collected voice.

As soon as he said that, I started to try and get out of his grasp not wanting to know what the King had in store for me, especially not in front of a hundred people. I heard that nothing good ever comes from discussions like this. The throne room is where the King decides one's life, a place where he chooses if you get to live or not. A place where he gets to decide if you will serve him for the rest of your life if you must serve the rest of your life in the Northern Mountains, or if you're free to go. Usually, no one is ever free to go, so I want to try and be free for as long as I can right now.

While struggling to get out of Aleksandr's grip I made sure to pull myself in the opposite direction he was walking in to make it harder for him as well. Instead, he tightened his grip causing me to struggle and pull more. Eventually, I stopped walking altogether and just fought to get my hand free. That's when he also stopped walking. I calmed down for a split second thinking he chose not to take me to the throne room. Unfortunately, that thought was thrown out the window when he threw me over his shoulder and continued walking. I punched his back wanting to be let down but when after a few moments of doing so, a loud smack resonated throughout the hall, causing me to let out a gasp and quit struggling for a moment.

"Did you just smack my ass?" I asked in an angry tone and started to struggle to get down again.

Instead of responding right away, he smacked me again which once again caused me to stop, however this time I didn't begin struggling again as he began speaking and I needed to know what he'd say.

"Yes, I did, and if you want to keep struggling, I'll keep doing it. So, stop" he replied in a flat voice.

At this point, I was pissed off because one I didn't ask to be here, and two I do not enjoy being manhandled. So I could only hope that he's ready to endure the consequences of doing so.

I didn't listen to him, instead, I continued to struggle to make it harder on him. However, instead of slapping my ass as he had in the past, he threw me onto the ground and pinned my arms above my head. His legs were straddling my waist as he stared into my eyes with a deadly look. However, instead of shying away or turning my head in fear, I stared right back at him with the rage I have for him right now.

"If I were you, I would calm the fuck down." He whispered in a deadly tone, but before I could respond to him he continued. "I'm trying to do you a favor by getting you to the throne room on time because if we don't then we'll both get punished and I don't think that's what you want." He whispered to me in the same deadly tone but with a tint of fear as well.

"I couldn't care less about being punished. There isn't a single thing that bastard could do to me that would make me hate him any less. I have nothing left so there is nothing he could take away from me anymore!" I shouted back at him with all the rage I have in my body.

I tried again to pull my arms from his grip but he just tightened them even more around my wrists. He maneuvered his hands around so that he was able to hold my arms in one of his before lowing his hand down to grip my chin allowing one of his hands to grip my chin and make me look him dead in the eye.

"Trust me he knows how to punish you. And if you think for even a second that he doesn't know about everyone you've come in contact with since I've caught you then you're more naive than I thought." He said in a dark voice almost making me tremble.

When he said that, all I could only think about was Barric, but there was no way the King could have him. I mean I left him in that room alone in the morning when I got caught. I didn't even have a conversation with him so there's no way the King could have him. I would know.

Right?

"So quit acting like some child and get your ass to the damn throne room!" He said whilst letting go of my chin aggressively before standing back up.

Instead of throwing me over his shoulder this time, he reached a hand out to help me up off the floor. I looked from him to his hand in front of me before sighing and reluctantly intertwining my hand with his. When he pulled me up I let go of his hand and dusted myself. Once I finished that I looked up at him before kicking him in the shin and attempting to run away.

"Bitch." I heard him grunt as I made it halfway down the hallway.

Unfortunately, I didn't get farther than that as Aleksandr didn't seem to be in much pain from my kick and instead, he gripped my wrist before throwing me over his shoulder. I didn't bother struggling when he did that, as I knew it was bound to happen I just wanted to see how far I could get before he managed to get me, which to my surprise wasn't very far.

As he walked down the halls with me over his shoulder, I could feel his shoulder blade jamming into my chest at every step he took which had me wanting to release a groan in discomfort, but I held onto it because I didn't want him to give me a smart ass reply. Fortunately, after a few long agonizing minutes, he stopped walking and when I turned my head over my shoulder, I saw that we were now standing in front of a double door.

Once he was sure I wouldn't fight I assume, he threw me back onto my feet and held me in place to make sure I wouldn't fall or stumble. He looked down at me for a second before fixing my hair slightly and nodding to himself. I suppose he was making me look decent enough to be in the presence of the King. When he finally deemed me ready he gripped my shoulders, turned me around, and whispered in my ear.

"Remember the consequences." He whispered while pushing a stand of my hair behind my head causing shivers to run down my body.

And with that, he pushed the doors to the throne room open.

Chapter 19

I looked around the throne room taking in all the designs trying to zone out all the people who are now staring at me as Aleksandr holds my shoulders in a tight grip so that I couldn't attempt to run and escape. The words he whispered in my ear right before opening the door were replaying over and over again in my mind.

'Remember the consequences.'

'The consequences.'

'Consequences.'

I couldn't help but wonder what the consequences would've been. Could the King have Barric in the castle, and if so where? I mean he could likely be held in the dungeon right now, or Aleksandr could've been bluffing and Barric probably isn't even here. Regardless, am I willing to take that risk?

As I looked around the throne room I took in how stunning it was with modest braziers encircling each of the twelve soapstone columns, lighting up every part of the throne hall, and blanketing everything in a warm glow. The large mirrors on the oblique ceiling danced in the flickering light while statuettes looked down upon the oaken floor of the radiant hall. A lilac rug ran down from the throne for a few meters before coming to an end while rounded banners with burnished crowns hung from the walls. Between each banner hung a torch, almost all of them have been lit and in turn illuminated the room even more. Humble, tinted glass windows are enclosed by drapes colored the same lilac as the banners. The curtains have been adorned with decorated tips and emblazoned edges. A grandiose throne of porcelain sits behind a lavish gate of gilded wood and was adjoined by a single similar, but undecorated seat for the Queen. The throne was covered in hallowed crests and fixed on the backside is a diamond head of an extinct Abolystic that the King had wanted gone. The soft pillows were a light lilac, and these too had been adorned with adorned fringes.

Those waiting to see the King can do so on the countless modest, yet comfortable stone benches, all of which are facing the throne. Those of higher standing can instead take seats in the gilded mezzanines overlooking the throne.

The King sits upon the middle throne while the council members stand alongside a couple of steps leading up towards the throne. All facing towards me. The servants and everyone else who lives in the castle are all sitting on the stone benches. However, rather than staring at me, they're all either looking down toward the ground or they are staring straight ahead toward the King probably thinking about what is about to happen. As I looked up, I could see a few people from other towns as well as the King's coven of Witches standing in the mezzanines overlooking the throne. I tensed at the feeling of being tortured by them, but I knew I could do nothing with Aleksandr standing behind me, so instead I looked back down and stared ahead of me.

I noticed how the King was staring straight back at me with a calm and collected look, opposite of me. I'm sure if I could see myself now, my eyes would tell me just how terrified I am at this moment. I'm trying to stay calm, but it all went down the drain once Aleksandr started pushing me toward the King.

I wanted to fight against him and run out of the room fearing whatever it was that the King was going to say. However I knew I could face the reality of the consequences that would come with my defiance, so instead, I looked back at him begging with my eyes for him to help me. Yet instead of getting the help that I wanted he didn't even bother to look back at me as he looked straight ahead toward the King. Telling me that I had no way of getting out of this without someone else getting hurt in the process.

Once we reached the correct stop in the room, Aleksandr let me go and went in front of me bowing down to the King before saying, "Your majesty."

He then went to go stand in the back by the door where we had entered. I wasn't sure exactly what to do while standing here, so I looked around avoiding all eye contact with the King trying to find a way to escape. Unfortunately, everywhere I looked that could be a possible escape route was guarded. In every corner, by every door, and by all the windows there was a guard. The only other way to escape was the way I came into the room, but that was guarded by Aleksandr and I'm not really in the mood to be manhandled by him again. I could tell that I had zero to no chance of escaping the room without getting myself killed in the process, or without getting someone else killed. When I finally came to terms with the fact that nothing I could do would get me out of this situation. I closed my eyes and let out a breath before turning and looking straight into the eyes of the monster who destroyed my entire life.

We stared at each other for a moment before he nodded to someone in the back. He then stood up and started to speak to everyone in the room. I heard the back door close slightly before he spoke telling me that someone had left the room, but they will be returning.

"Everyone in this room here today is here to witness a groundbreaking moment in our lives." He spoke loud and clear so everyone could hear him. "For the past twelve years, my guards have been searching for someone who has been on the run day and night to find this person that stands before us today." He stopped for a moment to take a breath and looked around the room.

As I looked around the room, I saw people with wide eyes however they quickly reverted to look towards the ground when they noticed me staring at them. While others had their arms crossed over one another with squinted eyes and their bodies were slouched slightly. As I looked towards the witches, I could see them already staring at me, some with the same expressions as before, while a few, specifically a woman with shoulder-length strawberry blond hair squinted at me before she turned and left my range of sight. I saw another witch leave to follow her, but I figured it was out of confusion as she drew her eyebrows together before leaving.

I wasn't able to get a look at everyone's expression such as the guards or the Lords as my attention was drawn back towards the King as he began to speak again.

"This girl before you is known as Seraphina. Her mother had lived in a small village and was on the opposite side of a forest from Coldvalley." The King continued while looking at me.

It upset me that he was telling everyone about my home and my mother, but it also brought up the question of why any of this was even important anyways.

But once again, I was taken out of my thoughts by King Taeg.

"Now you all may be wondering why I brought up Seraphina's mother or even why Seraphina is here in the first place. Well, that's what you're all here to find out." He looked over at me for a moment, but nothing showed on his face.

Not a single emotion.

"About twelve years ago I got word of some important information. Now you're probably wondering what kind of information would be so important for any of you to hear about." He says while continuing to stare into my eyes.

My breathing started to become uneven because I didn't know what the King was going to say. However, I felt that it wasn't going to be anything good. I looked around to see if I could get any clues from anyone for what the King may say next, but I got nothing but confusion and questions in everyone's eyes, which didn't help settle me.

The King began to walk down the stairs toward me while continuing to talk about the information he had discovered.

"The information I had found out was where my wife, your Queen, had been hiding when she had chosen to run away." He started with an impassive look.

Everyone in the room gasped and looked wide-eyed toward the King. I, on the other hand, was anything but okay. I was trying to come up with a reason why any of this was relevant. Why him saying that he knew where the Queen was, was so important, but I couldn't come up with anything. Maybe if I was calm and my nerves weren't all over the place, I could think right but right now I can't seem to think straight at all. I looked back towards the door where Aleksandr was and stared at him begging him to help me, but he just looked at me for a second before looking straight ahead once again. I felt a soft hand touch the hair that was falling onto my shoulder and softly push it back. Which caused me to look in front of me again to notice that the King was now directly in front of me.

"The information also happened to inform me that your Queen had had a child." He said and everyone gasped again but this time my eyes went wide in utter shock and my heartbeat started to speed up. "Yes, yes I know it is all a shock to you as it was to me at the time. But what shocked me, even more, was that this said child of mine happened to be about seven years old." He said calmly while looking friendly into my eyes.

This caused wheels to turn in my head as I tried to wrap my mind around the information, but before I could he continued speaking.

"I had found out that not only had I found my wife, but that I had a child I didn't know had existed for seven years." When he said that last sentence, he gave me a small smirk before walking up towards his throne and standing there to face everyone else in the room.

I could now see all the raw emotions he had been holding since I'd been here, I could see relief, pain, misery, happiness, and sadness, I saw it all mixing in his eyes. And then it all came to me.

All the paintings kept calling to me in his office and the hallway. The way he hasn't killed me yet and how he offered to have me eat with him in the dining hall with no guards around. Everything is rushing through my mind trying to make sense of all this. I couldn't believe what he was saying.

What he was saying couldn't be possible. If it was then that would make him my dad, and I refuse to believe that my dad is a monster. I will not be told lies about how my father wasn't my real father. Why would my mother leave? Why would she lie to me about this? My dad was a kind man. My dad didn't torture and kill people out of boredom, and he didn't go around making people suffer for no reason. No, my dad loved and cared for me as well as everyone he was around.

"No" I mumbled to myself quietly as I stumbled backward slightly, I could feel my eyes watering and the tears pooling in the crevices of my eyes.

I continued to shake my head slowly in denial and I looked the King in the eyes. He nodded his head to someone as I continued to shake my head back and forth. Within a few moments of me still backing up a few steps at a time, I felt arms wrap around my waist and I instantly started to struggle against them wanting to be let go but it only caused them to grip me tighter. I could feel my breathing start to become uneven as I fought to keep the tears in.

"Let me go!" I shouted whilst scratching at the person's hands before I fell limp in their arms exhausted from my earlier struggle against Aleksandr.

I looked up towards King Taeg waiting for him to continue with what he was saying. He looked at me taking in how I was waiting for him to continue and then nodded before continuing with the story.

"When I found out about this news, I was beyond livid. I was enraged. I wasn't thinking and sent my men out to the village to slaughter absolutely everyone and bring me back my child." He spoke fiercely while looking into my watering eyes.

I couldn't stand hearing him talk about how he found it right to kill my family. To slaughter everyone I loved. I couldn't just stand there and listen to it. But there wasn't anything I could do while being held against my will.

I was screaming at him through my eyes telling him that once I was free I would make sure to make him suffer ten times more for everything he's done. But he didn't seem to care as he looked at me for a short second before beginning to speak again.

"But when my men came back to me empty-handed, I was furious. I was told that my child, my daughter, had run away. Had escaped and they didn't know where to. So, I had to make a choice. Either I look for her and bring her back here unharmed, or I let her go and let her have a life of her own." He said, taking a few breaths in between each sentence.

He looked at me for a short moment before looking down and taking a breath. But then he looked up once again and began to say, "I decided to hunt her down and find her, and I did."

I watched as he pulled the picture frame from his office out from his jacket covering his body, his right hand held onto it tightly as his right thumb rubbed over it as if what he was seeing was something he wish he could have. I know whatever was on that frame had something to do with me, but I couldn't hold in the anger that was boiling inside me as I felt tears falling down my cheeks. So instead of thinking rationally to see what picture was in the frame, I screamed at him with every bit of anger I had inside me.

"You're a liar! My mother would never marry anyone such as yourself. She would never give her soul up to a monster!" I exclaimed back at him.

He looked at me with an almost pained yet shocked look. Almost like he didn't expect me to deny him to be my father.

"You are no father of mine! My father was a kind man far better than you'll ever be. And he was there for me! So don't you dare stand up there all high and mighty and claim to be my father! Because you'll never be him!" I shouted once again before he or anyone had the chance to speak or say anything back to my first claim. I managed to shake myself out of the person holding my arms and walked forwards slightly tilting my chin up towards the King.

At that point, he looked pained, his eyebrows curved downward and his eyes were looking toward the picture he was holding in his hand. It only lasted a moment though, as he washed it all away before placing the frame back inside his jacket. All his emotions were back to being hidden behind his mask. It almost made me stand back down in fear by thinking about what was running through his head. Maybe I had finally crossed the line because we were in a room full of his people and he didn't want to appear weak. Or maybe I finally pissed him off enough that he's done with me.

"Well Seraphina, if I'm the monster you claim that I am, then I guess you won't mind what comes next." He said gruffly while walking down the steps towards me once again before speaking. "I was planning on discussing and getting your opinion on this beforehand, but since I'm a monster I guess I can do whatever I want." He spoke with strong authority causing everyone in the room except for me to shiver and turn their heads down toward the ground.

I looked at him with a questioning look, but he just continued walking toward me until he was directly in front of me. I could hear the doors to the room open again before hearing some muffled sounds. Before I could look to see what it was the King began to speak again.

"Just so we have witnesses to this current moment in time, I want everyone to hear me say this now." King Taeg said calmly and then he said the words that will haunt me for the rest of my life. "I declare that my daughter Seraphina North shall marry Aleksandr Ashbrook in a week." He said in a deadly voice before looking directly into my eyes to see the blood drain from my face and my eyes widen in horror.

He turned around to walk away but before he could get far I responded to his statement.

"No!" shrieked out as I jumped forward away from the arms that were about to grip me.

When I turned my head to see who it was I saw Aleksandr standing there with a look of understanding, yet he didn't do anything to try and stop this. Behind me I could hear people, servants, mumbling in surprise and curiosity as they seemed to not know what was happening or why it was happening. From the corner of my eyes, I could see the Witches' bodies tense as some lifted their arms and the others who were sitting from perhaps boredom stood slowly with anticipation.

"I will not marry someone just because you declared it so. You cannot control me, you have nothing and you could do nothing to make me agree to this!" I screamed at him and went up to attack him, but before I could I felt my body being pulled back and I could feel the warm breath of the person holding me on my neck making goosebumps rise. And then they whispered in my ear telling me exactly who it was.

"I told you to remember the consequences," Aleksandr said ever so softly into my ear whilst pulling a strand of my hair away from my face.

I tried processing what he meant when suddenly I remembered and my entire body tensed.

Barric.

Before I got the chance to think too much about it, my chin was gripped tightly, making me look the King directly in the eyes. I knew he could see a slight fear that they held and I'm almost positive that he enjoyed it too. But before I could say anything he started speaking again. Only this time he continued to tighten his grip on my chin causing me to let out quiet whines, but he ignored it and made his voice as deep and as rough as he could.

"I tried to be nice to you Seraphina, but you just have to make it so difficult. You're like your mother in that way." He said striking a nerve in me when he brought up my mother which he ended up smiling at before he continued. "Now I don't care how much you fight or how long you do it for, because I know I could never let anyone lay a hand on you, not even myself. So I found another alternative to punish you in your advances of defiance." He said roughly and made sure that I was looking him directly in the eyes before he turned my head over to the side of the room.

And that's when I saw him.

Barric was standing there with bruises covering his body from head to toe. His clothes were torn from the shirt down almost as if a wolf ran its claws through his clothes. I could see blood seeping from his forehead and I knew that it had to hurt like a bitch. He looked as if he was going to pass out at any minute and I knew he wouldn't be able to handle any punishment any time soon which meant that I had to stay in line just a little longer because if there was anything I could do right now, that's making sure that Barric stays alive. I had to at least save someone in my lifetime. Even if that meant losing myself in the process and giving the King what he's wanted since the beginning.

Me.

I sighed before letting my body relax against Aleksandr before the King turned my face back towards him. This time he looked proud that he had found a way to make me submit to him. But only I knew that this was only the beginning of the fight and I'm not going to quit until I either win or I die trying.

Unfortunately, before I could say anything to the King to let him know that I would follow his rules, I felt a sharp prick in my neck. I knew if I could see myself right now I would look defeated as I felt my eyes begin to get heavy and I felt Aleksandr pick me up off my feet before walking out of the throne room.

And yet the only thing on my mind before I completely passed out was how I was going to save Barric and everyone else in this broken kingdom even if it's the last thing I do.

Chapter 20

I woke up gasping for air while my hands clawed at my neck. It felt like my mind was going a hundred miles an hour and I couldn't think straight. I threw the blanket cover off of me and stood up from the bed before getting light-headed and collapsing onto the floor. It took several minutes before my breathing calmed down and I stayed where I was lying on the floor trying to get it to become even. I lay on the floor staring up at the ceiling before I closed my eyes when my breathing stabilized. After a few moments, I opened my eyes again and turned my head toward the painting in the room, and just stared at it.

I didn't have the energy to get up or get myself ready for the day. Not that I could do much as I knew I had the same cuff around my ankle, and I wouldn't be able to move far around the room anyways. So there was no point in even trying to get up.

I thought about the last thing I remembered before blacking out, but then I remembered it all.

The King is my father.

My mother lied to me.

The marriage.

Barric.

The needle.

I kept repeating the same words over and over in my head while also thinking about how I'm supposedly getting forced to marry Aleksandr in a week. Which wasn't even enough time to plan a damn wedding. Besides that, I couldn't seem to find a single thing that could be good about the entire situation.

Every time I tried to think about something good that could come from it my mind took me right back to how the King could get into Aleksandr's head and mess it all up.

I wondered how different my life would've been if my mom hadn't run away when she found out she was pregnant, but I couldn't help but think that maybe she had a reason for doing it. Maybe she reasoned that I'd have a chance at a better life away from this castle, away from the King that parents tell their kids about. Or maybe she didn't even know she was pregnant until she had already run away. So maybe her reasoning was different. Maybe she wanted a way out and when she found one she took it.

On the other hand, I thought about what my life could've been like if I lived here. How I would've grown up with my mom as well as my real father, the King. Maybe he would've been an awful man to others but maybe, just maybe he would've shown his caring side toward me. Regardless, I'm not sure I'll ever get to see a different side to him now that he's shown me how awful he could truly be. There was a tiny spot in the back of my mind that kept nagging at me and just giving me all these things that could've happened if my mom never ran. I could've had a happy childhood and not one that was traumatic. I could've seen the entire country and not just peaks of them in a room or early in the morning. I could've even made a friend possibly and had someone to talk to while growing up. I might've not been alone.

Either way, I'll never find out because I didn't get an option on what my mom wanted to do. She did it without a second thought. Or maybe she did have second thoughts, I'll never know. One thing I do know is that I could never blame her for her decision as it was probably the best decision for her at the time. I wish she could've told me before it was too late.

One thing I do want to know is how she escaped the castle back then, and if I can figure that out, maybe I can escape the same way she did. But that's not likely. They probably sealed up every hidden exit this castle has anyways, so I wouldn't have a chance of escaping. Either that or they have hundreds of guards blocking every exit even the one she escaped from back then.

Instead of thinking of ways to escape, I continued to lie on the floor and stare up at the ceiling thinking about how my life could go from great, to messed up, to a bloody fucking mess. I couldn't even think about all the *what if's* because even if I did it doesn't matter as I couldn't change anything about my situation. No matter how hard I try I won't be able to change anything.

So I let my mind drift off to whatever thoughts it wanted to and didn't bother to move a single inch. I stared until my eyes hurt and I was forced to blink and then I went back to my staring contest with the ceiling.

Eventually, I got bored of all the thoughts and decided to start counting numbers in my head until someone entered the room. I looked over towards the door and noticed Aleksandr had walked in. Instead of acknowledging him or talking to him I rolled my eyes and turned back to stare at the ceiling continuing with my counting.

6789, 6790, 6791....

I could hear him walking towards me before he stopped and stared down at me, but still, I didn't acknowledge him. All I did was continue to stare at the ceiling. I heard him sigh before he sat down beside me on the floor. He didn't say anything, he just sat there.

6817, 6818, 6818....

Unfortunately, the silence didn't last that long.

"I wasn't expecting this to happen to Seraphina," he said with a distressed sigh. "I'm sure he wouldn't have made that decision if you hadn't agitated him or pissed him off as you did." Aleksandr tried to explain in a soft voice, but all I heard were excuses.

All I heard was him blaming me for all of this like I could make the King come to this decision.

6823, 6824, 6825....

I heard him sigh before he looked around the room laying down on the ground completely with me and stared up at the ceiling as well. Then after a few moments, he started talking again.

"Look, I know you don't want this Seraphina and to be frank if I knew this would happen, I wouldn't have brought you here." He paused probably hoping I would respond but when I didn't, he continued talking. "I don't want you to hate me. But if it makes you feel any better then hate me all you want because if there was anything I could do to get you out of this I would. But unfortunately, I can't. So, we're both stuck in this mess." He said once again.

Everything he had said made sense to me, but I couldn't find myself to speak to him. If I spoke to him, that would've given him a chance to get to know me, and I didn't want that. I'm not someone who needs other people in their life. More importantly, people don't need me either and if they do then they'd be begging for death. Then again I guess if we're to be married in a week I'm not going to live with him calling me Seraphina for the rest of my miserable life. So, when he stood up and walked towards the door, I said my name.

"Sephy," I spoke in a quiet, almost whispered voice.

He stopped for a moment before turning around and looking at me slightly confused.

"What?" He asked in a questioning tone.

I turned my head slightly to look at him for a quick second before answering and turning my head back toward the ceiling.

"My name, if we're getting married, call me Sephy," I spoke in a tone that said that I didn't want to talk anymore, and I wanted to be left alone.

Instead of responding, I saw him nod his head before walking towards the door and exiting the room.

Before he closed it on his way out, he said a soft goodnight. I could tell that he waited a moment for me to respond when he noticed I wouldn't, he closed the door softly. After the door closed, I continued my counting until I fell asleep while staring up at the ceiling. I could feel my head fall and before I fell asleep I saw the moonlight shining in through the window lighting up the entire room.

6853, 6854, 6855, 685.....

Once again I was back in the endless oblivion of darkness. I'm kind of getting used to it at this point, but I think I'd be more comfortable if the voices were back in my head telling me I deserved this. I wish they were telling me that this wasn't even the worst thing that the King could do to me. That's what I needed, I needed to feel as though I got off easy, but I didn't get that and it made me feel much worse.

I didn't bother to look around for anyone or anything in this darkness. Instead, I sat and waited for the voice to contact me again. I mean that's how it usually happens, and every time I'm in this darkness the voices either torment me or the one voice helps me. And since the voices weren't tormenting me, it could only mean that the voice wanted to help me. Whether that be giving me peace for a little while or even just saying a single word to me. It would help. Then again, the last time I listened to the voice in my head I ended up here and I not only found out that the King was my father, but that he was forcing me to marry a guard who harassed me on the ground the second we met. I mean seriously what's his deal? Who just decides to take time out of their life and worry about a kid they've never even fucking met before. Only to marry them off like nothing as soon as they get them in their grasp. Like the only reason he even wanted me here in the first place was so that he would have someone to take over the throne when he was done with it. If anything, he'll control Aleksandr and make him do everything he wants him to. So really, I see no point in him marrying me off like some pawn.

Instead of thinking of all of those problems, I decided to forget about them and let my mind rest in this oblivion of darkness.

I sat there in the dark, waiting for the voice hoping that it would say anything to help me get through everything happening, and then wake up to another day of counting and not moving. That is unless Aleksandr plans on dragging me somewhere or the King or I guess my dad decides that he 'requests' my presence. Which would be stupid but what could I do, deny him? No, because then he'll get someone, probably Aleksandr to drag me to him, so I'd have no choice but to see him. Or he could end up punishing Barric in front of me so that I would learn my lesson that I shouldn't defy him. Either way, it's a lose-lose situation.

As I was thinking, I suddenly felt a cold burst of wind pass by me causing my hair to fly behind my head. I opened my eyes and turned my head to the right to see what it was, but what I saw not only confused me, but it also shocked me in a way I'd never been before.

All I could see was color. Red, green, purple you name it and it was all I saw. All of the colors were spiraling around me and flew all over lighting up the darkness. It reminded me of the Wisps in the forest I used to hang and mess around with when I was younger. All they did was fly around me getting faster and faster until it all became clear.

I could see trees swaying, leaves flying, and then landing on the ground. I could hear laughing in the distance filling my ears as I watched a child run through the leaves causing them to fly in the air again. The Wisps were following close behind her, almost as if they were keeping an eye on her. Eventually, I saw that she was about to run straight into a tree so I screamed and warned her, but nothing came out.

I tried to remember what happened next, but I couldn't seem to remember because of how long ago it was.

I was taken out of those thoughts when I saw a flash of black light enter my vision, and I noticed it was a Black Wisp which surprised me because they never come out. I stared at it as it blew wind towards the girl causing her to miss the branch and continue running until she turned her head back backward and fell into a pile of leaves laughing. It made me smile knowing that this girl has someone there for her. Even if I have no one.

I was taken out of those thoughts when I felt another strong gust of wind go past me and the scene in front of me vanished into darkness until I was back in the darkness alone. I turned my head as the wind pushed me toward another scene in front of me, and I realized quickly that it was Shilo and me. And that's when it clicked, the little girl in the first scene was a younger version of myself as well. Only it was one that I wouldn't be able to remember. Once I realized it was Shilo and me, it instantly brought tears to my eyes. Out of everyone and everything I wouldn't have expected my head to torture me like this, with my past.

I watch with tears slowly falling down my cheeks as a memory of Shilo and me was shown. When I realized it was the last moment of us together it made me want to cry even more. I placed the palm of my hand over my mouth to stop the sobs from coming out, but it was no use.

I watched as we packed up everything important to us and how he placed his necklace of a snowflake around my neck saying that if anything were to happen, I'd always have him with me. It caused me to reach for the necklace which was still wrapped around my neck and grip it tightly.

I watched as we heard screams of people in the city as guards start banging on doors searching for me. I watched as Shilo and I escaped through his backdoor, slipping into the forest not knowing what would happen beyond those trees. I watched everything happen again like it always does in my head, but this time I could see all of it, and every second of it I begged for it to stop so that I didn't have to watch how he died all over again. But it didn't stop, it kept playing, breaking my heart all over again.

I was frozen and forced to watch as the second night came with us still in the woods. I tried everything to turn and look away, but it was as if invisible hands were holding me hostage and there was glue holding my feet to the ground. I was forced to watch as my face scrunched up when I smelt the scent of death. I know I should've said something, but I didn't and that cost me everything. Maybe that whole night would've turned out differently if I had known, but I wouldn't ever get to find out.

I watched as day turned into night and within seconds Shilo grabbed me and we started to run for our lives not even knowing what was chasing us. We ran until we could see the end of the forest when I heard Shilo trip over a tree root letting out a groan as his knee hit the ground.

I watched as I turned towards him, but before I even took a step forward he screamed for me to run. I tried to take a step towards him anyways as I didn't want to run again, but before I could the creatures jumped from the trees landing on top of him and tearing the flesh from his body. I walked forward hoping to save him as he did for me, but he screamed at me to run and save myself, but I couldn't. I wouldn't let myself be free knowing I would never see the only person I had left ever again.

I couldn't do that to myself.

I watched as the younger version of me tried to fight those monsters off of the only person I cared about. All the while listening to his screams of agony and telling me to save myself. But I couldn't leave.

I wouldn't leave.

I watched as he took his last breath while staring me into my eyes and whispered his last words. Which were for me to run and save myself and that he would always love me as if I was his child, and that time I listened. I watched as I ran from the beasts behind me. I watched as one of the beasts chased after me wanting more blood. I watched as everything went dark before she woke up to nothing and was surrounded by a field of flowers all alone. Shilo was nowhere in sight which told me that it wasn't a dream. I listened as the younger me screamed as loud as she possibly could in pain. When I looked closer, I noticed multiple black and blue Wisps hiding in the background in the trees.

Blue for pain and grief.

Black for purity and happiness.

I wish now that I had noticed them in the past because then I would've known that I wasn't alone. But it doesn't matter now, because I haven't seen any Wisps or been near any in years. They're all too bubbly and wild for me and I can't handle any of them right now. Especially not when I'm not sure if the King would kill them or not.

After a few moments of watching myself break down and cry, the memory began to fade into blackness and nothing showed up afterward. I managed to quickly wipe the tears that were still sliding down my face away. After doing so I then blink a couple of times erasing any excess of any other tears that were threatening to escape. I turned around in all directions trying to see if there were any more memories that my head wanted me to see but there were none. Instead, I fell to the ground and closed my eyes hoping that when I opened them I would no longer see the endless darkness. I hoped that I wouldn't have to see any more painful memories.

However, when I opened my eyes, I was still trapped in the darkness only this time a light came from behind me. I didn't want to turn my head, so I didn't. I shook my head and shouted 'no' to whoever was listening. But clearly, they weren't having it because soon enough a gust of wind came by and pushed me to face the light and that's when I realized it wasn't my memory.

Instead, I saw something that made me choke in shock. It was a memory of my mom.

Chapter 21

I woke up with sweat sliding down my forehead, breathing heavily. I could tell that I was no longer on the ground as my back wasn't sore and I felt like I was sinking into the mattress. I quickly sat up and looked around checking to see if there was anyone in the room with me, but there wasn't. I let out a relieved sigh and flopped onto my back letting my head hit the pillow, and closed my eyes.

I thought back to the memory I got of my mother, and I couldn't believe it. I mean it would make sense with everything going on now, and I understand why my mother left, but I don't understand why the King, my father, wouldn't tell me the truth. I mean he probably was going to tell me in private but considering he's pissed at me, I doubt he'll tell me. Then again he probably didn't want me to see him as someone worse than he already is, so he more than likely was never going to tell me the truth which is why the voice in my head showed me it. Still, I could ask him about it later and see if he tells me the truth or not.

I rolled over onto my side so that I was facing toward the window and opened my eyes to see the moonlight shining into the room. I looked at the light for a while before I suddenly got the urge to get up and stand directly in the light of the moon.

I slowly rolled out of the bed and walked towards the window before staring out into the endless horizon. I could feel the light feeding my body almost as if it were my source of life and I didn't feel so drained anymore. I sighed and let the feeling go through as I knew it was probably my body beginning to wake up. As I looked out the window, moved my eyes toward the moon, and stared at it allowing my thoughts to spiral through my mind. I could, I would sit on the windowsill and hold my knees to my chest but I couldn't with the chain wrapped around my ankle. If I were able to, I would map the star constellations that I was able to see until all that was left to do was to make my own.

Unfortunately, because I wasn't able to do either of those things, I chose to sit on the ground with my arms crossed over one another and stare up at the moon to see if I could find any weird shadows hiding inside it that were trying to tell me a story. The longer I stared the more I seemed to stare into the light the more relaxed I became. Until eventually my vision somewhat blurred and I zoned out; I couldn't hear anything around me or see anything but the light taking over my vision, I felt calm.

Unfortunately, my time relaxing didn't last long as I suddenly felt a hand touch my shoulder softly causing me to flinch. It also caused me to focus back on my surroundings which was when I realized that the moon was no longer out, instead the sun was now rising making the sky light up with a variety of colors. I looked at the colors for a while before remembering the hand on my shoulder causing me to turn around quickly to see who the hand belonged to. That's when I saw Aleksandr standing directly behind me. He was staring down at me observing me I assume but when he saw I was looking at him, his eyes met mine.

His eyes held an unknown emotion in them as he stared into my eyes. I could almost feel how he wanted to start a conversation with me but was arguing with himself over it. Which was fine because there was a high chance that I wouldn't even continue the conversation. Thankfully he let go of my shoulder and turned around walking towards the bed which was when I assumed that he had made up his mind and didn't want to start a conversation.

He sat down slowly before resting his elbows against his knees and looked at me for a moment. I stared right back at him and we were both left in a staring contest with each other waiting for the other to break it or ask something.

After a while though, I couldn't seem to take it any longer and raised my eyebrows waiting for him to say whatever it was he came in here to tell me. Whether that be that my newfound father wants to speak to me or that he came here of his own free will during his own time to try and get to know me. Which is doubtful. I'm guessing he wasn't sure if he wanted to tell me what he was going to tell me as he placed his head in his hands and began to massage his temples.

I didn't feel like waiting and staring at him so I turned back around towards the window and began to stare out at all the different colors once again. I could see a light purple coming from just behind the Northern Mountains and to the East of them, and I could also see orange and pink hues. It was nice to see the different colors as they reminded me of the Wisps and my freedom, but that all came to an end when I heard Aleksandr stand from the bed and begin walking toward me once again. I turned my head towards him and saw him standing a few steps behind me and like usual we linked eyes and just stared at each other.

We did that for a while before he walked the rest of the way over toward me and offered me a hand. I gave him a questioning look before I looked down at his hand and back to him before softly sighing when I realized he wouldn't let up on this. So I grabbed his hand and instantly felt my body being pulled up from the floor. Once I was off the floor I turned my body a little away from him and walked toward the bed. As I was about to sit down I felt Aleksandr grip my arm harshly and pull me back towards him, which ended with me crashing into his hard chest. Which in turn caused me to let out an 'oomph' sound.

I looked up at him with a scowl on my face, but he smiled back at me which pissed me off even more. I attempted to get out of his arms, but that only seemed to make him tighten his hold on me. So, instead of fighting I let out a sigh in defeat and rested my forehead against his chest waiting for him to tell me whatever it was he wanted to tell me.

We stood there for a couple of minutes before I got annoyed and ended up looking up into his eyes. He stared back at me with an emotion that sparked confusion in me as it looked like he was either amused by my actions, or he was relieved to see that I wasn't fighting him. Thankfully it didn't last long as the emotion soon vanished into nothing and he had a blank face once again.

After a few more moments, he loosened his hold on me slightly allowing me to take a small step back away from him before speaking.

"I came in to ask if you would like a tour of the castle since you've pretty much been locked in this room since you've been here." He asked softly before turning his head towards the window for a moment before turning back to face me and continuing. "But if you're more interested in staring out the window or lying in bed that's fine with me." He said in an amusing tone while looking straight into my eyes.

I thought about it for a few seconds trying to think of a good enough reason for me to stay in this room. To be quite honest I could think of a million reasons to stay in this room. One of them being that I'm safer in here than out in the halls. Another was that Barric is safer as long as I'm not causing any havoc which I'm not by staying inside of this room.

When I thought about a reason to go on this so-called 'tour' I could only manage to come up with one. Which was that it would help me to find an escape from the castle, which was what I needed. I let my mind work through the pros and cons of what could happen in every scenario as I immediately put my attention toward the window. I let my thoughts wander for a moment and didn't think about Barric or anyone else except for myself. I wondered if this 'tour' would be beneficial to me or not. In the end, I couldn't help but think that this could help me find my way out of this horrid place. So, as I stared out the window for a moment longer I sighed and nodded my head whispering a soft 'sure' to Aleksandr, and almost instantly I could feel the excitement radiating off of him at a thousand miles an hour.

Before we left the room, Aleksandr had called Mabel to bring breakfast to us and we ate in my room in complete silence with him looking at me from time to time. Probably thinking I would find a way to stab him with the fork that was in my hand, which I did think about doing after he looked at me for the fourth time. After eating I had asked him to take off the stupid ankle cuff so I could go to the bathroom and bathe before taking this so-called 'tour' around the castle.

Afterward, I changed into the outfit that he had asked Mabel to bring in, which was a simple black dress that went all the way down to my toes which I was grateful for.

As soon as I exited the bathroom, Aleksandr looked over at me which caused me to lift an eyebrow at him, but he shook his head and looked down towards the floor. I rolled my eyes in response and walked towards the door. Only for him to follow and grip my arm harshly while pulling me out of the room.

We walked down the halls in silence, and every so often Aleksandr would look over his shoulder to see if I was still following behind him. If it wasn't for the fact that this was a tour and not a trip to my apparent father's office then I wouldn't have even acknowledged him when he invited me on it. Unfortunately, it was a tour he invited me on, and I need it if I want even the smallest chance at escaping this horrid place.

"You know I'm not going to disappear every time you look away right?" I said as I walked forward so that I was walking right beside him instead of behind him.

"Can't be too sure when it comes to you Sephy." He responded back after a while.

He wasn't completely wrong, we both knew that if I could I would escape at any given opportunity. However in order to escape I'd need a way out which means I needed to know the layout of the castle. Which in other words means I needed to go on this tour.

"I'm sure you wouldn't be able to catch me if I planned to escape. I know you too well now," I said, glancing at him out of the corner of my eye. His body tensed slightly, and for a moment, I caught the flicker of something in his expression—maybe uncertainty, maybe a hint of something else—but he didn't respond.

We walked in silence after that. He only spoke when he needed to show me a new room or a hallway I hadn't seen before, his voice clipped and distant.

As we turned down another hallway, something about it struck me as oddly familiar. And there, once again, was the painting of the King and Queen—the one I had first seen with Mabel. The same painting that had haunted me ever since Aleksandr had dragged me away, before the truth of my marriage had come to light.

I stopped mid-step, a strange sensation creeping over me. It was as if something, someone, was trying to get my attention, but their voice was muffled—just out of reach. The feeling lingered, unsettling but undeniable.

I turned back to the painting, searching its surface, desperate for something that could explain this strange pull. But there was nothing new, nothing different. My gaze landed on the woman in the painting—my mother—and I stared into her eyes.

But what I saw wasn't the warm, vibrant woman I remembered. There was no spark of life, no trace of the joy she used to show when Dad would make her laugh. Instead, all I felt was an overwhelming emptiness, a dullness that made my stomach twist.

In that moment, she felt more like a stranger than my mother. The woman who had been so central to my life suddenly seemed foreign, cold, unrecognizable. And I wondered, for the first time, if that was always the real her—the one I never truly knew. Had I spent my whole life growing up beside a stranger, not the woman I had thought she was?

The thought hit me hard, like a punch to the gut. What if the two people I had always trusted, the ones I thought loved me—my parents—had been deceiving me all along? What if my father wasn't even mine, the person I had mourned so deeply? The realization was like a wave crashing over me, leaving me gasping for air, more isolated and lost than I'd ever felt before.

"You know, you kind of look like her in a few ways," Aleksandr whispered, his voice low as he stepped up beside me, his gaze fixed on the painting. "Like how your hair is straight and black, and you two have the same nose—if you look closely enough."

He stood there for a moment, his eyes lingering on the image of my mother, and I could feel his presence beside me, strangely quiet. His words, however, hung in the air between us, somehow heavier than they should have been.

I shrugged, unsure of how to respond. People used to tell me I looked more like my dad—*my real dad*—than anyone else, but I guess that was a lie. Not that I could exactly call them out on it; I didn't look much like my mom, and definitely not like the man who raised me. Sure, he wasn't my biological father, but my mom sure did a good job of finding a convincing stand-in.

He had the same green eyes I saw in the mirror every morning, the same eyes I used to think were the only thing I truly shared with him. My mom, on the other hand, had brown eyes, so I knew I didn't get them from her. His best friend used to say I had his "contagious smile," which always made me laugh, because I didn't think I could inherit something like that. But now, I guess I was wrong. I didn't inherit anything from him at all. Nothing of real substance, anyway.

I was taken from my moment of almost crying as I felt Aleksandr place his hands on each of my shoulders, squeezing them gently causing me to look behind me and up at him in confusion. In response, he looked down at me slightly before looking back up at the painting and crossing his arms over his chest, and asking a question that made my heart skip a beat.

"What was she like?" He asked softly.

I opened my mouth to reply before closing it trying to decide if it was alright to tell him or if I could trust him with it. But I guess it couldn't hurt me or anyone if I told him.

"She was great," I said while looking back up towards the painting. "Whenever I would come home crying, she would hold me for hours if needed and would wait until I had calmed down to ask what happened." I let out a small laugh and smiled at the thought of it before continuing. "She would also make breakfast every morning and sometimes it would be something new or something we've had in the past," I said and paused for a second while looking towards the ground thinking about my mom's famous waffles that she used to make.

I kept thinking about it, letting my thoughts take over before I felt Aleksandr turn me around and lift my head with his finger on my chin. We looked at each other for a second and he went to open his mouth to speak but before he could I continued talking again.

"She would also tell me stories before going to bed about her best friend from when she was a kid who lived in another village. But she said something had happened and they weren't allowed to see each other anymore." I spoke softly with a smile on my face until the last sentence wondering who that best friend was and if they were still alive or not. If so then maybe they're my way out of this hell hole.

Aleksandr smiled lightly at me before he responded.

"She sounds like she was an amazing woman. Although I've never met her, I've heard stories from my dad about how the King and Queen met. I'm not sure if those stories are true." He said quietly while closing his eyes before looking back up at the painting again. "Your mom, what was she? I heard stories about what she was but there's so many that I don't know what to believe." He said as he turned his attention back to me completely awaiting an answer from me.

I looked at him before looking back towards the painting staring into my mother's eyes hoping to get an answer from her on if I should tell him or not, but there was nothing. I closed my eyes and let out a long sigh before turning back to face Aleksandr. We stared at each other for a while, but I stared directly into his eyes to see if I could see anything behind his eyes to make sure if I could trust him or not. Then again I guess it doesn't matter, considering the King – my father – married my mom anyway so he must know what she was. Then again maybe my mom asked him not to tell anyone what she was, though I see no harm in me telling anyone considering she lied to me my entire life. So, I mustered up the courage and told Aleksandr.

"My mom," I started with a sigh before looking towards the picture again. "She was a Phoenix, if you knew her or ever met her at least once you would know that. She was the kindest, most caring person you could have ever met." I paused for a moment, closing my eyes and looking toward the ground before continuing. "She cared more about other people's happiness and well-being than her own," I spoke barely above a whisper, but I knew he heard me.

I heard him let out a soft sigh before speaking again as we stood still in front of the painting with my biological father and mother, yet I still couldn't believe that she had lied to me. Whether or not she was my best friend for several years of my life she will remain one of the only people I will ever have trusted with absolutely anything. And yet, she still lied to me the entire time. It makes me feel as though I can't trust anyone if I couldn't even trust my mother. So when I really think about it, I am alone and have been for a while, only able to trust myself with my thoughts and feelings because everyone else is either a liar, gone, or someone holding me away from my freedom.

I was taken out of those thoughts though when I heard Aleksandr ask another question, one that had me taking a deep breath and letting out a shaky sigh.

"What about your dad? What was he like?" he asked in a tone that seemed to carry sadness.

I smiled at the question, but there was an unease that crawled under my skin. It wasn't the question itself that made me nervous; it was the way he referred to him as *my dad*, without hesitation, without trying to make it sound like something lesser. That brought a real smile to my face—one that wavered slightly, tears welling up but quickly blinked away before they could fall. I faced Aleksandr and replied, the weight of my emotions settling into my chest.

"He was the best dad I could have asked for," I said with a small smile, briefly meeting his eyes before glancing at the guards in the hall. I could feel their presence, and knew they were listening. It didn't matter, though. I had no reason to hide who my father was or what he meant to me. He was *my* dad, and nothing anyone said would change that.

"He was always there when I needed him—whether it was for a hug or a little boost of confidence to try something new." I paused, taking a slow breath before continuing. "One time, I wasn't sure if I could climb this tree. Everyone else was doing it, but I was scared I'd get hurt. I just sat there, watching them, feeling like I couldn't keep up."

I exhaled, letting the memory unfold. "But my dad came over. He told me that even if I fell, at least I tried. And that if I fell, I should get back up and try again. And you know what? I kept falling—*a lot*—but each time, he was there. He'd help me up, telling me I could do it. And eventually, I did. I climbed that tree after all those falls."

My voice carried pride, but my eyes began to mist over. I blinked quickly, trying to hold the tears back, but the memory was powerful.

We both fell into a quiet, shared silence for a while. Finally, Aleksandr spoke, breaking it.

"He sounds like a great guy. I'm sorry for what happened," he said, his tone somber.

I shook my head, unwilling to let the sorrow settle in. "It's okay," I replied, turning away as I began walking down the hall, needing space from the conversation. I knew how this story would end—if we managed to survive the night and were taken to the castle, my father would never leave it alive. And my mother... well, I had no doubt she would face a cruel fate, too. The King would never forgive her betrayal, no matter the truth of it.

I heard Aleksandr's footsteps quicken behind me, and I slowed my pace, letting him catch up but still not stopping. He was panting as though he had just run a race, but his breathing steadied after a moment. We continued in silence, and I was grateful he didn't bring up my parents again.

After a while, we passed more guards and entered a room. I closed the door behind us, pausing as I took in the surroundings. I realized we had ended up in the library. A sense of calm washed over me, and a small, genuine smile tugged at my lips. For a brief moment, I felt at peace. I glanced at Aleksandr, who had no expression on his face—just an endless void, an emptiness that reminded me too much of my father's influence. I couldn't help but wonder how much of that void he already held within him.

Rather than linger on the thought, I reached out and gripped his arm, pulling him down one of the aisles. As we walked, he asked another question. It caught me off guard, and I drew in a sharp breath before I responded.

"What was your dad like, if you don't mind me asking?" He asked, lifting a hand to scratch the back of his neck.

I spoke softly, dragging my fingers along the spine of a book as I thought about how to answer. "My dad was a Wolf. Nothing special," I said, glancing at the titles on the shelves. "Our village was a mix of all kinds of people. Most were Wolves, thanks to my dad's pack. The rest of the village? A big mix of other beings."

I paused when I spotted a book that seemed useful, pulling it out to read the title. Flicking through the first few pages, I placed it back carefully before continuing.

"Some Fae, a few dragons, and maybe two or three lone Witches," I added, my voice soft. I reached for another book and blew the dust off its cover, preparing to check it as well.

As I read the title, I realized it wasn't what I needed. I put it back and kept searching.

"There were also a bunch of Wisps living in the forest that separated my village from Coldvalley," I said, a faint smile touching my lips. I had finally found the book I was looking for and moved toward a nearby table, continuing, "They were my best friends. I used to run around that forest with the Wisps every day. They were the only Abolystics who didn't mind my presence."

I set the book in front of me, sat down, and pulled out a chair, gesturing for Aleksandr to join me.

He hadn't said anything in response to my story. He had followed me silently to the table, eyes full of curiosity, though he didn't ask questions. I ignored the quiet look he gave me and opened the book titled *Order of the Ancients*. It was filled with the names of all known Abolystic creatures and their abilities. I hoped it might help me figure out what I was—or, more accurately, what I was *becoming*.

Aleksandr sat beside me, still silent. I flipped the book open to the first page, where it listed the names of the creatures, from the rarest to the least rare. There were three pages of names, so I knew this would take a while.

Out of the corner of my eye, I saw Aleksandr glance at me with a confused look. He didn't hold back for long.

"Why are you looking at a book of all Abolystic creatures, Sephy?" he asked, his voice laced with suspicion.

At the question, my heart skipped a beat. I froze, realizing I couldn't tell him the truth—not without risking my life in the process.

Chapter 22

I didn't answer him—not because I didn't want to, but because I didn't know what he would do with the information if I did. Instead, my mind raced as I tried to think of a plausible reason for reading this book. When I glanced at him, I saw the confusion on his face, which made it easier to come up with a lie. There were so many possible reasons for me to be reading this right now. I could say I was bored, or that I was reading to figure out his weaknesses. The options were endless. The only thing I was sure of was that I wouldn't tell him the truth.

Once I had a reasonable lie in mind, I turned my attention back to the book, brushing off the dust with a deliberate motion before speaking.

"It's been ages since I've read up on all the creatures of the world," I said casually. "Figured I might as well do it now, since I don't have anything else to occupy my time." I paused, placing my finger on the spot where I had left off. Then, I looked up at him, my expression calm. "Why, do you have a problem with me reading?"

I could see his confusion shift to something like shock, but after a moment, he just shook his head and said nothing.

I hummed in response, allowing a small smirk to play across my mind. Turning back to the book, I resumed flipping through the pages. This time, I focused on the one that discussed the rarest creatures in the world, the ones most people never even bothered to mention anymore because they were thought to be extinct.

The truth was, if anyone dared to speak of them, a disturbing pattern would likely emerge. Their deaths were often linked to three common factors: the witches and their dark dealings, the Kings—and all the Kings before them—or the possibility that they never even existed in the first place, and someone made up these creatures to create a myth. In most cases, the blame often fell on the witches, though in recent years, that wasn't always the case.

As I flipped through the pages, I noticed that some had been torn out completely, and others were so badly damaged that it wasn't worth even trying to read them. But after a few more moments of flipping, I came across a page in good enough condition to study.

The first creature listed was an Oni—basically, a demon. They were described as terrifying beings with one eye that glowed a brilliant diamond blue and the other a blood-red. Their teeth were described as sharp as sword edges, and they would eat almost anything... except other creatures. Their reputation was built on punishing those who broke their rules within their lands, and honestly, if the King weren't a Basilisk, I might have assumed he was an Oni himself. Given how many people he'd punished and killed, it wouldn't surprise me.

Fortunately, I inherited a few of my mom's genes, so I didn't turn out to be some evil monster. My eyes are a mix of brown and green, so I didn't have to worry about being an Oni. At least I could thank the gods for that.

But before I was absolutely certain, I kept skimming through the page, gathering more details on the Oni. Apparently, they only came out at night to hunt, so if anyone had ever seen one, it would have been during those rare, quiet hours when no one else was around. After absorbing the rest of the information, I concluded that I wasn't some twisted version of an Oni, so I continued my search.

Turning to the next page, I was relieved to see the top of it read *Phoenix*. That made sense. Though they weren't extinct, sightings were rare because so many had died in the past few years. That probably explained why my mom had kept her true nature a secret. I'd only ever met one other Phoenix in my life—Shilo.

Before I let the memories pull me under, I quickly flipped to the next page. But what I saw wasn't what I expected.

Instead of continuing with the next creature, the page seemed to be an extension of the Phoenix section. Upon closer inspection, though, I realized the words had been written over, and the handwriting was unfamiliar. I glanced over at Aleksandr, but he was over by a bookshelf, looking through other books, distracted. I took the opportunity to lean in closer and squinted at the text. The words were simple, just the name of another book, with the number 305 next to it.

That was all I needed. I stood up quickly and headed toward the aisle where the book should be. It took a while, but I eventually found it, tucked behind a pile of Phoenix ashes. I assumed it was some kind of joke, since many believed a Phoenix could come back to life from its own ashes. That myth had been disproven years ago when their population started dwindling, but the superstition had lingered. I shook my head, pushing those thoughts aside, and focused on the task at hand.

I dusted off the book before opening it to page 305. As soon as I did, a piece of paper slipped out, drifting toward the floor a few steps away. I let out a sharp gasp in surprise, quickly closing the book with a loud *bang* before shoving it back into place.

I grabbed the note from the floor, tucking it into the neckline of my dress, hoping Aleksandr hadn't seen. When I turned around, my breath caught in my throat. Aleksandr was standing behind me at a distance, watching me closely. I froze, wondering if he had noticed the note or if he had just arrived.

"What was that bang?" he asked in a low, concerned voice as he walked toward me.

I glanced around, momentarily confused, before remembering the loud snap of the book slamming shut.

"It was nothing," I quickly said, offering an excuse. "I just dropped a book and put it back when I found it." I hoped he wouldn't push further.

He furrowed his brows, glancing at the floor, then following the trail of my hands before finally meeting my eyes. I held my breath, praying he believed me and would drop the subject. Fortunately, he did.

I exhaled with relief as he turned around and walked back to the table where I had been sitting before, picking up his book and resuming his reading without another word.

A moment later, I glanced back at the spot where the note had fallen, shaking my head, trying to convince myself that there was no way he could know about it—or at least, I hoped he hadn't noticed. I walked back to my seat at the table, sitting slowly beside Aleksandr and stealing a quick glance at him. He seemed oblivious, or at least I thought he was. I turned my attention back to the book, taking a few deep breaths before turning the page to the next creature.

This page was about Harpies. I didn't know much about them, given how long they'd been in the world, but as I read through the information, I found some strange similarities to Phoenixes. For one, they were said to be beautiful, always wearing smiles and exuding an infectious energy, ready to celebrate life. They were musical beings, known to carry music wherever they went. That thought made me smile inwardly, hoping they were truly as happy as they seemed—though I knew from experience, anyone could hide their true feelings behind a smile, if they tried hard enough.

For a moment, I almost thought I could be a Harpy, but then I reached the end of the page, where they described what they actually looked like. It said that most Harpies had golden amber eyes that gleamed when the sunlight touched them, and long, wavy dark hair that shimmered in the wind. But the most distinct feature of a Harpy was its wings, which were key to identifying the different types of Harpies.

There were Snow Harpies, with wings as clear as ice and cold to the touch. If I had to guess, I'd say they could easily disappear into the Northern Mountains, but then again, it was only their wings made of ice, so I wasn't entirely sure about that.

Then there were the Fire Harpies, whose wings were aflame, though they never caused harm unless someone touched them. I don't know about anyone else, but I certainly wouldn't be foolish enough to touch fire. As I read more about them, I learned that Fire Harpies had a peculiar challenge: if someone could touch one of their wings without screaming, the Harpy would grant them any favor they wanted—whether that favor was requested immediately or years down the line. It sounded fascinating, but I wasn't entirely convinced. After all, touching their fiery wings would likely result in losing a finger—or worse, an entire hand.

Next were the Wind Harpies, whose wings were soft and white, capable of controlling the wind itself. They played a key role during the crowning ceremonies of Kings, where they would summon leaves and snow to swirl around the newly crowned monarch, symbolizing peace and freedom. Unfortunately, that tradition seemed to have faded with the Harpies' disappearance. I wouldn't be surprised if King Taeg had something to do with it—he was hardly known for fostering peace and freedom.

The last Harpy mentioned was the Earth Harpy, whose wings were made of leaves that changed color with the seasons. While that was beautiful, it came with a downside. If their wings died, so did they—slowly, but inevitably. Unlike the other types of Harpies, the Fire Harpies thrived in warm areas, the Snow Harpies lived in the Northern Mountains, and the Wind Harpies, who could control the wind, moved freely, often residing near the Selkies in the mountains.

As I read further, I tried to find any explanation for the disappearance of the other Harpies, but all I found was one glaring weakness they all shared: a dagger forged from ice and the blood of a cursed witch could kill them. There was no word on where such a dagger was now, but it was clear that no one had seen one in years. The mention of cursed witch blood piqued my curiosity—why not just the blood of an ordinary witch? But I didn't bother dwelling on it; after all, cursed witches had been extinct for as long as anyone could remember.

When I finished reading about the Harpies, I let out a soft breath, feeling the weight of their fate. Aleksandr noticed, but only shook his head and returned to his reading, seemingly uninterested. I turned the page, hoping for something that could finally help me understand what I was before it was too late.

Unfortunately, the next page was damaged beyond recognition. It was almost impossible to make sense of any of the words without straining my eyes. I flipped through the pages until I finally reached one that was somewhat readable.

The next page was about Elves, a topic I knew all too well. A few years ago, the King had them all killed after their eldest member devised a plan to ambush the castle and kill him. I couldn't say I disagreed with the plan, but not everyone was in agreement. When someone betrayed them and spilled the plan to the King, well, he made sure to silence them permanently, cutting off their heads and wiping out the rest of the Elven. Though I hated the King's cruelty, it did assure me that I wasn't one of them. And honestly, I wasn't sure if I'd ever see one again.

Unfortunately, just thinking about Elves brought back memories of my time with Shilo. I remembered him teaching a young Elf how to make a flower bloom within seconds. The boy had struggled for months, but he never gave up, and one day, he did it. I'll never forget the giant smile on his face when he succeeded, how he jumped on Shilo, thanking him over and over for not giving up on him. I knew Shilo too well—he never would have given up. I'd seen his "wall of memories"—a collection of photos of people he'd helped. He always tried to get me on that wall, but every time he did, I'd take it down, convinced I was beyond saving. And, sadly, I was right. He never had the chance to add me to that wall.

I squeezed my eyes shut for a moment, pushing away the memories before continuing to read about the Elven to make sure I wasn't one of them. When I reached the section on their physical characteristics, I knew for sure. My ears were perfectly normal, not pointed like theirs, and while my right eye was green, it wasn't the same as theirs. Elven green eyes changed with their emotions—dark green when sad or upset, and bright green when happy or excited.

Relieved, I flipped to the next page with an internal groan.

The page showed a black-and-white illustration of a dragon-like creature. It looked beautiful, but I had never seen anything like it. I glanced beneath the image to find the name: *Etoirir*. I wasn't sure if I was pronouncing it correctly, but I didn't care enough to dwell on it. I read on, hoping to find some answers.

According to the book, the Etoirir was a type of Dragon, but unlike the typical dragons that had fiery orange eyes and hair that sparked when they got angry, this one was different. The Etoirir was an Ice Dragon that could control all forms of water. It was said that depending on the type of Etoirir, it could even create ice from its own hands. There were some downsides to being an Etoirir, but the text was difficult to read. Some words were faded, while others had been scribbled out entirely. If the downsides were significant, it would explain why they were so rare. After all, any creature found to be "too human" often met an early death.

The book went on to say that these creatures felt most at home in cold environments. Even though they could get cold, they couldn't die from the freezing temperatures. This made me think that if there were any Etoirir left, they might be hiding in the Northern Mountains, never wanting to leave. If I were one of them, banished to the mountains, I don't think I'd want to leave either.

I paused for a moment, contemplating the idea that I could possibly be this creature. However, it didn't make sense. My father was a Basilisk and my mother a Phoenix. There was no way I could be an ice creature. If I were, then at least one of my parents or some relative would have to share that lineage—and I highly doubted anyone in the royal family was linked to ice, water, or anything cold. On the other hand, it was possible that my mother's bloodline had a distant descendant who was a creature of ice, but to be sure, I'd have to ask the only person who would know.

I slammed the book shut, making Aleksandr jump in surprise. I quickly stood up, placing the book back exactly where I had found it. As I turned around after putting it away, I noticed Aleksandr standing in the opening between the shelves, eyeing me with furrowed brows. He opened his mouth to speak, but I beat him to it.

"Take me to his office. He and I need to talk," I said sternly, locking my gaze with his.

He hesitated, glancing back and forth between me and the book I had just returned. Finally, he sighed, nodding slightly before turning toward the door. I followed closely behind him.

We walked through the halls in complete silence, turning left, then right, then right again. Eventually, we arrived at his office. Aleksandr told me he'd find me later, as he had training to attend to, and after that, he left.

Now, I stood in front of the King—my father's office door—trying to summon the courage to knock. After a few seconds of hesitation, I exhaled softly and knocked. Standing in the hallway, staring at the door, would only delay the inevitable.

I heard a low, gruff voice tell me to enter. I took a deep breath, exhaled, then gripped the door handle, twisting it open and stepping inside.

When I closed the door behind me, he looked up. His face was unreadable until he saw it was me. Then, he smiled slightly, which sent an involuntary shiver racing up my spine. He smirked at my reaction before looking back down, motioning for me to sit. I walked over and took the chair closest to the painting on the wall, glancing at it briefly before turning my attention back to him—my tormentor, my father.

He was already watching me, leaning back in his chair with his fingers steepled in front of his face.

"What can I do for you, Seraphina?" His voice was casual, a stark contrast to the dark, menacing tone I had heard the previous day in the throne room.

It calmed me slightly, but not enough. I knew just how ruthless he could become in an instant.

I didn't speak right away; instead, I locked eyes with him, watching his expression. He raised an eyebrow in question, but I didn't break my gaze. I stood up slowly, walking over to the bookshelves, my fingers gliding over the spines of the books as I took my time, deciding how to phrase my question.

"Why did Mom decide to leave you when she knew she was pregnant?" I asked, turning around to face him. My hands were clasped behind my back, my posture calm, but my tone was firm. Before he could respond, I quickly added, "Because I know my mother, and there's no way she would have left without a reason. So why?"

He closed his eyes for a moment, and I squinted, wondering if what I had seen in my dream was true. When he sighed, I kept my focus on him, waiting for his answer.

He finally stood from his chair and walked to the window behind him, his back to me. "I don't know why your mother left," he said, his voice heavy with a sigh.

I opened my mouth to call him a liar, but he raised his hand, silencing me before I could speak. He continued.

"All I got from her was a note telling me she was leaving. She couldn't live in this castle anymore, surrounded by everything and everyone. She asked me not to look for her, but of course, I didn't listen. I searched for her until I finally found her."

His voice softened as he spoke, and my chest tightened, but I said nothing.

"Unfortunately," he continued, "when I did find her, I discovered she had remarried and had a child. A seven-year-old."

His words were calm, but there was a sadness in his tone, almost as though he regretted it. I could see the shift in his expression when he said she had remarried, and I wondered if he had hoped she would've stayed for him. He took a breath, turning his gaze to the painting on the wall before glancing at me.

"She took you away from me. And for that, I had to take you away from her. It wasn't supposed to happen the way it did."

His voice almost sounded sincere, but I didn't believe a word of it. I couldn't.

I needed to get the truth from him somehow, but I wasn't sure how. The voice in my head had led me here to see one of my mother's memories, and I needed to know if it was real. If it was, everything I thought I knew about my past would be shattered. But for now, I had to get through this conversation, get what I needed, and then return to my room to read the note that had fallen from the book.

I glanced at the painting of my mother on the wall. It was almost as if she were staring at me, silently pleading for me not to bring this up. But I had no choice. I took a deep breath, closed my eyes, let it out slowly, and then turned back to my father.

"I will ask you this one time," I said, my voice steady as I fought the stinging in my eyes, "and only one time."

I saw his eyes narrow, a muscle in his jaw twitching, but he remained silent, the air around us thick with the tension that crackled between us.

"Did she leave because she discovered what you intended to do to me—your own child—just to prevent an heir from being born?" I asked, my words barely a whisper, the weight of them making my throat tighten as I stared at him, trying to hold back the tremble that threatened to break through.

I didn't want to believe what I had seen in the memory, but when I saw the flicker of realization in his eyes, my heart shattered. It was as if he couldn't believe I knew the truth—and that she had known it too.

His response, however, only made my anger boil over.

Chapter 23

We stared at each other with anger in both of our eyes, only I know why I have anger in my eyes. I have no idea what he was angry about. I mean sure it could've been because I accused him of something I know nothing about, but I wanted to know the truth. The truth was all I was asking for.

After a couple more minutes, he finally let out a breath, I knew he was still pent up with rage as he turned his head to the painting on the wall and dragged his hands down his face before turning back to face me. When he saw me still staring at him in anger he turned back around so that his body was fully facing towards the painting.

"Your mother and I met each other in Newmore when we were both young." He started in a low but saddened voice.

I wanted to open my mouth and say that this wasn't what I asked as it only made me angrier but before I could he continued.

"At the time my dad was still the King, and I didn't have many things to worry about. But your mother's family, on the other hand, weren't as well set as mine was." He said with a low soft voice taking in a breath before continuing. "Her parents had had many children so they would work to get money for the family. I ran into her in the middle of the street on one of her free days which caused her to drop the food she had just bought for her family." He chuckled slightly when he said this but I furrowed my eyebrows questioning what this had to do with my mother leaving him.

"It probably would've lasted them about three weeks at most. So, when she dropped it she started to freak out saying how she had no more money to buy anything else, and I just stood there watching her." He said.

This angered me more because he didn't do anything to help my mother, but before I could interject and call him an asshole for it he continued talking.

"I figured since I didn't need anything, I could help her. So, I did, I gave her about half the money I had on me at the time which for her family was a fortune." He paused for a moment to look back at me and I could've sworn I saw his eyes beginning to swell with tears but before I could be sure he turned back around to face the painting. "My father found out about the incident and told me that I wasn't to waste such things on unimportant people," he said and scoffed as he did so.

I'm sure if it had happened today he wouldn't think twice about it as I'm pretty sure he would tell the guards to put the women in the cells for ruining his clothes.

"So, I did as he said only, I made her an important person. We hung out in secret for years until finally the crown was passed down to me when my dad fell sick and passed away." He said as he brought his hand up towards his face and wiped his eyes before turning towards me and continuing again. "And almost six days later I declared her my Queen and a Queen she was." He spoke with adoration which brought a smile to my face as he spoke proudly of my mom.

I guess we could agree on at least something. Then again we could agree on more than that if I opened up to him, like how we're both pissed at my mother for lying and also running, but I didn't let that go to my head like he had.

After a little hesitation, I walked over to stand next to him by the painting and just stared at it.

"This was the first portrait we had done of us together. We were young at the time and didn't know what we were doing." He said as he looked at the floor slightly before he looked back up at the painting. "Time went on obviously and things happened between us that I wish I could take back. One of those things was what I said to her the night before she left. I guess I can only blame myself for her leaving me like that." He said as he turned towards me and stared at me silently with regret in his eyes, but it still didn't mean anything to me. "But I will continue with my plans, you and Aleksandr will be married in three weeks." He said in a determined tone while walking back to his desk.

Another thing I noticed when he said that was how his face went from despair and regret to almost nothing in only a few seconds.

I didn't respond to him when he said that, as I knew I wouldn't be marrying Aleksandr.

Instead, I looked back towards the painting to see my mother looking at my so-called father in the eyes with nothing but admiration and happiness. I'm not entirely sure where it all went wrong as I knew somewhere along the way my mother lost that spark that she had in her eyes. Every time I looked at the painting in the hallway it bothered me, and maybe now I know why. Maybe it's because I could tell that my mother wasn't happy anymore. Or maybe it was because I could see my pain through her eyes. Either way, I knew she wasn't happy, and what he said to her that night was the final straw and for that, I'm thankful that she left.

My attention was taken from the painting to my 'father' when I heard him start talking again.

"Do you need anything else Seraphina, I'm a busy man." He asked in a low tone.

He didn't bother to look at me as he signed a paper before he placed it on a stack of other papers that I assume to be signed by him as well.

I took a breath and let it out before speaking, "Do you know of anyone in the family who had power over any form of water by chance?" I asked in a cool and collected voice.

This caught his attention as he looked up from the paper he was reading and looked over towards me with a questioning look before shaking his head. After that, he looked back down at his paper and continued to sort through them. He didn't say anything so I assumed he was thinking about it. Once he signed another paper and placed it on the other stacks of signed papers, he placed his pen down and looked over at me before he gestured for me to sit. So, I walked over and sat in the same chair I always sit in when entering the office.

"Why do you suddenly have an interest in the family?" He asked questioningly with suspicion showing slightly in his eyes.

I shrugged in response and answered his question, "Well figured I'd ask because it would be weird to have the castle built somewhere cold without having someone who could control the snow." I said in a calm tone that instantly erased the suspicion in his eyes as he leaned back in his chair and hummed to himself.

"Well, if you're interested, I guess you would be happy to know that the first King himself was a snow harpy, nothing special, he was probably the last of his kind to be completely honest, but other than him there is no other person in the family that had anything to do with snow." He said bluntly, trying to end the conversation there.

After that, he waved his hand at me and told me he had things to do so I rolled my eyes and left the room. However, before leaving I asked if I could borrow a book off of his shelf, before he responded he looked at me with squinted eyes before raising one hand as if to say 'Sure, just get out.' So after grabbing the book I saw earlier, I walked towards the door and left the office. Once I closed the door I turned to the left only to see Aleksandr standing right there leaning against the wall with a smirk on his face.

"Get what you needed princess?" He asked with a cocky tone.

He looked towards the book in my hands which made me roll my eyes and walk past him mumbling that I wasn't a princess.

"What was that princess?" He asked with amusement laced in his voice, which caused me to turn towards him with anger coating my eyes.

"I said I'm not a fucking princess so quit calling me one you cocky bastard," I said in an aggravated voice before I turned back around not waiting for his reply, and walked away.

After finishing the conversation I had with the King, Aleksandr decided to show me the rest of the castle. Which I only agreed to after he apologized. He showed me places like the music room which had a piano and a few harps in it. He also showed me where all the servants lived in the castle which was in the West wing on the first floor. My favorite part of the tour was when he showed me the portrait room which was a room filled with portraits of every King and Queen from the past starting with the very first King and Queen.

In between each portrait was a glass casing on top of a stone pillar and inside each case was a different set of crowns. One for each King and Queen from each time they ruled. They were all different from the other, each one of them probably built for each different Abolystic each of the Kings was. I guess If I had continued the tour with Aleksandr instead of going to my 'father', I could've found out who had power over snow and all of that by just looking at the crowns. Even then, I still would've had to ask him about the real reason why my mother left him in the first place.

I walked down the line of portraits admiring them and analyzing each portrait and seeing each person's qualities as well as how they acted during the portrait. The first one I saw was of my mom and dad which would mean we had entered the room from the back entrance and not the front entrance which I didn't mind much.

When I looked at the King and Queens portrait from before my parents, I could see the resemblance of my 'father' to the King. I mean other than the eye color they were almost twins. Which was strange, but I didn't put too much thought into it.

I continued walking down the hall until I reached a specific portrait that intrigued me. When looking at it I noticed how the King during this time had different colored eyes such as myself. Only his left eye was green, and his right eye was brown, opposite to mine. He looked a lot like me I would say, except for his chestnut-colored hair, we were identical which brought a smile to my face. I liked knowing that I look more like a King who cared about how his people were treated compared to my actual father who couldn't care less about anyone else's feelings.

While staring at the portrait I made a small promise to myself and all the Kings before my 'father' that I would fix everything and make this world right again. Even if that meant getting more blood on my hands than I could handle.

I could see that each portrait had some type of hidden piece in them as each one was different than the one before it. However, at the bottom of the painting where the signature was, the person who painted each painting was from the same family. The Sandbecks. Of course, the same person didn't paint each one, but it seemed that everyone from that family had a skill for the arts as no one else had ever painted any of the King and Queen's portraits.

After a while, my feet started to get sore so Aleksandr walked me back to my room. We walked in silence and didn't say much to each other other than Aleksandr asking me every so often if I'd prefer to be carried to my room if my feet were bothering me. I declined his offer each time with a simple 'no,' but he still didn't stop offering it which began to annoy me the more he kept asking. When we finally made it to my room I was planning to shut the door in his face, but before I could he told me he'd be back to get me for dinner and walk me to the dining room. I responded with an 'ok' before I closed the door and walked to sit on my bed, and placed the book next to me on the side table.

I sat for a while thinking about everything I learned today in my head. First about the Etoirir, then the note I had found in the book, and finally, about the conversation I had with the King. It took a long time for the realization to come that I had found a note in a book.

I quickly pulled the note out from my dress and unfolded it to read it.

To Seraphina,

I'm not sure if you're the one reading this, but I do hope it is as I made sure to hide it where your father would never look. I know I lied to you, but I also knew he would catch you and when he did I hoped that you would find this. I made a promise today that I would do my best to protect you, but if you're reading this then I guess I have failed. I wanted to tell you that I never meant for this to happen. I wanted you to have a good life, a happy life. But unfortunately, that couldn't happen in this castle, not with your father around. So I tried to find a way out. One of the guards had found out what I was trying to do, but thankfully they decided to help me after finding out I was pregnant. Though the night before I was going to go through with the plan I became very guilty and I wasn't sure if I should've gone through with it. But I made my decision after what your father said to me. He told me that he wanted to change the rules and that he didn't want to hand the crown down to anyone. He had decided that if I were to get pregnant he would kill the child. But I couldn't let him kill you. So I went on with the plan.

I snuck out of our room one night and went to the hallway with our painting on the wall. If you look while passing by you won't see anything. This is why you have to see it up close and you have to pay attention to detail. There is a specific spot on the painting that won't glow when touched by light. And if found you can open a door on the other side. I'm not sure if your father found out about it, but if not then that is your only chance at escaping the castle. Be aware though that there are always people watching.

I hope you do come through and change this country. The people no longer need a dictator, they need a savior, someone who will protect them and not look down upon them. I'm not asking you to fight alone or be the only one to do this. I'm asking you to find people to help you and I'm sure if you look hard enough they'll be right in front of you.

I had asked a witch who visits the castle now and again to place this note in a book in the library, hoping you'd find it. And if you did just know today is your fifth birthday and I couldn't be more proud to see you flourish in this world. I wish I was there to see you now.

Your mom

Aurora North

After reading I noticed how some of the words were almost scribbled as if my mom had been shaking while writing it and I couldn't blame her. It was as if she knew this would happen sooner or later, but she didn't care. Instead, she spent the time she had with me making sure my life was as great as she could make it. I know she lied to me and she knows she lied to me, but she did it to protect me, and for that, I couldn't hate her or be mad at her.

I didn't notice I was crying until one of the tears dropped down onto the note causing me to quickly place the note elsewhere and wipe my tears away. I didn't want to ruin the words I would read from my mom so I grabbed the note again and folded it back into a square before placing it inside my dress once again.

My thoughts were spiraling after reading the note my mother left for me. I wasn't sure if my 'father' knew about the passage or if it was blocked off. All I knew was that there was a way out and all I needed to do was find a way to escape. It's going to be tough considering all the guards in that specific hallway. So maybe my 'father' did find out and now has the hallway guarded, or he wanted to be cautious and make sure every hallway was now guarded. Either way, it's going to be difficult to make an escape plan.

Instead of giving myself a headache with the thoughts I decided to rest until Aleksandr came to get me for dinner. So I laid back and took a well-needed nap.

My 'father,' Aleksandr, and I were eating dinner in the dining room where I first sat with my 'father' the first day I had gotten here. I was sitting to the right of my 'father' as he sat at the head of the table, and Aleksandr was sitting in front of me, or better words, to the left of the King. We were all sitting in silence not daring to start a conversation or even look at each other. I was hoping that this dinner was going to go by fast so that I could leave and head back to my room to stare out my window into the stars above. Unfortunately, this dinner was taking forever as my 'father' and Aleksandr kept bringing up a topic and having a conversation about it. I figured out after a few of their conversations that they would look at me from time to time almost like they wanted me to put in my input, but I never did. Thankfully after the food came their conversation died down a bit but they would still talk every so often.

I was taken out of my thoughts when the King – my 'father' – coughed, catching both mine and Aleksandr's attention. However unlike Aleksandr, I didn't bother to look up, instead, I continued to eat as I thought it was another attempt to get me to talk to them. Unfortunately, I was proven wrong when my 'father' cleared his throat once more causing me to finally look up at him with an eyebrow raised. When he saw we were both looking at him, he started to speak.

"It has come to my attention that some important business needs to be taken care of in three weeks." He said and paused to wipe his face with a cloth that was laying on his lap.

I was confused by this statement and so I looked over toward Aleksandr while furrowing my eyebrows to see if he knew anything about this, but he shook his head. So we both turned back to my father and waited for him to continue.

"So, I and the other council members had gathered earlier this afternoon after you left Seraphina and decided that it would be best if we moved the wedding up to the end of this week." He said while standing up.

I could feel my eyes bulge out of my face, it was almost as if I had frozen and I could hear the cutlery in my hands fall to the floor. My heartbeat had increased and I could feel my thoughts swirling through my head and my breathing had become uneven. I stood up quickly, almost causing me to fall over as the room was spinning, but eventually, it stopped and

I looked at my 'father' with confusion and anger swarming through my eyes.

"The end of this week is in three days; how do you expect a wedding to come about in only three days? This is absurd!" I shouted at him and looked toward Aleksandr hoping he would agree with me.

Instead, all I got was a shake of his head before he stood up and stood next to my father. This caused me to scoff as I knew better than to expect a different reaction from him as he's my father's perfect little puppet.

"Don't argue with me Seraphina, I can simply accuse you of killing the Queen and everyone would believe me. So, if I were you, I would just do as told." He started with a sinister look in his eyes.

My body filled with rage knowing this was more than likely what he did to my mother as well and why she ran away. I wanted to fight him and yell at him for everything, but I didn't want to get myself killed by doing something stupid. So instead, I looked towards Aleksandr letting out another scoff, before walking out of the room and slamming the door shut behind me.

As I walked down the halls in anger I could feel the guards' eyes watching me as if they were worried I would do something reckless and they wanted to be prepared for it. However, I did none of that and waited to get back to my room before I released a scream and pulled out the braid in my hair allowing my hair to flow freely just like the tears in my eyes. I walked towards the window, my tears still flowing freely, feeling my eyes burn as mascara slid inside them. As I sat on the alcove I brought my knees to my chest and laid my head on my knees turning my head sideways to look out the window.

When I looked out I could see snow falling slowly and the windows fogging up with every breath I took. The moonlight was the only thing lighting up the sky as well as the room. I let myself go back to the note my mother had left me and I knew I had to continue fighting for her so I stood up and walked over to the table by my bed.

I picked the book up and read the title, The Mysterious of the Extinct Abolystics. I wasn't sure if the Etoirir would be included in the book, but if they were, I would like to know a bit more about them, that is if the page isn't damaged or destroyed.

I opened the book to the index and looked for the creature's name and saw that they were on chapter thirty-two page two hundred and forty-nine all the way to page two hundred and seventy-five. I assumed I would be staying up all night reading up on them. So I began reading.

I stayed up for hours reading until I eventually got to page two hundred and sixty-seven. I took notes on the things that intrigued me as well as the things that made them unique such as their strengths and weaknesses.

Eventually, my eyes began to flutter as I struggled to keep them open, and before I could control myself or move, the book slipped from my hands and onto the floor and my breathing evened out.

Chapter 24

It's been two days since I last left my room. I wanted to wrap my mind around the fact that I'll be forced to marry Aleksandr even though we've barely even known each other for a month. While I've been in my room I've also been reading about the Etoirir.

I've learned a lot about it mainly that it could live in very cold temperatures, which made me think that some of them could still be alive and were living in the Northern Mountains. I'm not completely positive because even though they could live in very cold temperatures, the book said they could survive up to a certain extent and once passed that extent, their wings would freeze and fall off causing them to die if they didn't find a warm climate. I also read that they, unlike the dragons, could shift into dragon-type creatures only their scales were made of ice and could break at the slightest touch. I suspect that they didn't transform very often for that specific reason as it could cause them serious injuries that would take a long time to heal. The most important thing I found out about them was that they were able to control snow like the snow Harpies, only they could do it faster as well as more efficiently. Another important piece of information that the book gave me, was that when the other half of the Etoirir shows itself, it would be a shock and it would be noticeable right away. Though it's only noticeable because once they wake up their abilities also awaken causing them to freeze things sporadically, and without cause. This was why they needed to learn and gain control over their abilities quickly, otherwise, someone could get seriously injured or potentially killed.

I wish I could find out more about them, but it was hard to even get a little out of it with all the words being scribbled over or they are fading away making some letters look like other letters.

I spent an entire day reading up on them trying to figure out other weaknesses as well as strengths that they had, which wasn't much since no one has ever seen them or heard of them. They're basically a myth waiting to be found. Which isn't much help to me. I did however find many similarities between myself and the creature which has me almost thinking that I could be one of them, but I'll have to wait and find out.

I've been sitting on the alcove for the past two days, occasionally getting up to go to the bathroom and doing everything needed before coming back to my spot. I would change positions when I would get uncomfortable or the wood it was made out of made my butt too sore. Each day a new servant would walk in to bring me food, and I realized after the first day that it was probably so that I couldn't ask one for help escaping because they'd just switch out with another person. I didn't eat breakfast and I barely ate lunch anymore as I had lost my appetite when the King told me that the wedding would be happening sooner rather than later. The only time I had eaten was when the last servant brought in my final meal until the next morning. Which was when it would start all over again.

What I've noticed in the past two days is that the snow would fall from the sky for a few hours each morning, but would stop in the afternoon to let the sun come out to melt some of it away. Then when the sun goes down it would start to snow again until the following afternoon. I've also noticed the guards changing shifts throughout the day, and it always happened at the same time every day, so If I had any chance of escaping it would need to be tomorrow. I also noticed how every now and again the same witch I had seen a few days ago would walk out to the guard in a fur jacket with the hood covering her head. I'm not entirely sure why she goes, but then again it's also none of my business.

I was staring out the window waiting for the same witch to walk out at any moment, when I heard the door open. I knew it wasn't a servant because it was too early for them to bring in lunch as it's only been around an hour and a half since they brought in breakfast. I didn't bother to turn around and give the person any of my attention because they have yet to ask me anything. Instead, I continued to sit in the alcove and watch as the snow fell from the sky still waiting for the witch to come out.

"You know it's kind of sad how you've just been sitting there for two days not wanting to talk to anyone or do anything." I heard Aleksandr say from behind me.

He sounded far back behind me probably by the door or sitting on my bed watching me. I, however, let out a sigh and continued to stare out the window before responding with a quiet voice.

"And it's sad how I used to believe that I would grow up and marry the man who made me smile until my face hurt and laugh until tears pricked my eyes as my mom and dad had," I said softly knowing it had to have at least some effect on him, but I didn't even bother to turn my head to get the satisfaction of it.

I heard him sigh quietly and for a while, we sat in silence with me still looking out the window. While staring I finally saw the witch walk out towards the garden, however, she stopped midway causing me to furrow my eyebrows before she turned and look up straight at me. I was confused but didn't get a chance to do anything before she turned and ran back inside the castle looking flushed and worried.

I wanted to get up and find her to see what was wrong, but before I could, I suddenly started to see the edges of the window start to freeze and it started moving closer toward the center of the window. My eyebrows furrowed once again as I wasn't exactly sure what was going on, but when I went to touch the window with my hands, I was in shock to see the tips of my fingers had turned a light blue. If Aleksandr weren't here I more than likely would've jumped off the windowsill in confusion and excitement knowing that I finally discovered what I am and knowing that made my fight for escape come back to me within moments.

Unfortunately, I was taken out of my short-lived excitement by Aleksandr speaking to me once again.

"You can still have that you know, I'm not a bad person Sephy. If you just give it a chance maybe, we could work out-" Before he could finish his sentence, I quickly cut him off by turning my head towards him in anger.

"Are you kidding me!" I shouted at him as I stood up in anger. "We could never work out, no matter how hard you try to make it work it would never work out! My dad only chose you because you're like his own puppet. He'll use you to do his bidding until he's sure he won't need to control you anymore. So no, it will never work out between us so quit trying to make it work!" I all but screamed in his face in rage.

He looked at me in complete shock and confusion which caused me to let out a scoff and go back to sitting on my windowsill.

"If you have nothing else to say, then please leave Aleksandr, I'd like to be alone," I said in a calm and quiet voice once again.

I didn't move or turn my head until I heard the door open and close, which was when I was sure that he was no longer in my room.

When I was sure that he was no longer there I turned my head and stood up heading towards the bathroom. When I got to the bathroom, I looked behind me and quickly shut the door, being sure to lock it so no one would interrupt me.

I quickly went towards the tub that was filled with now cold water and moved my hands towards the water only for nothing to happen. I let out a sigh in frustration thinking that I could have quite possibly been wrong about what I thought happened. However, When I thought back to what the book had said, I calmed down knowing I wouldn't be able to control it all right away. So, I took my hands out of the water and turned around in an attempt the calm myself down as I knew that once I escaped this castle, I would have time to learn and practice my skills to gain control over my abilities. However, when I turned around, I felt as if something was off so I turned back around and what I saw made my heart skip a beat.

Right in front of me was the water from the bathtub floating in the air just above the bathtub. My eyes widened, but I'm sure if I were to look in a mirror right now there would be a huge smile on my face for the first time in a long time. I lifted my right hand slightly and moved it to the left, and surprisingly the water followed my hand movements causing me to let out a gasp in shock. I decided to see if I could make the water freeze, so I thought of sharp pieces of ice and held my hand steady. After a lot of concentration and effort, the water started to break apart and build itself into sharp shards of ice. Sharp enough to cut through the skin, to be honest. I knew it had done this partially because I was new at this and couldn't control as well, but the water still froze meaning I had some sort of control or idea of how to do this.

I turned my body while still holding my right hand up and steady and then put all my concentration into having the shards crash right into the wall in front of me. When I was sure I could do it, I pushed my right hand forward and as I thought, the shards attached themselves right to the wall. There wasn't any damage done, as the wall was made out of brick so when the shards hit it, they broke into tiny pieces covering the floor. Unfortunately, once on the floor, they turned back into water causing the floor to be soaking wet.

I let out a curse as I tried to lift the water back up with again, but when I couldn't seem to do it I dropped my hand and let out an aggravated sigh. Not realizing that I had controlled the water from the bathtub instead and all of it fell on top of my head soaking me from head to toe. I let out a gasp as the cold water hit me before pulling my hair from my face I don't have to use a towel to get all the water off the floor. I realized that controlling the shards was probably a spontaneous moment of control, so instead of attempting to control the water again, I opened the cabinet to my left and pulled out two bath towels. I unfolded the towels and threw them onto the ground before getting on my knees and trying to clean up as much water as possible before I hung the towels up to dry.

After hanging them up I grabbed the third towel from the cabinet and began to dry myself off and walked out of the bathroom, thinking about all the new things I could do with my newfound abilities. Although I have a lot of practicing to do before I have them completely under control, and I have no one I trust enough to teach me, I still have something that could help me when I go against the King.

I smiled knowing how I'm going to get out of this marriage, and castle, and how to survive without anyone coming after me. For once I'm going to live my life and I'm going to live it for everyone I've met throughout all my years of life who didn't make it. Now I know that I can accomplish this promise for once in my life. I've carried all these promises with me for years and I've carried all the pain of seeing my loved ones die and even though I know I'll see them again, I didn't want to yet, not without fighting and destroying the person who took their lives.

My revenge starts now, and it starts with that wedding.

I walked over to the window and decided that I would sit and wait for the moon to rise. I wasn't sure if what I felt from the moon the other day was anything at all, but if it was then I want to know. Just to be sure.

I sat in the same spot for hours waiting patiently for the moon to rise. I remember hearing the door open and close letting me know that lunch had been brought in, but even then I didn't move from my spot. Eventually, I heard the door open again alerting me that dinner had been brought in which made me realize that I had zoned out for most of the day. I'm sure that if the maids are informing my 'father' about my eating habits then he doesn't care as he hasn't shown up to yell at me and although Aleksandr did come in here earlier, he didn't ask about the food. So I know my father didn't tell him to come in here, or at least I don't think he did.

Eventually, the moon began to rise and the room was slowly getting lit up but it was light. I didn't move to try and bring myself into the light, I waited for the light to cover my body on its own. When it did I was slightly disappointed when I felt nothing happen. I sighed in disappointment, but I still didn't move. Instead, I raised my right hand and focused on the snow forming above it, but unfortunately, nothing happened. Regardless I didn't give up, instead, I tried harder and let my mind think of nothing except for that.

At one point I began to get a migraine, but I still pushed myself to figure it out, and that led me to pass out into complete darkness.

When I woke up I realized I was back on the horizon of darkness. I couldn't see or hear anything, and I haven't been in here in a while so I had no idea why I had woken up here again. Usually, I would find myself here every night, but recently it's gone away and I thought I wouldn't show up anymore. I thought that the voices were done tormenting me as the King finally had me in his grasp, but I guess I was wrong. The last time I had woken up here was when I was shown my memories from the past, but other than that I haven't woken up here in a while.

I sat and waited for something to happen, as I wasn't sure why I was here. It felt warm and I couldn't see anything as my eyes hadn't adjusted yet. I felt as if I'd been here for a while and still nothing happened. I felt like I was brought here to be left in isolation for a while, but I'm not sure.

Eventually, I got bored of waiting so I stood up and turned to the left, and began to walk in search of whatever it is I was brought here for. As I walked I noticed how it began to get colder almost as if the temperature was decreasing, but I ignored it and continued walking. That was until I heard a voice. Well, not just a voice, that one specific voice.

Seraphina...

I heard it whisper from behind me causing me to jump and turn around. Only I didn't see anything, and I didn't hear anything after that. I did however feel a cool breeze from behind me so I turned back around and continued walking again. Only I heard the voice once again.

Seraphina...

This time the voice echoed throughout the whole of the endless abyss and I couldn't figure out where it came from.

I was going to reply but I was cut off when a huge gust of wind came and shoved me to the ground. I gasped in surprise before attempting to get up, but I couldn't as it felt like I was being held down. I started to freak out and I went to yell out for help but nothing would come out, which freaked me out even more. I couldn't move, I couldn't scream out for help, I was paralyzed.

That was until I felt like I was drowning and there was nothing I could do. Only it lasted a couple of minutes before it all stopped and I was breathing heavily. I brought my hands up to my throat and sat up quickly as I felt the pressure on my chest and arms release. I turned my head left and right but I saw nothing. It was almost as if I was imagining all of it, but that couldn't be true because this has happened before. Only that time it was worse. This time it felt like someone or something was trying to warn me or at least scare me. In either case, they succeeded, but I wanted to know why.

"What do you want!" I shouted from the ground with my hands shaking as I tried to calm myself down.

I could feel sweat dripping down my forehead, as well as goosebumps running along my entire body. I sat and waited for a response, but there wasn't one. It was just quiet and I didn't know why. Until I finally got my response.

You need to leave...

I was confused about what the voice meant. I needed to leave. Leave where? The castle, my room, this darkness. What do I need to leave?

"Leave where?" I shouted back as I stood up from the ground and turned my body at a three hundred degrees angle.

I was expecting an answer to my question, but I wasn't expecting the answer I got.

LEAVE!!!

The voice shouted once again, but much more violently as I felt the gust of wind come back and shove me to the ground. Only this time the pressure didn't let up and it felt as if I was being drowned underwater. I was struggling and trying to get back up but nothing seemed to work. I couldn't breathe and the pressure in my chest started to become painful. It became so painful that I finally had to let go and when I did I felt my eyes close and I was no longer drowning.

I woke up the following morning with a jump almost toppling over the side of my bed. I was confused about how I got in bed, to begin with, but excused myself when I saw a bunch of servants scurrying around in my room, and that's when it hit me, today was my supposed wedding day. I let out a sigh before I looked for Mabel who I spotted standing by the window, but before I had the chance to say anything to her, I was dragged out of my bed and thrown into the bathroom being told to take a bath before having the door slammed in my face.

To say I was shocked would be an understatement.

To get it over with, I took a quick bath before stepping out and grabbing a towel being sure to wrap around my body tightly. Once feeling like it was secured to my body and wouldn't come off, I walked out of the bathroom only to see only three servants in my room now and no longer fifteen of them in here. I took a calming breath and let my presence be known in the room.

When they saw me, they all stopped what they were doing and stood there frozen before rushing over towards me, gripping my arms and pushing me into a chair harshly. I attempted to get up but that only caused them to push me back down onto the chair. So, I sat there while they did whatever it was, they were doing.

I felt my hair being dried and then felt it being brushed through which bothered me a lot because I don't usually enjoy it when people decide to brush through my hair without my consent. Though it's not like I could stop her without getting my hand slapped away and I'm not really in the mood for that right now. So, I sat there in a very uncomfortable chair waiting for them to finish.

Eventually, after what felt like hours, I was pulled out of the chair and a dress was forced into my hands. I was rushed into the bathroom by all three servants rather harshly before they pushed me inside. I scowled at each of them before shutting the door and turning around holding the dress out in front of me.

I have to say it was definitely something. The dress was a beautiful slim dress which I'm sure will fit perfectly on my body. There was no puffiness to the dress and the sleeves were long and plain white similar to the sleeves on my black dress. The dress seemed to look tight until it gets to the waist, and then it began to fill out, so I didn't have to walk with small steps. Which made it easier to run away thankfully. I know for a fact I'm more than likely going to be wearing heels so when I get the chance, I'll be sure to throw them off before making my escape. The only thought running through my mind right now other than running was what I was going to do with my shawl as I won't have time to run back to my room and then make my escape. By that time the King will have everyone coming after me and I can't risk that.

I shook those thoughts from my head when I heard knocking on the door, I turned my head towards the door before shouting for them to give me a moment before taking a breath and sliding the dress on. Like my original thought, the dress fit perfectly and flowed down once it reached my waist making it easy to walk in. I would happily get married in this dress if the circumstances were different, but unfortunately, that's not how life wants to work for me.

I quickly took a breath and let it out and woke out of the bathroom only to be welcomed by the King himself which caused my breath to hitch and my body to shudder.

He took note of the small action and smirked wickedly before walking over towards me with a pair of beautiful black heels in his hand. He bent down on one knee once he reached me and reached out to grab one foot. I hesitantly placed my hands on his shoulders and allowed him to put the heels on my feet before he stood back up smoothing out the wrinkles on his tux.

"You look just like your mother did on our wedding day, absolutely stunning." He said just barely above a whisper.

The compliment made me blush and I whispered out a small 'thank you' in response.

"Shall we?" He asked as he stretched his arm out for me to grab.

I took a deep breath and counted to three before letting it out and nodding in response. I grabbed onto his arm for dear life hoping that I wouldn't fall from walking in these heels. Before we walked out of my room, I looked out the window and prayed that my mom would help me make it out of this wedding alive.

We walked down hallway after hallway which made my feet ache from having to wear heels. We passed the hallway with the painting and when I looked at it carefully I almost thought I saw the latch to open the door. I didn't see many guards around the halls as usual as they were probably all in the throne room. Which was a good thing for me. Although there may be guards hiding in secret passages that I don't know about, so I'll still need to keep my guard up when escaping.

Thankfully after walking for a couple more minutes, we made it to the door of the throne room and I could hear nothing. It was almost as if no one was in the room and I was about to walk in on my death. I took in a breath ready to do what I was planning, but before my 'father' opened the door he turned towards me and whispered in my ear.

"If you defy me and this wedding today in front of these people, your little friend will be dead before you even get a chance to leave the room." He whispered menacingly, causing goosebumps to rise on my skin.

I had completely forgotten about Barric in my plans to escape, but even then I can't let it stop me. Even if I'm being selfish, I need to leave so that I can come back later to help everyone. So I let the thoughts of Barric leave my mind as I watched my 'father' reach his hand out towards the door knob and open it with great force.

And the music started.

Chapter 25

My hair was swept behind my head as a gust of wind blew past me as the doors opened. I let my eyes close not wanting to see any of the people inside the room who stared at me waiting for me to walk. I took a deep breath and let it out before I opened my eyes only to be shocked by the sight in front of me.

The throne room had been decorated in the most beautiful way I could have imagined. With benches on each side of the room and candles hanging from the ceiling. It was as if a witch had conjured a spell as I could see the snow falling from the sky and landing above us. The windows were open as well allowing light to seep inside and brighten the room a little more. The floor was covered in white rose petals and stopped at the stairs where Aleksandr stood waiting for me. There were torches on the sides hanging off the walls lit with fire to brighten up the room even more and bring little warmth as well. On each side of every bench, was a bouquet of white roses adding to the stunning outlook of the room. I saw guards lining the walls taking away the feeling of amazement, but I couldn't deny that this wasn't perfect. The only thing that wasn't perfect was the reason behind it all.

Power.

I looked up and saw Aleksandr standing up ahead right in front of me. He was wearing a black suit with a white undershirt, his hair was left with its usual curl and he had a smile planted on his face. He stared straight at me with a look that screamed adoration, but I knew it was all fake. It was all for the show.

I was taken out of my thoughts when I felt a pull on my arm, I looked down at the person lightly pulling me by the arm and looked up, noticing it was my 'father.' He had a soft smile on his face which again was just for show, and I know for a fact that most of the people in this room know that as well. But unlike me, no one was willing to speak up about it because they feared the punishment it would bring them and their families.

I placed a small, but fake, smile on my face as well and then nodded my head toward him telling him I was ready even though I know I'll never be ready for this. We both turned forward with him on my left and me holding onto his left arm so that I wouldn't fall on my face, but also for him to hand me off to the guy he chose for me to marry. I looked ahead of me and held my head up high showing my confidence as well as the power I hold in the room, but it was also to show that something as horrible as this wouldn't bring me down even the slightest. It would take more than a forced marriage for me to crumble and break into a million pieces, and I'll be damned if I let my father control the decisions that Aleksandr makes. I'll make sure that I'm always there with them when they decide for our people. Too many have already been hurt because of my 'father' and I won't have another version of him ruling over me for the next few years to come. I couldn't live with myself if I allowed that.

I plan to make sure that he stays as ruler for a while because only I have the power to make Aleksandr King. If I don't marry him, he can't be King. On the other hand, if he does happen to become King without marrying me after everyone has found out about me, then he and my 'father' will be executed. As it would break the law of the first King and all Kings after him. So either way, it's a win-win on my part.

As we walked down the aisles of benches and bouquets of white roses people stared at us with fear and their eyes filled with pity directed towards me. It made me know that there were people in this world who still understand right from wrong but couldn't do anything about it. Which means that I would have to be the one to do the fighting for them. *And I will.*

For them and for all the ones who have been lost along the way because of the cruelty in the world.

As we walked, I could feel all sorts of emotions running throughout my body, I felt rage and anger the most, while other parts of me felt guilty for knowing how this night would end. As I looked around the room I saw how many people were excited for this wedding while others seemed to be uninterested, but no one seemed to be ready to fight. I felt a pinch on my arm causing me to look up only to see my 'father' with a stern look on his face as he held his head up high. I could see the stumble from his recently shaved beard coating his chin and his long eyelashes hitting his cheeks every time he blinked. I knew when he pinched me that he wanted me to act the same and face forward with my head held high, but in all honesty, I just wanted to hide away in a cave and never come out. Regardless of those feelings, I let out a low sigh and turned my head forwards. I held my head high and didn't show any emotions as we walked the rest of the way.

Once we reached the stairs Aleksandr walked over and reached his hand out towards me, I looked towards my father, and he gave me a nod signaling for me to go. I raised my right hand to Aleksandr and he slowly helped me up the stairs so I wouldn't fall. I smiled slightly at him to which he reciprocated back to me.

When I was finally up the stairs, we stood in front of each other and right next to us was the Royal Advisor, or I guess he's more of the Royal Pastor. He was holding a book in his left hand that seemed to be old and worn out so I assumed it was the book that every Royal Advisor had used before him to marry the new King and Queen. He looked like he was ready to speak which made me breathe in deeply once again before shakily letting it out.

I could feel my legs shaking from all the nerves I was feeling and I couldn't help but be thankful that Aleksandr was holding my hands as he kept them from shaking. I wasn't entirely sure if I'd be able to pull this escape off, but before I could second guess myself, the Royal Advisor began speaking.

"Today we gather here to witness this ceremony of marriage between Aleksandr Ashbrook and Seraphina North." He started in a strong, loud voice. "A ceremony in which you come to be united as one and is one of the first and oldest ceremonies celebrated in Karsindel, as well as in the presence of the Gods themselves. This marriage is a gift from the Gods claiming that you give yourselves totally and completely to one another." He continued looking at both Aleksandr and me before looking back up and continuing. "I believe that marriage is a gift given to comfort the sorrows of life and to magnify life's joys." He said in a calm and steady tone, yet loud enough so that everyone in the room could hear him.

I looked over Aleksandr's shoulder and saw my 'father' standing on Aleksandr's side of the room staring right at me. His stare made me shiver a bit, but before I could turn my attention toward the pastor, my 'father' looked over his shoulder causing me to follow.

I almost gasped at what I saw.

Barric was covered in purple and black bruises, hunched over almost as if he couldn't stand on his own. If it weren't for the guards holding him up by his underarms, I would imagine that he would crumble to the floor in seconds. I wanted to run and help him, but I knew if I did that, my father, my horrible no good father, would kill him without a second thought and force me to marry Aleksandr with Barrics corpse hanging from the ceiling. I could see his chest rising and falling slowly assuring me that he wasn't dead, but a part of me wishes he was so that he wouldn't have been suffering so much pain because of me.

Chains were wrapped around his feet and went up to wrap around his wrists before finally attaching themselves to a collar that was wrapped around his neck. I couldn't stand to see him like that and I felt a tear slide down my cheek, but my line of sight was taken from me as Aleksandr moved in front of the way and directed my eyesight towards him before wiping the tear away.

He looked at me softly and his eyes held guilt, but for what I have no idea. He didn't seem too quick to stop this wedding and he definitely wasn't hesitant about it either so I knew he wasn't sorry about forcing me to marry him. Maybe he could've been sorry about me having to see Barric so broken and bruised, but I'm not sure.

I did know two things though. I knew that I had to come back and save Barric, and I also knew that the likely chance of him still being alive was zero to none. On the other hand, that is only if my 'father' follows through with his threat and I don't doubt that he will. Regardless I couldn't let myself focus on that. So I brought myself back to the wedding and focused on what the advisor was saying.

"This marriage will signify the sharing of power, trust, and honesty between these two people who stand before you. It will bring equality back between two rulers placing a barrier between what can and cannot happen. They will make decisions collectively and wisely as it will affect the entire kingdom as a whole." He said while looking between Aleksander and me quickly before looking back down at his book and continuing. "This equality however does not stand if King Taeg and Aleksandr decide on something together and the Queen declines it as she sees it will not benefit her, and vice versa." He said which made the anger inside me rise knowing that my father only made him say that because he knew I would fight him tooth and nail if it hadn't been said aloud to everyone in the room.

This would mean that because all the King's advisors were in the room right now, I would have zero chance of getting anything I want. Which gave me even more of a reason to leave.

I looked around the room doing a sweep of everyone in the room, taking into consideration how many people could die from my burst of emotion. As I looked around I spotted the King's Coven of witches once again in the same place as before, and I spotted the witch that had been going to the garden at the same time every day. All of the witches except her seemed bored and uninterested in everything happening, but she seemed terrified. Her body was stiff and she watched me intensely as if ready to make a run for it as if she knew what was going to be coming. I ignored her however and turned my head back toward Aleksandr as I knew that if she did know what was coming, then she'd be smart enough to leave before it happened.

This wasn't the way I wanted this to end, I didn't want to hurt innocent people, but I knew at this point that I had no other option. I've had reason after reason to escape this place, as well as a way to escape. So I have to go through with it. My 'father' has too much control over the people in this castle and I have no one to turn to or trust.

I had to.

Although Aleksandr said I could trust him I know I couldn't as he's with my 'father.' He's fully committed to him, so I know I can't trust him. The other reason was that I made a promise to not only myself but to my mother, my dad, Shilo, and everyone else who had been caught in the crossfire. The only way to make those promises happen is if I leave, prepare myself, and come back stronger and harder. So that's what I would do.

No hesitation.

No guilt.

And no fear.

I would get this done. Even if I get hurt in the process.

I felt Aleksandr squeeze my hand signaling that I was beginning to zone out, so I quickly zoned back in just in time to hear the advisor talking again.

The advisor turned towards Aleksander first and asked him if he would take me as his wife and Queen to which Aleksandr responded 'I do." After that, he told him to repeat the words that he said. So, Aleksandr raised my hands while looking me in the eyes and recited the words to me.

"I, Aleksandr Ashbrook, take you, Seraphina North, to be my lawfully wedded wife and Queen. I promise to be honest and faithful to you through sickness and in health, in good and in bad. I will love and treat you as my Queen all the days of my life." Aleksandr spoke with a proud smile on his face and his eyes held nothing but softness.

I couldn't tell if he was being honest with me or not. If he wasn't then he sure was one hell of a liar, but if he was telling the truth, then it only made this hurt more than it had to. I didn't know if I could do it, but I knew I had to.

The pastor then turned to me and asked me the same words as he did Aleksandr, only I was more focused on something else. Or someone else. I kept thinking about Barric and if I could leave him behind to suffer for my decisions. I wasn't sure if I would be able to deal with his death in my hands. I could barely handle Shilo's death on my hands, so I wasn't sure if Barric's death would kill me or not. Regardless, I let it go and sighed before I decided that I had to speak those words. I had to speak words that went against everything and everyone. The words that would cause the deaths of many.

"Do you, Seraphina North, take Aleksandr Ashbrook, to be your lawfully wedded husband?" He asked while staring at me with a look that said if I didn't say 'I do,' something very bad would happen. A look that said it wouldn't only cause Barric's death but also everyone's death in this room.

I looked to my right and over Aleksandr's shoulder to see my 'father' sitting on the front bench sitting back with an unidentifiable look in his eyes and his arms crossed. Which made shivers run through me, he caught on to it and quickly had a smirk on his face.

I then turned my attention to everyone else in the room and they seemed to be waiting in anticipation of what my answer would be. I could tell some people were praying that I'd say no, while others were hoping for this to be over quickly. I could also see that some people were beginning to get anxious as their legs were bouncing up and down and others were playing with their fingers, but that didn't make me say the words any faster. I turned my head towards the witches again, only this time *she* was gone. I knew she knew what was going to happen, but I couldn't help but think 'Why didn't she tell him, why didn't she tell my father?'

I wanted to think about it longer, but I knew I didn't have the time to. So instead, I turned my attention toward Barric and I could see him looking right at me. He looked like he was in pain, but it was almost as if he didn't want me to do this. It was as if he was trying to tell me something through his eyes, but I didn't want to believe it. However, when he shook his head no it confirmed exactly what I didn't want to believe he was showing me through his eyes.

Tears welled up in my eyes and I could tell he noticed as he nodded his head yes as if telling me that it was ok and that he would be fine, but it still hurt. I assumed he put all his strength into his slow movements as his head dropped back down, and I noticed the guards shift their weight to hold onto him tighter so he wouldn't fall. I could feel a burning sensation in my chest as if my body was telling me not to go through with it and save Barric, but at the same time, another sensation was spreading through my body as if begging me to listen to him and do what I have to do.

I felt a soft squeeze on my hands which caused me to look down at my hands to see them still in Aleksandr's hold to which I then looked up at him. We stared into each other's eyes, and I let mine hold pain and regret right away when Aleksandr took notice of it, he looked confused and looked towards my 'father' for some sort of answer which he could not give him.

And then I said my answer which made Aleksandr flick his head back in my direction and look shocked, but it only lasted for a few seconds because what happened after that brought tears to my eyes as I could feel the burning sensation inside of me grow until it was all I could feel. I heard gasps in the background and shouts from other people, but I let it all go through the other ear as I remembered the words I said.

The words that caused havoc in death, and all I could feel was an icy feeling clawing its way through my body and out into the room and all I could hear were the sounds of pain and misery before I ran.

Acknowledgments

First off, I want to say thank you for giving this book a chance even if you didn't finish reading it you still gave it a chance and I am incredibly thankful for that. When I came up with the idea for this book, it was nothing like how it turned out. In fact, the entire plot was supposed to be entirely different, but I made the decision to change its course and create new characters and new outcomes. While writing this I have come to know my characters very well, even the minor characters which will help me to make book two of this series the best it can be and I hope for you readers to continue following me in my journey of learning and creating.

I am incredibly thankful to all my friends for pushing me to finish this book and telling me that even if I felt like it was the worst thing in the world, I still accomplished something that most people my age haven't. Moreover, I'm especially thankful to my best friend for never giving up on me (even when he didn't think I would finish it like all my other books) and celebrating the achievements that have come with this book. He's been there with me from the very first draft of this book all the way to the end of it and I couldn't be more thankful for that.

I would also like to acknowledge everything I've learned during this journey and know that imposter syndrome is nothing to be afraid of and will only hold me back if I allow it to get to me. I'm thankful to all those I've met through TikTok/booktok and how they helped me learn new things while editing my book. I'm incredibly thankful for them boosting my confidence by telling me that no matter if you are the best author in the world, there will always be someone out there who doesn't like your book and that it shouldn't matter what they think. All that matters is if I wrote the book that I wanted to write, and I did just that and I'm so incredibly happy that I did.

I'd also like to thank the amazing artist that did my beautiful cover! It's truly stunning and I couldn't have pictured it any better than what it is. So big thanks to SelkkieDesigns she can be found on Instagram.

Finally, I would like to acknowledge my dad and sister for being my biggest supporters by not only wanting to stay up to date on how everything was going but for finding an artist to create my book cover and for helping me market my book as well. If it weren't for both of them I might not have finished this book, to begin with and it could be sitting in google docs along with all my other unfinished drafts.

King of Frostbite

BLURB

The war for the throne is coming... and Seraphina is the key to winning it.

After barely escaping with her life, Seraphina has found refuge in the Northern Mountains, a place as deadly as the past she's running from. But survival isn't enough—she needs control. Of her power. Of her destiny. And of the truth buried deep within her blood.

As whispers of war echo across the land, allies and enemies alike move against her. The father who stole everything from her tightens his grip on the throne, and an old foe hunts her from the shadows. But the greatest betrayal may come from within, from those she trusts most.

With her abilities changing in ways she can't explain and a voice in the void calling her toward something unknown, Seraphina must decide: will she embrace the monster she fears she will become, or will she rise and reclaim the power that was always meant to be hers?

The fate of the kingdom rests in her hands. But in a game of deception, power, and war... will she be the one to survive?

Coming 2025

www.ingramcontent.com/pod-product-compliance
Lightning Source LLC
Chambersburg PA
CBHW052021240626
47153CB00006B/1903